Shameles

The Autobiography of a Bimbo

Stella Linden

SIMON & SCHUSTER

LONDON • SYDNEY • NEW YORK • TOKYO • TORONTO

First published in Great Britain by
Simon & Schuster Ltd in 1989

Copyright © Stella Linden, 1989

Simon & Schuster Ltd
West Garden Place
Kendal Street
London W2 2AQ

Simon & Schuster of Australia Pty Ltd
Sydney

British Library Cataloguing-in-Publication Data available
ISBN 0–671–65316–4

Typeset by Selectmove Ltd in Palatino 12/13pt
Printed and bound in Great Britain by
Billing & Sons Ltd, Worcester

Shameless

Chapter One

What you'll read in this book is the truth and nothing but the truth. Not 'the *whole* truth', a certain gentleman will be relieved to know. His lawyer managed to fix that, so he can sleep easily. The others – the men who've been begging me to leave things out and even offered me a lot of money to do so – can start worrying right here. For this is my story, but it's about *them*.

Men. How I love them all. I love them when they have lean, hard young bodies that can make love for hours without flagging, and come and come again. I love them when they're older and have learned variety and subtle technique to surprise me. I love them as instruments for my pleasure, their cocks huge and hard and all for me, driving into me, filling me, overflowing, their loins melding with mine; their tongues teasing between my legs, thrusting into me with supple skilful movements.

But the man I loved first and most was Steve.

I met him when I was fifteen and still at school. Steve was one of my teachers, but like no school teacher you ever saw. He was twenty-seven, maximum, with dark wavy hair, a lean muscular body and a voice that brought me out in goose pimples. He wasn't really a teacher but an archaeologist. He had an expedition all planned but it had been held up because someone had broken a leg. So while they waited for him to get well Steve filled in by teaching geography.

I was coming up to sixteen and longing to leave school. I dreamed of a life of beautiful clothes and exciting places, but I didn't know what else I wanted until the day this Grade A, solid gold, twenty-four carat mixture of Robert Redford and Don Willis walked into the classroom and said, 'Hallo everyone, I'm Steve,' in the most beautiful deep voice I'd ever heard. And suddenly my school blouse felt too tight across the bust.

My breasts have always been too big for the rest of me. I have this tiny little waist and hips that are rounded but not huge, topped off by a bosom that's at least a size larger. In time I came to be glad of it because my shape has been responsible for most of the fantastic things that have happened to me, but in those days I was so self-conscious that I didn't even mind the Iron Maiden which was what we called the confining cotton bra we had to wear.

But the day Steve came in I got the strangest feeling, and when I looked down my nipples were pushing against my blouse hard enough to be seen, even through the Iron Maiden. I could feel a little pulse going in my throat too. It had never happened before, but just looking at Steve and hearing him speak had done it to me.

He began walking round the class asking our names. He knew a lot about names and told everyone about the meaning of theirs. My name was Melissa and I hated it. When it was my turn I stood up

2

and frantically crossed my arms over my chest because I was sure what was happening to me must be obvious.

'And you are?' he said.

I could hardly speak. He was standing two feet away from me and he was the most wonderful sight I'd ever seen. I managed to gasp, 'Melissa Hawkins.'

He smiled. It came from deep inside his eyes which were very dark brown and warm. Sensations I'd never known before took possession of my body, filling me with excitement, as if someone had just made me a present of the whole world. I could have stood there looking at him forever, feeling his smile go through me.

'Melissa,' he repeated, and from him it was beautiful. 'Did you know that means "honey"?' I shook my head, dumb with delight, and he went on looking at me in a way that made me feel as if he was touching me in places where I'd never been touched by a man.

'Why are you crouching over like an old lady?' he asked me.

I couldn't answer because something had happened to my breath. 'Come on,' he said. 'Uncross those arms, head up.' As he pulled my arms apart his fingers brushed lightly across my breast and I felt as though an electric charge had gone through me. Suddenly my whole body was 'live', and when I dared to look down my nipples were even more prominent.

Steve's attention was fixed on them too, and he became completely still. I saw him give a quick glance down as though he was afraid he'd forgotten to do up his flies, then he hastily marked my name off the list, and passed on. My legs were jelly by that time and I sort of collapsed back into my seat. I knew I'd passed a turning point in my life.

I kept saying 'Honey' over and over to myself. It was the most beautiful name I'd ever heard, because

3

Steve had given it to me, and from then on I always thought of myself as Honey.

I began going to school without a bra. I wasn't ashamed of my breasts any more because they'd made Steve look at me like that, and I wanted him to do it again. I never skipped a geography lesson and I kept my eyes fixed on him. I can't say I learned much because I didn't pay any attention to what he actually said, just the way he said it. That lovely deep, rich voice always made me feel breathless.

Sometimes I caught him looking at me, but he always turned his eyes away quickly. At night I used to lie awake dreaming of what I'd like him to do to me, and plotting ways to get him alone. But when I finally managed it, it was by chance.

The games master was off sick and Steve took over. We were doing athletics on the playing field that day, all lined up in our white vests and shorts, and I wondered what Steve would think of my figure now there was more of it on show. My tiny waist gave me a nice hour-glass shape but I wished I was a bit taller than five foot three.

Steve was in a track suit that made him look more fabulous than ever. I was clumsy that day because I was trying to watch him instead of what I was doing. And that was how I fell and twisted my ankle. Steve said he'd help me back to the locker room and we went off together, with his arm round my waist and me leaning on him. I could feel his body through the thin material of the track suit, his hip moving against mine, and all the fantasies I had about him at night came back to me and made me stumble again.

'If you can't walk I'd better carry you,' he said, and lifted me up in his arms.

'If I'm not too much of a weight for you,' I said. But I knew I wasn't. He was so strong.

He laughed. 'A little girl like you doesn't weigh anything.'

I couldn't bear it any more. I had to know. 'Is that how you think of me, Steve? As a little girl?'

'It's how I *ought* to think of you,' he said after a moment.

'But I'm not really a little girl,' I insisted.

I was pressed close up against his chest and he had only to glance down to see that my nipples were pushing hard against my T-shirt. I could feel his heart hammering. 'No,' he said. 'You're not, are you?'

He carried me into the locker room and over to the couch. As he was about to set me down I tightened my arms about his neck and pulled his head close to me. I knew I *had* to make something happen now. This might be my only chance, and I'm a girl who believes in never letting a chance slip by – as several people could tell you.

He made a half-hearted attempt to resist me, tightening his neck muscles so that his lips stopped short of mine, but not putting me down. 'Melissa,' he growled, 'you stop this.'

'I'm not Melissa,' I said. 'I'm Honey. And you don't really want me to stop.'

I must have been right about that because he lowered his mouth to mine and started to kiss me. Straight away all sorts of terrific feelings coursed through me, like being hot and cold at the same time. They were the most delicious sensations I'd ever known and I wanted them to go on forever.

Steve's arms were trembling as he lowered me on to the couch and sat on the edge. Something strange was happening to him. I felt him give a violent jerk as though he'd had an electric shock, his arms tightened around me and suddenly everything was different. His mouth crushed mine and I could feel his tongue trying to get between my lips.

5

I let him in and at once his tongue plunged down my throat, then withdrew and plunged again, and again. Each plunge started off tremors that went right down through my body and exploded between my legs, as though there was a direct connection. It excited me unbearably and I moaned with pleasure.

He pulled up my T-shirt from the waist and began caressing my breasts. It was devastating. The rest of the world simply stopped existing. It was just Steve and me.

No man had ever kissed me like this before, but although I was so inexperienced I felt, even then, a powerful urge to please him as well as have him please me. Some people say that's the secret of my success, and I'd like to think so because there's nothing more satisfying than knowing you're giving a man the time of his life, something he couldn't find with anyone else.

I didn't know what Steve would like but I guessed I could find out by a bit of exploration, so I began to run my hands over him, which was something I'd always wanted to do. I could make out his shape under the track suit, his back which was long and lean and his thighs which were hard from the tautness of his muscles. Then I moved round to the front and found the huge bulge in his trousers. At the feel of it I got a tingling between my thighs and I hurried to pull the cord open. He surged right into my hand and I closed my fingers, enjoying the pulsating of the hot, rigid penis, and the feeling that *I* was making this happen.

He slipped his hand into my shorts and eased his fingers down between my legs. As soon as he touched me there violent tremors of pleasure began to go through me. They mounted quickly until I couldn't stop shuddering, while everything spun round me and I wondered how I'd reached the ripe old age of fifteen years and eleven months without ever discovering something so fantastically enjoyable. I felt as if 'they' had been keeping a secret from me, but now I'd found out and it was just great.

Steve was shuddering too, and I could feel a wetness on my hand as he went limp. I wanted to tell him how pleased and happy I was but I didn't because he looked desperately upset. He turned away quickly and began pulling himself together. When he looked back he couldn't meet my eyes.

'I ought to be shot,' he groaned. 'I must be crazy. Melissa –'

'Honey,' I insisted.

'Yes, Honey. It's what you are – pure honey. The most sweet and desirable girl I've ever met, and I've no right even to say that. You're just a child.'

'I'm sixteen,' I protested.

He gave a smile that made my heart turn over several times, very fast, and I could hardly breathe.

'You won't be sixteen for another four weeks. I checked.'

I knew the significance of sixteen and I guessed why he'd checked. It meant he felt the same as I did and I was so happy I could have danced. But Steve was backing away from me.

'From now on we keep our distance,' he said.

I jumped off the couch and ran to him, but he took hold of my wrists and held me off. '*No*,' he said firmly. 'Stay away from me, Honey. I ought to be strong, but I'm not.'

He rushed out, leaving me standing there. I felt bleak and miserable, and suddenly my ankle was hurting.

But I soon cheered up. I told myself what Steve had really meant was that we must stay apart until

I was sixteen. I lived for my birthday. Night and day I thought about Steve and me together, and what we'd do with each other. I tried to imagine being naked with him, feeling him running his hands over me, touching me everywhere, coming inside me. My body grew more fevered until I thought I'd explode. He didn't come near me any more at school, but when he took a lesson I'd often find his eyes on me. They had a hot look that told me he was thinking the same as I was and it was torturing him too. But it was a delicious torture that was going to end in ecstasy. I just knew that he was going to be a fantastic lover.

When my birthday came I was full of eager anticipation. I didn't see him in assembly. I decided he was just a bit late. Nothing to worry about. But when the geography lesson arrived I kept my eyes fixed on the door, and my heart was beating painfully. And to my horror, instead of Steve, Miss Hadway, the headmistress came into the room.

'I shall be taking your lesson today,' she announced in her sharp voice.

I wanted to burst into tears, but managed to ask if 'Mr. Lanson' was ill. She gave me a piercing look. She was in her fifties, with a dried-up appearance, and she looked as if she'd never in her life felt what I was feeling then.

'Mr. Lanson has left the school permanently,' she said. 'His expedition was ready to depart and they flew out this morning.'

I sat staring into space. Steve had vanished without a goodbye, which meant he was deliberately avoiding me. I'd been fooling myself. He didn't love me after all. My heart was broken and I wanted to die of grief.

But later that day I found a note among my things in my games locker.

Darling Honey,

I'm sorry I had to go like this, but I didn't dare tell you. You're so lovely and sweet that I know I couldn't resist you, and I must. Even though you've reached sixteen (which I'm sure seems very old to you) you're still just a baby really and I have no right to snatch you. Forget me, grow up and discover the world. Men are going to fall over themselves for you, and you can take your pick. I hope you find someone worthy of you.

Steve.

For a brief moment I was deliriously happy. He did love me. But then I realized he was gone and I might never see him again, never feel the fulfilment I was sure only he could give. That night I cried myself to sleep in an agony of despair and frustration.

I sleep-walked through my exams, not knowing whether I was doing them well and not caring. When they were finished I went on a school trip to London because it was a chance to get away from everything that reminded me of Steve. But I soon regretted it. We wore uniform and Miss Hadway came with us, yakking on about the museums and art galleries we were going to see. While we were going round the Natural History Museum I managed to fall behind. Then I slipped out of the building and made a run for it.

I caught a bus and let it take me round the centre of London. I'd never been there before and even though I was so unhappy I thought it was a wonderful, exciting city.

I got off on the Embankment and wandered by the Thames. I was so preoccupied I nearly bumped into a young man who was moving backwards, looking into the viewfinder of a camera. He was taking pictures of a girl leaning against a rail with the river as background. She was glamorously made-up and wore the

9

most fabulous clothes I'd ever seen. I stopped and stared, wishing I could afford to dress like that.

The young man kept calling, 'That's beautiful sweetie . . . perfect . . . and another one . . .' He didn't see me until he stopped to change the film, and then he scowled. 'Shoo,' he said, 'go and look at something else –' He checked himself suddenly and an interested look came into his eyes. 'Who are you?' he said.

'Mel – Honey,' I corrected myself quickly,

'Honey.' He seemed to roll the word round his mouth, tasting it. Then he smiled. 'Lovely. I'm Clive Ronnell.' He said his name with a kind of tentative flourish, as though he was hoping I'd recognize it but wasn't too sure. I'd never heard of him.

'Are you a famous photographer?' I asked.

He shrugged. 'Not *that* famous, evidently. But I'm a professional.'

'I'm getting stiff over here,' the girl on the railing complained.

'Sorry Jane. You can go now.'

'Aren't you going to give me a lift home?' she said indignantly.

'Sweetie, the place is crawling with taxis. You don't need me. 'bye.' He turned his back on her.

She grumbled but vanished and I was left alone with Clive. I noticed he was looking me up and down, so I did the same with him. He was as thin as a rail with blue black hair and an unshaven face that would have been saturnine if it hadn't had so much crumpled charm.

'Let's go back to my studio and talk,' he said.

I couldn't believe it as he showed me to his car. It was a sports car, not a stuffy family saloon like my Dad's, and I was going to a real professional photographer's studio. It turned out to be in a mews. It looked tiny from the outside, but it was huge inside.

The whole ground floor was a studio with lights hanging from the ceiling and bits of equipment scattered about. I was fascinated by a contraption that consisted of two metal uprights, about twelve feet high and ten feet apart, with seven crossbars, each one holding a roll of coloured paper.

'That's to give me different backgrounds,' Clive said, and pulled one of the rolls down to the floor. It was vivid blue. He stood me in front of it for a moment and surveyed me. 'Nice,' he grunted, 'but let's try something else.'

He wound up the blue roll and pulled down a red, then a yellow, then a green, all the time studying me. At last he decided on the green, settled me in front of it on a high stool and began to snap away. He made me put my school hat on, and take it off, then he told me to pull forward my hair, which I kept pinned back. I shook it to make it fall round my face and he clicked the shutter madly.

'How old are you, Honey?' he asked, still looking into the viewfinder.

'Sixteen.'

'Really? Sure you're not having me on?'

'I was sixteen three weeks ago.'

'That uniform's deceptive.' He stopped clicking and came towards me. 'Stand up.'

I got off the stool and he put his hands on my waist. 'You've got a fantastic figure,' he said, beginning to move them around, down over my hips then up to the sides of my breasts. 'At least, I think you have, but how can I tell through all that stuff?'

I couldn't answer him. His touch was making my breath come in little gasps and I was astounded. I thought only Steve could make me feel like that, but here was this stranger, the touch of whose fingers so close to my sensitive breasts was giving me a delicious tingling feeling all over.

'What – what did you say?' I managed at last.

'I said I'd like to see what you look like without that uniform – just for the picture. Don't worry, you're just light and shade to me. Why don't you pop into that dressing room over there?'

He was urging me towards the door while he spoke, seeming to take my agreement for granted. He deposited me in the dressing room and left me. I stripped down to my slip but I wasn't going any further. I thought about it for a long time and when I returned to the studio Clive was just coming in through the front door.

'I nipped out and got you these,' he said, tossing a little packet at me. 'Go and put them on.'

The packet contained a skimpy pair of panties made of satin and lace, a tiny bra, a suspender belt and a pair of stockings. They were all in delicious, sinful black and suddenly my inhibitions deserted me. I just knew I was going to look great in them and I couldn't get them on fast enough. There was some make-up in the dressing room and I used it to make myself look older and more glamorous. I was thrilled with the result but when Clive saw me he shook his head.

'Scrub that lot off,' he ordered me. 'I want you the way you looked before.'

'But I don't want to look like a kid,' I protested.

'Do as I tell you,' he yelled. It was amazing how fast charming Clive turned into bossy Clive.

He came into the dressing room and hovered round me, nagging, 'Do it thoroughly . . . you've missed a bit . . . make sure your neck's completely clean.' It was worse than being at school. I was so cross I forgot to be embarrassed about the fact that I was half naked.

'Good,' he said when he was satisfied. 'Now let's get your hair right.'

I'd pulled it about my face to look slinky and sultry. Would you believe he told me to pull it all back and do it in plaits? When I refused he started plaiting it himself.

'I look about fourteen,' I wailed when he'd finished.

'That's how I want you to look,' he insisted. 'Now put your school hat on.'

I was beyond arguing, so I put it on. He switched on his CD player and the studio was filled with heavy rock music. That was great because it really made me want to move. Clive hauled down the roll of yellow paper so that it went over the floor and told me to lie down on it. But as I passed him he suddenly grabbed me and pulled me against him. Before I knew what he meant to do he was kissing me hard, forcing my lips apart and driving his tongue inside. It was what Steve had done, yet different. Clive's tongue was harder, more aggressive, invading me forcefully. He was doing what he wanted without caring much for my feelings, but the sheer physical excitement of having him deep inside my mouth made me oblivious to everything else.

His fingers brushed the tops of my thighs, found the satin of my panties and slid inside. I moaned as I felt him caress me lightly between my legs, and repeatedly forced myself against him to the rhythm of the music, wanting more . . . and more . . . and more . . . But just when I thought he was going to make me burst with excitement, the way Steve had done, he stopped and withdrew his hand, leaving me aching and unsatisfied.

'Don't stop,' I pleaded. 'You haven't finished.'

Clive grinned. 'Oh yes I have. I've got you to just the state I want you.' He whirled me round by the shoulders until I was facing a mirror, and showed me to myself. At once I could see that I was different. My lips were swollen and my face flushed with excitement.

'Now lie down on the floor and do just as I say,' he ordered in a voice that crackled with authority. The erotic power that had possessed him a moment ago had vanished. I was too dazed to do anything but obey.

I lay on my stomach, then on my back with one leg raised, with Clive dancing round me, glued to the view-finder, yelling, 'Gorgeous darling . . . that's it . . . let me have it . . . roll over and over . . . fantastic . . .'

Then I had to sit on the floor and change the angle of my hat while he crawled this way and that, sometimes distant, sometimes coming close. The music pulsated through me and I soon found I could anticipate what he wanted. We seemed to have perfect rapport. I felt good. This wasn't Melissa Hawkins, schoolgirl. This was Honey, the person I'd always known I could be.

And then it was all over. He switched off the music, said, 'OK, you can get dressed now,' and walked off into his little office, taking the film out of the camera as he went. I was left sitting there on the floor like a lemon.

I put my uniform back on and went into the office. Clive asked for my address and I gave it to him, but I could tell his attention was somewhere else.

'You'd better go now,' he said. 'I've got someone coming. I'll be in touch, OK? Nice to meet you. 'bye now.'

And I was out in the street.

I had to hurry. The school party would have left the museum by now and be in the National Gallery. I managed to find a bus that was going there and arrived just as they were coming out. I slipped in among them and it was a few minutes before Miss Hadway saw me.

'Ah, Melissa, I thought I hadn't seen you for a while. Where have you been?'

'I'm sorry,' I said demurely. 'I got lost.'

For the next few weeks Mum and Dad couldn't think of anything except wondering how well I'd done in my exams. Dad worked in the accounts department of the Town Hall and Mum did part time in a library. They were determined that one of their kids was going to have a brilliant career and we all knew it wasn't going to be my brother Ricky.

He's five years older than me and the sort people call 'carefree', which means he's got the common sense of a newt. He got chucked out of one school for never doing any work, and out of another for 'corrupting' the girls. He always said they corrupted him, but I shouldn't think he fought very hard to keep his virtue.

Ricky was OK. He could make me laugh and we got on fine, but I was fed up carrying all my parents' ambitions just because he was such a dead loss. He used to say, 'I can't hold a candle to you, Mel. You've always been the brainy one.' And I used to kick him, partly because I was having enough trouble with Mum and Dad without him making it worse, and partly because I hated being called Mel.

I told you I went through those exams on 'automatic', didn't I? Well, my subconscious must have known a lot more than I did because I passed everything with flying colours. The results came with a letter from Miss Hadway talking about my dazzling future. Mum was over the moon, and Ricky was making the most of it to distract attention from his latest spot of bother. Only Dad was a bit quiet. I wondered why until Mum said something about, 'My daughter, the professor!' and Dad roared, 'Professor be blowed! Look at this.'

He held up the tabloid he'd been reading, open at page 3. And there I was in tiny little bra and panties with my hair in pigtails and my school hat on. The caption read, 'This is Honey, and she's a real sweetie.'

'Blimey!' Ricky said, studying it. 'Is that hot little piece really you, Mel?'

Dad shut him up, then turned on me, and within seconds we were all at it, hammer and tongs. I won't go into the details of what everybody said. It was very vulgar and I've always disliked vulgarity. In the middle of the row the phone rang. Dad answered it and found himself talking to Miss Hadway. At least, she did most of the talking. The words were a bit muffled but I could hear her squawking from the far side of the room so I reckoned she'd seen page 3 as well. I think it was my wearing the school hat that really bothered her.

I left them to it while I studied the picture, and as I looked I felt a rising excitement. It wasn't the same kind of excitement Steve had made me feel. It had more to do with realizing what I was capable of. There was a different person in that picture. Her name was Honey, she had a fantastic sexy figure, her mouth was provocative and her eyes were an invitation to bed. And she was *me*.

Dad had put the phone down and was talking without pausing for breath. He'd got past the bit about, 'That any child of mine. . . .' and had just reached, 'Do you realize the people at the Town Hall know you're my daughter?' when the front doorbell rang. I went to open it and found Clive on the step.

'You really landed me in it,' I hissed, indicating the kitchen.

'Don't tell me you mind looking like that, Honey.'

'I mind that you didn't tell me first,' I told him indignantly.

'OK. In future I will, I promise.'

'Future?'

'You've got a *big* future – if you want it.'

'I want it,' I said at once. 'What do I do?'

'Come to London with me.' He seized my hands. 'We can go places together, Honey.'

Before I could answer my parents came out into the hall. When I told them who Clive was Dad took a swing at him, but he missed because Clive hopped out of the way, smartish.

'Don't murder me,' he told Dad, grinning. 'I'm the man who's going to make your daughter a star.'

'You're a dirty little so-and-so,' Dad roared and took a second swing. Clive hopped again and took my hand.

'We'd better be going before your old man gets third time lucky,' he said.

'You're not going anywhere,' Dad told me.

'I'm going to London, Dad. I'm going to be a model.'

'You're going back to school to take your A-levels.'

'Dad, if I weren't a lady I'd tell you what you can do with A-levels. And Miss Hadway can do it too. And I hope the two of you have a lovely time doing it together. *I'm* going to London.'

'Have your breakfast first,' said Mum.

'She's going back to school,' Dad repeated.

'I shouldn't suppose they'll take her after this,' Mum said reasonably. 'Drop me a line when you're settled, love.'

'I will,' I promised.

'If you go,' said my father ominously, 'you need never come back here.'

I couldn't help giggling. He looked so much like a

Victorian patriarch. 'All right,' I said. 'I won't come back, and you can tell the people at the Town Hall that you've shown me the door.'

I kissed Mum goodbye, winked at Ricky and followed Clive out to his car. He handed me in ceremoniously and we zoomed away. My life as Melissa was over. My life as Honey had really begun.

Chapter Two

Clive was a monster: a cynical, calculating, cold-blooded monster who'd do *anything* to get the picture he wanted. He also had the charm of the devil, which was how he got away with it.

But I learned all that later. As we drove to London together I felt like Cinderella after they found that the slipper fitted.

It was lunchtime when we arrived and Clive took me to a little Italian restaurant, where he demanded a table by the window, 'So that I can take a good look at you.'

After studying me for a while he said, 'Honey's a marvellous name for you. You're pure honey: honey hair, honey skin,' his voice softened, 'and I'll bet you're honey all through.'

'What do you mean?' I asked, although I had a suspicion.

'You'll find out,' he promised with a smile.

Something about that smile filled me with pleasurable anticipation. Of course I could never love Clive as I loved Steve, but he *was* very attractive.

He told me he was twenty-six and a Welshman. I reckon that accounted for his Celtic charm. He had pale skin as though he spent a lot of time indoors, and against it his black hair and dark blue eyes made a devastating effect. And while other unshaven men merely seemed scruffy, Clive's designer stubble gave him the look of a sexy bandit.

'I was right to make you wear school hat and pigtails,' he said. 'You had a "touch-me-not" face and a "come-and-get me" body, and the contrast was fantastic. You've made a great start, but if you're going to get to the top you've got to be properly looked after.' He gazed into my eyes as though trying to hypnotize me. 'You must promise to put yourself in my hands, Honey.'

'I promise,' I said in a daze.

'It means signing a contract that makes me your manager as well as your photographer. You've got to trust me completely!'

'Of course I trust you,' I breathed. 'You've been so good to me.'

Which was a pretty dumb thing to say, but I was innocent then.

We went back to the studio and he showed me the flat above it where he lived. It was a lovely place with polished wood floors and white walls covered in huge photos of gorgeous girls, with madly affectionate captions. While he took the messages from his answering machine I wandered round, looking into rooms, growing more wide-eyed. He had a small bedroom with a huge double bed that left no room for a wardrobe.

I sat tentatively on the bed, bouncing slightly. Then I looked up to find Clive leaning against the door jamb regarding me with a grin. 'You'll have to be patient for a while,' he said.

I felt myself colouring. 'I wasn't – I just wondered – where I'm going to sleep,' I said.

'Out here, on the sofa.' He reached out his hand to lead me back into the main room, but when I took it he drew me close to him and slipped an arm around my waist. 'Does that disappoint you, Honey?'

It did, but I wasn't going to let him know that. 'I guess I can take it or leave it,' I said, trying to speak casually, but my voice trembled a little with what his closeness was doing to me.

He laughed. 'That's good. Play your cards close to your chest.'

I stored that up for future reference.

He stood looking down at me with a smile, then slid his hand behind my head and leaned down to kiss me. It was a teasing kiss, meant to interest but not satisfy. My brief experience of explosive passion with Steve was enough to show me that Clive was fully in control of himself and meant to stay that way. He moved his mouth slowly over mine, flicking my lips with the tip of his tongue and then sliding it into my mouth, drawing it across the soft, moist flesh inside as if he were testing me for quality. I felt a quickening as though a vibration was starting deep inside me and pulsing out to the very ends of my fingers and toes. I wanted to go with that vibration and become a part of its rhythm, but Clive ended the kiss too soon. He drew back to look down at me and I could see myself mirrored in his blue eyes. I had a vague look. My eyes were hazy and my lips were slightly parted because I was breathing in little gasps.

'Oh, Honey,' he breathed, 'if only I could. . . .' He seemed lost for words.

'What?' I murmured.

'If only I could capture you on film exactly as you are now,' he said. 'What a picture that would make.'

My head seemed to clear. '*What?*'

He grinned. 'You're a photographer's model now. You'll have to get used to me seeing everything from that point of view.'

I glared at him, but soon he had me laughing again. Clive was like that. He worked to get people into the mood he wanted because gloomy faces bored him.

I slept on his couch that night and he didn't come near me. I was sure my frustration would keep me awake but it had been a big day and I dropped off quickly.

Next morning Clive drove me to another mews house four streets away and introduced me to Phil and Donny, who lived together and were a 'married' couple. Their home was a pretty little place, full of dainty cushions and Laura Ashley fabrics. Phil was fantastically houseproud and was ready to murder anyone who so much as dented a cushion.

Donny was the best looking man I'd ever seen. He had a gorgeous lean, muscular figure, curly fair hair and beautiful eyes. I thought his being gay was a terrible waste. Phil was the complete opposite. Although he was the house-keeper he was broad, stocky and butch-looking, the sort that makes you say, 'What *him*?' But beneath the look of an amiable gorilla he was very gentle and they were devoted to each other in a way that was rather sweet. They owned a beauty salon called *Revelations*, and Clive told me they knew everything about showing women at their best.

As soon as they saw me their eyes lit up. 'Glorious!' Phil breathed, looking me up and down. 'Stand there, darling. Don't move.'

Donny touched my hair, pulling it this way and that, but his hands were quite impersonal, and he murmured, 'I haven't had material like this to work on for years.'

'I'm not material,' I objected. 'I'm me.'

We all laughed and Clive brought some papers out.

22

'Before you start work, fellers, I want you to witness Honey's signature on this,' he said.

It was a contract, and it practically made me his property forever. I didn't care. This was what I wanted.

When Clive had gone Phil and Donny studied me some more and Phil told me to pout. 'Again,' he ordered, 'and this time let your lips fall open a little.' I did so and he sighed with pleasure. 'Now lick them,' he said. 'Get them really wet and pout again.' When I'd done it he exchanged a glance with Donny and they both nodded.

'Your mouth's perfect,' Phil said. 'I know models who would murder for large lips like yours. Poor dears, they have to rely on injections.'

'Injections of what?' I asked.

'Animal protein. It makes their lips swell up, but it wears off after a few months and they have to do it again at £150 a time.'

'But why bother?' I asked.

'It's more sensuous, darling,' Donny said. 'When people see that you have generous lips they'll think you're generous in bed too. Oh but you are *gorgeous*! I could go for you myself if I was that way inclined.'

'But you're not,' Phil said firmly, giving him a jealous look.

'No, I'm not, am I?' Donny agreed, winking. Phil winked back, they chuckled and harmony was restored.

'You've got other natural advantages too,' Phil said. 'Your eyes are big and widely spaced, which gives you a little-girl-lost look, and you have a nice heart-shaped face. Maybe it's the teensiest bit too wide over the forehead, but I can put that right.'

'Are you going to squash it in?' I asked, trying to joke.

23

'I'm going to use blusher and highlights to make it look smaller,' he said severely, for to Phil beauty was no laughing matter. 'Didn't you ever learn how to do that? My God, what do they teach you girls at school?'

'History and algebra,' I said.

'See how far history and algebra get you in front of Clive's camera. Now watch me and learn. I shan't use much foundation because your skin's so young and perfect it doesn't need anything heavy.' He stroked my cheek. 'Like velvet,' he sighed. 'Make the most of it while you've got it, darling, because it'll all be gone by the time you're twenty-five.'

'I shan't be old at twenty-five,' I objected.

'You won't be young either; not by the standards of this business.'

I watched attentively and saw a new me coming to life under his hands. He used shader under my cheekbones and highlighter on the sides of my forehead, and my face really did seem to change shape.

When I told him that I'd always used blue eye shadow on my blue eyes he wailed mournfully as if I'd done him a personal injury. '*Not* blue with blue, darling. Never the same colour on the lids and in the pupils. For you – silver and plum, I think.'

I thought it would make me look as if I had a black eye, but it didn't. By the time he'd put plum shadow over the lid, dusted it with silver and outlined with silver-grey I looked madly glamorous. Then he put peach lipstick on me and glossed it and I stared at myself ecstatically.

Clive returned and after a critical look grunted, 'She'll do. Be at my place at nine tomorrow morning, boys, and get her ready for the camera.'

That night Clive ordered me to sleep naked, 'Because nightclothes would leave marks on you.

24

Your body's got to look perfect tomorrow.' I lay awake half the night, wondering how he could lie just the other side of that door, knowing I was naked and not doing anything about it.

Next morning Clive made me have my breakfast wearing one of his loose silk dressing gowns, so that my unmarked state would be preserved.

Phil and Donny turned up early and Donny got to work on my hair. When he'd finished I was disappointed. My hair was all mussed and I thought I looked as if I'd been dragged through a hedge backwards, but he explained, 'You've heard of "windswept"? Well, I call this "bedswept". You look as if you'd just got up after a fantastic night in the sack. That will make men think of sex, which is what it's all about.'

'Don't put thoughts into the child's head,' Clive said languidly. I glared at him but he didn't seem to see me.

Phil took over and repeated what he'd done to my face the day before. As he worked he questioned me to see how much I remembered. He was pleased with the result, but I complained that it was like being back at school.

'You're in the School of Life now,' Donny proclaimed.

Clive scowled. 'If you're going to start talking about Life with a capital "L", I'll bring up my breakfast. Honey, are you learning anything?'

'Of course I am,' I said, and couldn't resist adding, 'Svengali.'

'Well just you remember that Svengali owned Trilby body and soul. OK fellers, if you've finished I want to start.'

Phil and Donny went off to start their day's work at *Revelations*. Clive led me down to the studio, where he'd pulled a roll of blue paper right down so that it made a floor covering as well as a background. On it he'd tossed a beanbag covered in black velvet.

'Are you ready?' he asked.

I nodded, my throat constricted with excitement. Clive pulled the dressing gown off me, leaving me completely naked, and pointed to the bean bag. I dropped down on to it, he turned on his CD player and we began.

We worked hard for an hour. I did everything he told me, but somehow the vibrations were wrong. I became nervous, sure that he was disappointed in me. I was all tensed up when he started to adjust my pose with his hands and his touch on my bare flesh made me gasp. I began to feel erotically alive and when his fingers brushed across my nipples I nearly jumped out of my skin.

Clive smiled at me in a way that made my heart skip a beat. I wondered what he would do next. I was burning with frustration and when he reached out to me I nearly threw myself into his arms. But he only took my hand and drew it up to his mouth, brushing his lips across the palm. The tickling sensation was delicious and made tremors go through me until my toes curled. 'Do you like that, Honey?' he murmured.

'You know I do,' I gasped.

'Not unless you tell me. I want you to like everything I do.' He flicked my palm with his tongue and it felt so good I nearly squealed.

He was watching my face, his eyes alight with curiosity and interest. 'Shall I do that again?' he asked.

'Yes please.'

The tip of his tongue began to trace whorls on my skin, touching off sparks that flashed along my arm, deep into my body and exploded again between my legs. I'd began to twitch pleasantly there in rhythm

26

to the pounding of my heart, and never wanted this to stop. I took a deep breath and threw my head back, losing myself in this wonderful enveloping experience.

'Stay like that,' Clive said excitedly. Dropping my hand he began to click away with the camera. I was burning all over with the sensations he'd roused in me and then left incomplete. I'd only just started to learn about desire and I couldn't handle frustration. (In fact I've never coped well with frustration, but that's another story.) I only knew I was furious at the cynical way he'd roused me just to get a good picture. I let out a scream of temper and tore at my hair which cascaded all over my face. I shook my head to get it out of my eyes and found Clive snapping away exultantly.

'That's glorious, darling!' he yelled. 'You look just like a frantic lioness. Give it to me, *give it to me*.'

I would have done gladly, but he didn't really want it. He just wanted the right look. With Clive the look was everything.

At last he let out a roar of triumph. 'We did it! Those pics will be fantastic. OK, you can get dressed now.'

He started to walk away but I wasn't having that. I was still on the bean bag but I managed to grab hold of his hand. 'Oh no you don't,' I gasped, 'you can't leave me like this.'

I tightened my grip, pulling him down beside me. He laughed and set the camera aside. 'I know what you want of me, Honey,' he said, but you've got to wait until Svengali says you're ready. I want plenty of pictures of you as a passionate virgin first.'

'You bastard!' I raged. 'I'm not just a piece of clay for you to shape.'

'Aren't you?' he queried mildly. 'I thought that was exactly what you were.'

27

'But you want me,' I pleaded.

'Sure I do,' he agreed affably, 'but there's lots of other things I want more, and you're going to help me get them, Honey.'

I growled with exasperation and lunged at him but he fended me off. Then I became aware that his other hand had slipped between my thighs and the fingers were drifting lazily upwards, triggering off fires wherever they touched. I gripped his shoulder, thrumming with excitement as he reached the electric place between my legs. I was already wet with wanting him, and he dipped his finger tips in the moisture, letting them glide back and forth, leaving trails of aching sweetness that I wanted to last forever. It was as though every sensation of which my body was capable was concentrated in that one little spot that throbbed with every touch he gave it.

'You get aroused quicker than any girl I've ever known,' he murmured. 'Don't rush it, little Honey. It'll be worth waiting for.'

'I don't want to wait just for your damned pictures,' I told him, speaking with difficulty as the pleasure mounted.

He grinned. 'See if you call them "damned pictures" when you see them.'

I wanted to argue but he was working faster and faster so that I came suddenly, groaning and clutching him as my body writhed against his hand. Afterwards as I lay back, gasping, I noticed that his smiled had changed. The calculating light had gone out of it and it was almost tender. He held up his hand, the fingers glistening wet from where he'd touched me. Then he deliberately curled his tongue around them. As though they tasted delicious.

'Nectar,' he murmured, 'from Honey. Sweeter than anything in the world.'

Then he gave me a long, lingering kiss that calmed me down, and I felt good again.

He was right about the pictures. When I saw them I forgave him everything. Even I could tell that I looked sexy and full of erotic invitation, half kitten, half lioness. Clive immediately sent them to the national tabloid that had featured me the first time, and he had a sale that very afternoon. By the end of the week I was in the papers again.

I had some money too because Clive paid me a modelling fee. He'd taken a hefty percentage as my agent, but it was still more money than I'd ever seen before, and I splurged out on some make-up and new clothes.

I got some modelling work straight away, showing off scanty underwear in a magazine advertisement. Since Clive had my exclusive services they had to give him the job of taking the photographs. They argued a bit but gave in rather than lose me, which made me feel terrific.

The pictures were in colour, so I got a new look at myself. Clive showed them to me one evening. I'd been shopping for new clothes and was wearing a thin silk dress and nothing else. He'd made me promise only to wear loose clothes so that I needn't bother with underwear.

When I saw the pictures I said I hadn't realized my skin had that lovely glow, but Clive said the effect was caused by the filter he'd used. He explained to me about filters and through them he taught me one of his maxims about Life (Clive wasn't above talking about Life with a capital 'L' when it suited him): that it all depends how you look at a thing. You can make yourself see anything you want if you're determined enough.

'You look different even to yourself, don't you?' he asked.

'Completely.'

'And you look different to me. It's only been a few weeks but that schoolgirl has vanished.'

He slipped an arm round my waist and looked down into my eyes. I wished he wouldn't do that because just being this close to him made me feel the moisture between my legs. Clive had never looked so handsome, his dark blue eyes blazing strangely against his pale skin and bandit stubble, but I wasn't going to give him the satisfaction of knowing what he did to me, so that he could reject me again.

But something had changed this time. He'd fixed his gaze on my plunging neckline. The heat that was rising from my body was making the thin silk cling to my breasts, outlining their size and shape and the fact that my nipples had peaked. Clive said softly, 'Let's go,' and took my hand, to lead me into the bedroom. It was late and the only light came from a small lamp. He placed my hand on the bulge in his trousers and I could feel his cock in there, huge and pulsating, inviting me. Without waiting for his permission I unzipped him and slid my fingers in, curling them round his organ, letting them enjoy the heat.

It felt magnificently good, throbbing there in my hand. Clive reached down and took hold of my dress, pulling it over my head in one movement. I helped him yank his own clothes off and was thrilled by what I saw. His cock was big and rampant, standing at a sharp angle, and I couldn't take my eyes off it.

Clive drew me down on to the bed and grinned at the direction of my gaze. 'Never seen one before?' he asked.

I shook my head. I hadn't really seen Steve's properly.

Clive didn't seem in any hurry. He sat astride me so that I had a grandstand view of his equipment, the massive penis that was strangely beautiful with its smooth, rounded tip, and the heavy balls beneath. I caressed them with my finger tips and they felt wonderful.

He lay beside me and began to kiss my body, taking each breast in turn. I wanted that because just being naked with him and thinking so many exciting thoughts was making them ache. He rasped his tongue across one nipple, sending violent tremors through me, and when he touched the other nipple with his fingers I trembled again. Then he started to work on both breasts together and I began to rock my hips back and forth uncontrollably because the lightning was forking through me and exploding in my loins and suddenly I was caught up in a violent rhythm that shook me again and again. As it ended I sighed with disappointment because I knew I'd come and I thought that was that for the night. And he hadn't even been inside me.

'Why that sigh?'

'Because it's all over and I thought there'd be so much more.'

'Who says it's over? he teased, sliding his hand down to my legs. 'I've never known a girl who came so easily. It means you're very highly sexed.'

'Am I really?' I said eagerly.

'And you can keep on for as long as you want, doing whatever you want.'

'Show me,' I begged.

But he already was. His hand was working between my thighs, touching me as he had before, making me ache with pleasure. Now I knew he was right and I would come again at any moment. But before it happened he stopped and slid one finger deep inside me, then two fingers. It was a little strange at first, but then the feeling of being full was marvellous. As he was withdrawing he paused and tickled me just inside and I went into instant convulsions of delight, writhing dementedly and thinking nothing could possibly feel as good as this.

Clive withdrew his fingers and let them trail up and down on the sensitive skin of my inner thighs. To my amazed delight I felt the excitement begin all over again. And now, at last, he moved over me to settle between my legs and suddenly it was happening. That great, powerful, beautiful thing was sliding inside me, feeling like the beginning of the world. I arched against him as he thrust, instinctively going to meet him. It felt so good, so natural. I'd been born for this and I couldn't understand how I'd lived without it for so long.

I could feel myself ready to come. I didn't want to. I wanted to go on and on feeling him inside me, but it was like trying to beat back a wave crashing on the shore. When the crash happened it shook me into little fragments and I was faintly surprised to find myself still in one piece. I groaned with lusty pleasure, arching against him violently, digging my nails into his shoulder.

But it wasn't over. Clive was still ramrod stiff and my own desire came surging back at once, demanding everything he had to give. I became a tigress, half demented with glorious craving, and also a little insulted at his control. Why wasn't he wild and raving joyously like I was? In my frantic determination to make him crave me as I craved him I did something that was wholly instinctive. I tightened my muscles where I was enclosing him, released them, then tightened them again.

I felt his jolt of surprise and saw the intrigued look that came into his eyes. I did it again – and again – settling into a rhythm, and soon he was breathing in time to that rhythm. He began to thrust deeper into me and with every movement the sweet aching pleasure in my loins grew stronger. He was thrusting faster and faster and suddenly his climax came. At the very same moment I gave a shriek of glorious, shattering, mind-bending, explosive lust, shaken from head to toe by what felt like an earthquake.

He rolled off me and lay on his back. I was too exhausted to move. My whole mind and body were taken up by the stupendous discoveries I'd just made. Life began here with the revelation of why I'd been created. And it was free to everyone. I couldn't understand why the whole world wasn't singing and dancing. Why did they waste time making money and having wars when they could be doing this instead?

Clive turned his head to look at me oddly. 'I could swear you were a virgin,' he said.

'I was. Why?'

'Then how did you know to do what you did?'

I shrugged. 'It was just instinctive.'

He grinned. 'If that was instinctive, Honey, you are going to have a *great* career with men. You're a natural.'

'A natural what? Whore?'

'No. More of a courtesan. You're going to specialize in love, and when you've had some more experience you'll be the best there is.' He got up. 'Now let's see how the pictures came out.'

'Pictures?' I shot up in bed. 'Do you mean you've been filming all this, you bastard?'

'Of course.' He pointed to the ceiling. 'The cameras are up there. The "lusty virgin" stage of your photographic career has run its course. I needed a new look.'

I aimed a swipe at him. He grabbed me and in a moment I was on my back with Clive between my legs, ramming into me, and I was ready for him all over again and, oh, it felt *good!* It felt so good that

33

I forgot I was mad at him, even forgot about the cameras clicking away overhead.

And that was how I learned that Clive's control was never so perfect as when he seemed to lose it. It's lucky I wasn't in love with him or he'd have hurt me, but I never reached that point. I became sexually fascinated with him and I learned an immense amount from him, but my heart wasn't involved.

He developed the pictures that night. It was fascinating to see myself in the throes of passion. In the following days he took more publicity pix and they were subtly different. Just looking at that woman's face you could tell she'd discovered a wonderful secret and was full of the joys of it. As Clive had said, I was on the edge of a great career with men.

Chapter Three

Let me tell you something: page 3 girls are ten a
penny. If you can't hit the headlines for something else as well you're finished in a year, and I
wasn't going to let that happen to me.

It was Phil who had the brilliant idea. You remember it, don't you? It was in all the papers and there was
even a question asked in Parliament. If you ask me I
was lucky not to end up in the Tower of London, but
it worked and after that I never looked back.

We managed it like this. Clive hired some antique-
looking panelling, and twenty feet of oak railing from
a firm that made theatre sets. They were to be the
backdrop for some very special pictures.

For this session I wore a pair of black silk stockings
held up by frilly garters, and over them a hired mink
coat. The railing was set up in front of the panelling.
Then I perched on it and let the coat fall wide
open. My leg was bent at the crucial angle to prevent
me showing too much because these pictures had to
be tasteful and artistic. Even so, they revealed a great
deal.

Clive had obtained a couple of tickets to the public gallery of the House of Commons for next day. There was a big debate about Social Security changes that would make it harder for married women to go out to work. The chief speaker was going to be Leonard Hawkburn. Yes, *that* Leonard Hawkburn. In those days he was a junior minister at the DSS, and at thirty-two that wasn't bad going.

He was known for his outrageously macho attitudes. He didn't believe in the equality of the sexes and he said so, loudly and often. According to Leonard women belonged in the home, bringing up children. Of course the lib sisterhood hated him, and I too sometimes got indignant, but the sight of him could make me go all reflective. He was built like a bull with heavy shoulders and neck, and a sturdy muscular body. His face was heavy and unimaginative, but in a coarse kind of way he was rather attractive.

On the day I dressed carefully, putting on a soft wool dress that buttoned in front, with stockings and garters beneath it and the mink coat on top. Clive and I bagged seats at the front of the public gallery, and I got to work. I buttoned the coat right up the front, pulled my arms in from the sleeves so that it hung on me like a tent, and undid the dress. The coat was several sizes too large so it was easier than it sounds. Then I slipped the dress right off under the coat, let it fall to my feet and put it in my bag.

The debate started. There was a lot of hot air flying around, and at last Leonard Hawkburn rose to add his bit. He spoke beautifully in a vibrant, deeply masculine bass. If only he didn't talk such bilge!

'We have gone too far,' he was saying, 'in encouraging women to put their homes second. Now we must say to them, "Your family needs you. You must think of what being a woman means, and use those attributes that only a woman has – "'

It was the perfect moment. My heart was thumping as I rose, pulled open the coat and sat on the gallery rail, just as I'd done in the pictures. I waited breathlessly for the reaction.

Poor Leonard Hawkburn couldn't understand why he'd lost everyone's attention. I'd put my hands on my hips, holding the coat right back so that the MPs had a grandstand view and, believe me, they were making the most of it. Some of them started to cheer and I swivelled round to give them a better look.

Of course it couldn't last. Two policemen hauled me away and I had a final vision of Leonard staring up at me as if a thunderbolt had hit him.

They took me to a police station and charged me with disturbing the peace. Gerry, a solicitor friend of Clive's, who'd been put on alert, appeared from nowhere. I spent the night in the cells. Luckily they let me keep the mink coat because no-one dared to take it off me. Mind you, one or two would have liked to.

In the morning Gerry turned up with my bag which had been rescued by Clive. I appeared in the Magistrates Court in the wool dress which was very tight and suggested everything underneath. The magistrate kept clearing his throat. I explained earnestly that I was so enraged by the Junior Minister's attitude that I'd felt obliged to do something drastic to make my point.

Gerry nodded and looked serious. 'In other words, you were making a political protest?'

'Definitely,' I said, fighting to keep a straight face. 'And after all, I was only following the Minister's advice.'

'In what way?' the Magistrate asked faintly.

'Using those attributes that only a woman has,' I explained sweetly.

I was let off with a fine.

Clive drove me home and told me what had happened after I'd left. 'Those MPs had never seen anything like it,' he chuckled.'One third of them had breathing problems, one third had their eyes out on stalks and the other third are going to have to do some explaining to their boyfriends – and I'm not talking about the women.'

That afternoon the phones hummed. Clive had passed the word round that he had photographs of 'what the MPs saw', which of course were the mock-ups we'd taken the day before. He drove the price up really high but everyone paid up and next day I was centre spread in all the tabloids, accompanied by captions like, 'Those attributes that only a woman has,' which must have made Leonard choke over his coffee. A journalist called Eddie interviewed me about my 'political protest'. It made a nice little story and looked terrific next to me displaying my birthday suit.

I got invited onto TV-am, and since I had to say something I chatted on about what a clown Leonard Hawkburn was and how he was a threat to nice simple girls like me who were only trying to make an honest living.

After that my mail got interesting. I received an invitation from a constituency party to stand as their candidate at the next general election. I got sheaves of hate mail from the sisterhood for 'degrading women'. And one of the animal lib organizations wrote to me, more in sorrow than in anger, asking if I knew how many minks it had taken to make the coat I'd worn? That made me think a bit and I asked for some of their literature. When I'd read it I was hooked. I became a paid up member and swore off fur forever. Their PR man called the papers and they made another story out of it.

I got invited onto TV-am again, plus a couple of

celebrity panel games. Me – a celebrity! I walked around on cloud nine for a week.

Mind you, I looked over my shoulder for a while. The Magistrate might have let me off but I had a feeling I could still end up in the Tower. They say the P.M. was fit to be tied.

I was sleeping regularly with Clive and life was terrific. I still went around without any underwear but now it was by choice because I wanted to be ready for sex at any moment. I didn't even wear tights. I had my legs waxed regularly at *Revelations* so they were always smooth, and at any moment of the day or night I was ready for Clive.

My whole view of life and people had changed. When I met a new man my first thought was to wonder how he'd look naked, how big he was, and what it would be like to do it with him. Well-known people began to look different when I saw them on television. Was *he* any good at it? Did *she* know the tricks I was learning?

I practised sex with the fervour of a recent convert. I couldn't get enough of it. Clive laughed that I was wearing him out but he was having a good time too. If I wasn't working I'd wait in the flat upstairs while he took his pictures in the studio below, and he'd rush up to me while his assistant changed the film. The more pushed he was for time the more we enjoyed these occasions. He'd burst in, trousers already open, cock rampant, muttering, 'Five minutes.' We'd jump on to each other and make every second count. I could come and come again and still want more. When he'd gone I'd lie there feeling my cunt still throbbing from his hardness, smiling to myself.

My pictures showed a woman who thought of nothing but sex, who lived for sex, woke, slept, breathed, dreamed sex. Clive doubled his price and increased my fee (although he didn't double *that*). Papers that had once referred to me as a 'sex poppet' now called me a 'sex bomb'. I liked that.

The life I was enjoying with Clive was perfect while it lasted, but all good things have to come to an end. That's how you move on to other good things.

I'd started reading books and discovering that there was more to sex than what we were doing, but when I wanted to experiment with Clive he wasn't interested. Svengali had his limitations. Sexually he was a plain, simple boy at heart. He liked what he'd always known. Him on top, me underneath, in-out-in-out and wham! It was wonderful, but I wanted more.

If I'd gone on living there we might have quarrelled, but Phil and Donny offered me their spare room. Clive said he'd be able to keep me under his eye. 'And they'll look after you like a pair of mothers.'

He was right. Donny welcomed me with a cordon bleu meal that he'd cooked himself and Phil had put flowers in my bedroom. As they were only charging me peanuts I pitched in with the housework but it wasn't a success. Phil thanked me very sweetly and as soon as my back was turned he went round dusting in all the corners I'd missed. Then he begged me with tears in his eyes to leave the housework to him.

One night I woke up thirsty and decided to go downstairs for a drink. But as I went out on to the landing I heard a noise below, and when I looked down there were Phil and Donny, stark naked, lying together on a fur rug on the floor. The only light was the moonlight coming through the window and at first I couldn't make out what they were doing, except that Phil had his head between Donny's legs, and Donny had his head between Phil's legs.

Then Donny lifted his head and I saw Phil's cock,

huge, engorged and glistening with moisture in the silver light. It was as thick and sturdy as the rest of him, throbbing with power and utterly beautiful. Donny's head went down again and the cock vanished into his mouth. He was sucking it passionately, making little pleased grunts as he did so. Or perhaps he sounded so satisfied because Phil was doing the same to him at the other end.

Every so often Phil's cock would emerge again, gleaming wet from the way Donny had sucked it. I watched enthralled, feeling the excitement start and the place between my legs get damp. I wanted a cock like that to tease with my lips. I wanted to play with it and encompass it, to release it and recapture it, torment it, love it.

They shifted position and now I could see Donny's penis coming out of Phil's mouth. It was like the rest of Donny, long, pretty and elegant, but it didn't thrill me as Phil's magnificent organ did.

I could tell from their sighs and groans that they were having a great time. They grew noisier and faster until at last they came together. I knew I should creep away before one of them saw me, but I was so fascinated I couldn't move. Donny was lying back on the floor with his arm over his eyes, his chest glistening. Phil relaxed beside him, watching him.

And then he looked up and saw me. I froze, expecting him to be angry. But he only gave me a huge wink. I winked back and crept away.

But what I'd seen had left me wound up. My cunt was throbbing with need and I knew I'd never go to sleep without some release. I slid my hand between my legs, rubbing myself hard until I came. And as it happened I fancied I could feel my mouth full, gorged, satiated, overflowing. But it was only an illusion and I realized I wouldn't rest until I'd tried this new experience for myself.

Next morning Phil made breakfast and smiled at me in his usual way. Not a word was said. It might never have happened.

One night Clive asked me to stay on for supper after a modelling session. He'd hired the video of *Blood And Fire* starring Randolph Berrick and we watched it together.

'Randy' as the newspapers called him played a 'freedom fighter', which gave him plenty of scope for heroic action which he performed grittily, and passionate love scenes which he performed smoothly. He was terribly handsome with a voice like old brandy. At one time the sound of it would have turned me to water inside, but that was when I was young and innocent. Now I thought a man should be young and have plenty of energy. Randy had narrow hips and muscular thighs, but the close-ups showed the lines about his eyes.

'I used to think he was gorgeous,' I said with a sigh.

'Some women still think so,' Clive observed.

'He must be fifty.'

'Late forties. And he's a big star. You should get to know him. A famous escort for you would be the perfect finishing touch.'

He was right but I was getting wise to Clive by now and my ears pricked up. 'What are you up to?' I demanded.

'Me? Up to? I don't know what you mean.'

'Stuff it, Clive, and tell me what's going on.'

'Look, Honey, I just want you to have a date with him, and be nice to him.'

'Why?'

'Why?' he echoed innocently – too innocently.

'*Why?*'

42

Clive sighed as if grieving over a wicked world. 'I've done a lot for you, Honey. Now I'm asking you to do something for me. I want to be in the big time.'

'But you *are* in the big time.'

'Snapping tits and bums for page 3 doesn't exactly put me in the Norman Parkinson league. I want to be *the* photographer for the rich and famous, and I need a start. Randy's sent a message to say he'd like to meet you.'

'And what do you get in return?'

'A photo session with him.'

'All right,' I said. 'I don't mind going out with him but I'm not making any promises for afterwards.'

Randy called to ask me to dinner. I accepted, and immediately wondered what to wear. It was Donny who chose my clothes for special occasions. He had a cousin who owned a garment hire shop and he got me things at a discount. I asked for something with a high neck. I wanted to look demure until I'd had a chance to make up my mind.

The dress he produced had a high neck all right, but the rest of it was shameless. It was peach silk, cut skin tight, with a lace insert that stretched up to my throat, then plunged between my breasts and down to my waist. The back was the same except that the insert went right down as far as my behind. There was no room for anything underneath except a pair of panty-tights. I felt safer when I had those on.

I had a polite little speech of refusal all worked out in case Randy asked me to go to bed with him, but perhaps he wouldn't. He was thirty years older than me and probably realized that it wasn't on.

He arrived in his chauffeur driven Rolls Royce. He was in a dinner jacket and I gulped a bit when I saw how staggeringly handsome he looked. Some big stars are a disappointment in the flesh, but not Randy. What you saw up there was what you got

43

in real life. He smiled when he saw me and my heart flipped. 'I'm so glad you dressed up,' he said, 'because tonight we're going to dine in style.'

In the car he poured me a sherry from the drinks cabinet. We clinked glasses and he said, 'Here's to a wonderful evening, Honey. I may call you Honey, mayn't I?'

'Of course.'

'And you must call me Randy. It's what my dearest friends call me. You don't mind my asking you for a date before we'd been introduced? The fact is I've seen you on television and I was dazzled.'

'I'm very glad you called me,' I said, meaning it.

He took me to a new French restaurant which was the 'in' place to be seen. As I sailed in on his arm people turned their heads to look at us and I felt proud to bursting point. There was no doubt that Randolph Berrick was the best accessory a girl could have.

I'd been afraid he might hurry me to a private room. Instead he'd reserved a table in full view of everyone, and I began to relax. Randy was a perfect gentleman, handing me to my seat and treating me as if I was breakable. He smiled at my look of surprise.

'I suppose I seem hopelessly old-fashioned to a child like you,' he said.

'I'm not a child,' I told him, a little indignant.

He laughed and it was a wonderful sound that went down my spine like warm treacle. 'You're a child to me. It's plain you're not used to these little attentions, but when I entertain a woman. . .' his voice caressed the word '. . . I treat her like a lady.' He took my hand and lightly kissed the tips of my fingers. 'For one thing, I never swear. To me, swearing in front of a lady is a desecration. You see, Honey, I learned manners a very long time ago, when women were regarded as precious.'

44

'Not that long ago,' I said quickly. 'You talk as if you were old. I don't think you are.'

'What a very sweet thing to say, but we both know the truth. I'm much too old for a charming, dewy young thing like you. All I ask is to bask in your light for a little while, to sit and adore you and carry away with me a memory that will sweeten the rest of my days.'

Yes, I *know* what you're thinking, but I was sixteen for pete's sake! Fell for it? Of course I fell for it. I listened, almost hypnotized, as he went on, 'I want to sit here looking at you and thinking how, if I were a few years younger, I'd remove that dress from you, inch by inch.'

'I'll bet you've removed an awful lot of dresses,' I said, trying to sound sophisticated.

Randy gave a little self-deprecating laugh. 'Perhaps I have. When I look at you, I find I can't remember.'

I gave what was meant to be a knowing laugh but it came out sounding tremulous. 'All those women you've romanced – what would they say if they knew you couldn't remember them – or pretended that you couldn't?'

'Pretended? So cynical so young? Wise girl. Doubt all men, my sweet Honey – except me. As I look at you I'm not sure the others even existed.'

'And yet you have a reputation as a Great Lover,' I teased him.

He shrugged. 'Tabloid stories. Ignore them. True passion is far more sensitive and subtle than a tinsel reputation.'

'Of course it is,' I said, hardly knowing what I was saying.

'The essence of passion is leisure,' he explained, holding my eyes with his own. 'Desire is an experience to be savoured slowly and with relish. A true lover doesn't come charging at a woman like a bull at a gate. He takes his time and begins by kissing her *very* slowly, all over. Have you ever been kissed all over, Honey?'

'Never,' I said, hoping my voice didn't sound strangled. My skin was tingling with the thoughts he was putting into my head.

'I hope the man who finally does so knows what he's about.' Randy took my hand and turned it so that the palm was almost against his mouth. The heat of his breath scorched me as he whispered, 'I hope he caresses those sweet breasts with his lips and tongue. . .'

On the word he drew my hand closer and traced circles in my palm with the tip of his tongue. I could feel my breasts straining at my dress. I could hardly breathe.

I won't bore you with the rest. You want to know whether I did or I didn't, don't you? Of course I did! With all that sexy talk he got me so that I didn't know whether I was coming or going. He described everything he wanted to do to me and there was no way I was letting him go until he'd done it.

In the car afterwards he gave the driver my address and held my hand chastely. I wasn't having that, so I pulled his head down to mine and drove my tongue between his teeth. I'd learned a lot from Clive by then, and when I felt his tongue come up to meet mine I teased and challenged it in a way I knew he'd find provocative.

By the time we drew apart we were both gasping, and Randy said unsteadily, 'Am I understanding you properly?'

Since he seemed slow on the uptake I gave him the treatment again and this time he came back at me, plunging his tongue deeply down my throat. I took his hand and placed it over my breast. I was aching for him to touch me inside my clothes but

46

there was hardly any way into the damned dress from outside. That'd teach me to make good resolutions.

Randy pulled himself free and hoarsely told the driver to go to his home after all. Then he returned to me and slipped his hand up my skirt. I groaned as I remembered how I'd insisted on wearing pantytights. It felt like having a chastity belt on. I heard a tearing sound as Randy ripped them apart and then his fingers were between my legs, teasing my cunt. I came three times on the journey and knew I could come again and again before the night was over. I was going to romp in the hay with the Great Lover and I was raring to go.

He had a fantastic mews house full of mirrors with erotic pictures all over the walls. Not that I noticed many details at the time. I couldn't wait to strip off and get to it. I noticed the bed because it was big enough for five people and had dark blue silk sheets. We fell on it together, tearing at each other's clothes. I'd have liked to see him naked but he kept the light off and I had to sense him out by touch. He felt good and smelt good, but when I tried to feel for his prick he caught my hands and said, 'All in good time. I have things to do first.'

He reached out to a bedside CD player and flicked it on. At once music filled the room. It was modern jazz, sophisticated, moody and intensely erotic. Randy may not have been the world's greatest actor but he knew a lot about getting the setting right. He began to make love to me with his lips and his tongue. As he'd promised, he kissed me everywhere. He started at the top, making me lie on my stomach and flicking his tongue against the back of my neck in a way that nearly made me jump out of my skin. I hadn't known I was so enjoyably sensitive there.

47

It got better still as he worked down my spine, making shivers of pleasure go through me and I heard him chuckle as I writhed at the feeling.

'Nice?' he asked.

'Mm, yes. Don't stop.'

He'd reached the small of my back, then my hips and down into the cleft of my buttocks. A growl formed itself in my throat at the feelings that gave me. This was something like! This was the kind of thing I'd read about in those books and had wanted Clive to try. Randy was a real artist in the way he used his tongue. Sometimes it was an erotic weapon, thrusting its way aggressively, sometimes it was like a painter's brush, making detailed, intimate little strokes, sometimes it became a conductor's baton, urging me into rhythmic movements.

I grew quickly attuned to him, arching this way and that to meet him, offering him new places that ached for the same sweet torture he was inflicting elsewhere. I wished he'd let me have his prick, but he kept just out of reach. I pictured it swollen and ready, looking like Phil's the night I'd seen him with Donny and I yearned to have it in my mouth.

Randy was kissing my inner thighs, working his way slowly to the top where my cunt was softly throbbing in time to the pounding in my blood. I gasped and moaned as he reached it and teased it with the very tip of his tongue, making me come twice in the space of a minute.

'You taste delicious,' he murmured. 'I want more of you . . . much more. . . .'

And he plunged his tongue deeply into me, thrust, thrust, like a cock but so much more flexible. The power and subtlety of that tongue was a revelation, an overwhelming experience that drove me deliciously crazy. I wanted to scream with pleasure as I came. I reached out for him and this time I managed to get what I wanted. My lips closed on his prick and I grunted with satisfaction.

It didn't feel as I'd thought it would. It felt smaller than the mighty, massive organ I'd imagined, and not nearly so hard. I worked on it feverishly with my lips and gradually I felt it stiffen and grow a bit larger. But just as I was getting into my stride it was snatched away. Randy twisted round and settled between my legs in the normal position and thrust into me. I began to flex my muscles as I was well practised in doing now, trying to give him the time of his life as a thank you for the fabulous new experience he'd given me.

And then it happened. For a few brief seconds he moved faster and faster, then he gave a groan – and came.

I couldn't believe it. He'd barely been inside me a minute and that was that. Now I could feel him getting smaller and slipping away. The performance was over for the night.

Randy was gasping as if he'd run a mile. He switched on a small bedside lamp and in its dim light I could see that he'd completely collapsed. It was a real little tiddler he had down there, rather sweet but definitely not inspiring.

'Well?' he said archly, and I wondered if I was expected to applaud.

Well I wasn't stupid enough to say, 'Is that all?' So I concentrated on what he'd achieved with his tongue, which really had been rather special and unexpected, and when I'd told him this about ten times he began to look relieved and I knew it was all right. It took me half an hour to ease his mind and when I'd finished I was exhausted.

He sent me home in his Rolls. I was glad he didn't come too because I had a lot of thinking to do. As we drew up outside the door I had a qualm about Phil and Donny, because I'd definitely told them I'd be home early. But surely they'd have realized what had happened and gone to bed?

They hadn't though. As I crept in the front door there they were, looking down at me from the landing like a pair of maiden aunts, their faces stiff with outrage.

'Where the hell have you been?' they chorused. 'We've been worried *sick*.'

Chapter Four

Randy and I became an established couple. He took me everywhere, film premières, theatre first nights, expensive restaurants. Wherever we went there were cameras clicking and the papers were full of stories about our 'romance'.

Clive had his photo session with Randy and the pictures were fabulous. I had to laugh because I knew by then that Randy's hair was grey and he had it dyed, but through Clive's lens it looked completely natural. Randy was delighted and insisted that Clive should take the publicity shots for *Force Field*, the new film he was starting. Word soon got round that Clive could knock five years off anyone's age and film stars began knocking at his door.

I was meeting a lot of famous people too. There was one woman – I won't give her name but she's a *big* film star – who dragged her new husband away as soon as she saw me. That made me feel terrific. The men would whisper things like, 'When you're finished with Randy. . .' which I stored up for future reference.

One night we went to the première of a film called *Crashing Out*. The sound track was heavy rock sung by Butcher. I'd always been fascinated by him in a naive sort of way. He had a very brutal image and an evil expression, and his songs, which he wrote himself, had cruel words – when you could hear them.

At the première Randy and I went round socializing, and suddenly there he was – Butcher! Standing right in front of me. He was dressed in black leather fixed together with nuts and bolts and decorated with chains and studs. A hacksaw dangled from one ear. I stared at him for a moment, trying to control myself, but I couldn't. Instead of appearing mean, moody and magnificent he looked like something that had been left behind in a scrap-metal yard! I began to laugh. I choked it off quickly but it kept breaking out again. Butcher scowled and I wondered if he was going to tear the hacksaw off and use it on me, but he only turned and stalked off.

Oh yes, I had some great times with Randy, but it wasn't all a bed of roses.

At first I loved listening to him talk. He seemed so world-weary and knowledgeable. But pretty soon I began to realize that he was repeating himself. He had a standard line which I think he'd worked out carefully and learned by heart. It was very effective to start with but when I was hearing it for the third time I began to understand that this was as deep as he went.

It has to be said that Randy wasn't the world's greatest intellect. The only subjects on which he could talk with real intelligence and knowledge were contracts and money. When I told him about my contract with Clive he was scandalized at how much it gave him and how little it gave me.

'But don't worry about it,' he added. 'You're a minor so it's not enforceable.'

'Are you sure?' I mused.

'You can walk out of it any time you like.'

That was useful to know. I listened carefully to Randy's talk of stocks, shares, and tax havens, storing up useful information, but at other times it was tough keeping a conversation going. Out of bed Randy could be a terrible bore.

In fact, he wasn't so hot *in* bed either. He'd developed that technique of using his tongue to counter the fact that his energy was flagging. He never came into me properly until the very last moment, and then it was all over in seconds. Sometimes he didn't come into me at all, but expected me to be satisfied with what we'd already done. At first I didn't mind too much. I enjoyed making love in this new way and, as I've said, Randy's tongue was a very special instrument.

But in the long run it couldn't replace a decent screw with a lovely great cock inside me, filling me up. I began to think nostalgically of Clive who might be unimaginative but boy! when he screwed you, you stayed screwed.

One night I couldn't stand it any longer. Randy had been off form that evening because his back was giving him some trouble, and now I was in dire need. The Rolls dropped me at Phil and Donny's house but as soon as I was inside I called a taxi to take me to Clive's.

I still had my key and I slipped in quietly, crossing my fingers that I'd find him alone. I knew he was dating a very starry theatre actress now but she came over after the evening performance and might not be there yet.

Clive looked out of the flat as I crept upstairs. 'Are you alone?' I demanded urgently.

'For the moment, but she'll be here in half an hour.'

'This won't take that long,' I assured him, ripping open his flies.

He saw at once that the situation was desperate, and pulled up my dress. We had each other standing there, leaning against the wall. It felt good! It felt great! It felt outstanding! His cock was enormous inside me, driving and driving me against the wall.

When we'd both come we stood locked together, him still inside, while we caught our breath. 'What are you doing to me?' he said frantically. 'She'll be here any minute. She's forty. She likes young men because of their energy.' He started to move against me again and I answered him in gasps.

'So be energetic.'

'How can I after this?'

'You'll manage, Clive. You're the best.'

'I'm damned well going to have to be.'

We came explosively and then collapsed against the wall, holding each other up weakly. Then Clive jumped.

'That's her car outside,' he said. 'I know the sound. You'll have to go out by the back way.'

I shot down the stairs. Clive hastily zipped himself up and went to the front door. To be strictly accurate, he tottered to the front door. As I slipped out I sent the lady my silent apologies.

I'll never forget the day Randy took me to visit the set of *Force Field*. I had the boys do a specially good job on me. We all agreed that this was no time for the sweet country girl look, so Donny gave my hair the tousled, bed-swept appearance and Phil made me up to knock their eyes out. It was he who chose my white skin-tight pants and helped ease me into them. They were so clinging that I couldn't wear tights or even the tiniest pair of panties underneath, but that was all right – I wasn't wearing a bra under the blue silk shirt either.

Randy called for me in the chauffeur-driven limousine that the studio sent for him every morning, and together we swept out to the studio. It was a bit early in the day for me, but we made up for it by drinking champagne.

The film was an action adventure thriller, all about how Randy saved the world by jumping out of helicopters and getting runaway lorries under control. Of course they got stuntmen to do those bits. The film company had to think of the insurance and Randy had to think of his back.

There were three women, all of whom he loved and left before climbing aboard his private Lear jet and flying off into the sunset. On the day I went he was filming a clinch with Delia Linnett, who was playing the 'mature' love interest. I was dying to meet her because she'd always been my idea of a star.

But when I got up close she was a bit of a disappointment. Her publicity biogs said she was thirty-three, but she must have been at least forty-five. It took a lot of cunning camera work to sustain the illusion of beauty. Her close-ups, for instance, were always shot from slightly above, to hide the fact that the line of her jaw was blurring.

But what caused her face the most damage was the fact that she looked so bad tempered whenever the cameras were off her. Or perhaps it was just me she didn't like. She kept looking daggers in my direction, and when Sax Kalloway, the director, said to me, 'My god, you're so young. I mean *really* young. I'd forgotten what the genuine article looked like,' I knew Delia would have liked to kill me.

Sax was about forty but his hair was completely white and the effect was devastatingly attractive. He hopped everywhere on the set like an agitated mosquito, and looked me up and down in a way I was getting used to by now. I didn't mind. I knew I could bear scrutiny. Then he called out to someone, 'Get a camera on her, *quick.*'

He made me pose, turning this way and that, murmuring, 'Beautiful. The camera just loves you. What's your name? No, don't tell me. Write it down, and your address and number.'

I did so. Delia, who'd been watching cynically, drawled, 'And that's the last you'll ever hear of it, darling. Sax papers his walls with those bits of paper, and sells the numbers to his friends who want a cheap lay. Don't you, sweetie?'

Sax cupped her face between his hands, gave her a lingering kiss, smiled deeply into her eyes, and murmured, 'If anyone should know about cheap lays it's you, darling. Now get your spiteful ass out of here.'

Delia flounced off. Randy appeared from his dressing-room looking bronzed and athletic, courtesy of the make-up girl, and Sax ordered them into place on the set. I stayed out of sight and watched avidly. I wanted to pick up tips for when I was being filmed.

Delia was playing the wife of the villain who was secretly in love with Randy. He'd just escaped from a murder attempt and his face had a discreetly placed bruise to indicate the desperate danger he'd been through. She was wearing a see-through négligé. Randy climbed over the window sill of her bedroom, crept up behind her and dropped a kiss on her bare shoulders. Their eyes met in the mirror and a glance of smouldering intent passed between them.

It took ten takes to get it right. Delia kept fussing about the lights and every time they started again Randy produced smouldering intent right on cue.

56

I noticed that however often they did it he always smouldered in exactly the same way, like someone turning on a tap. At last Sax shouted, 'Cut it and print it.' Delia stormed off in a temper and Randy looked as if a morning's hard smouldering had left him fed-up.

It was lunchtime. He beckoned me to follow him to his trailer and our meals were served there. Evidently someone had told him about Sax's interest in me.

'Is that what you'd like?' he asked. 'To get into films?'

I shrugged. 'It might be fun,' I said, remembering what Clive had taught me about not sounding too keen.

'There's a small part still going in this,' he said casually. 'It's only a couple of lines, but it would make a start for you.'

'Perhaps that's what Sax had in mind,' I mused.

He slipped an arm round me. 'Yes but sweetie, it's *me* who has to have it in mind, or no deal.'

'I don't understand. Sax is the director.'

'But I have casting control.'

I gave him a look that I knew turned his knees to water. 'You wouldn't refuse me one little thing, would you . . . Randy?' I put everything I had into breathing his name so that it carried memories of all our most successful beddings. I saw the heat come up into his face beneath his make-up, and he nearly dropped the coffee he was holding in his other hand.

'I can't refuse you anything, you know that,' he said hoarsely and slid his fingers into my shirt, caressing my bare breasts urgently. 'Do you know what I'd like to do to you?' he gasped.

'Mmm, but they'll be calling for you at any minute,' I whispered.

He got up and locked the trailer door. 'We've just got time if we're quick,' he said.

I was already stripping off my pants. The notion of a quickie really appealed to me, and it appealed to me even more when I saw how it had affected Randy. When he unzipped his trousers his cock was bigger than I'd ever seen it, surging out and standing proudly at an angle. I couldn't wait to get it into me and I leapt on to him while he was still standing. He placed his two hands under my buttocks, pulling me close while I wrapped my legs round him, squeezing him as hard as I could while his organ came up inside me and I bore down on it. It was the first time I'd ever had a man in this position and I promised myself it wouldn't be the last.

There was a knock on the door and the handle rattled. A voice called, 'You're wanted on set, Mr. Berrick.'

'I'm just coming,' he yelled back.

That struck us both as terribly funny and we choked with mirth while it was all happening. My body shook with laughter and excitement at the same time and the two sensations reacted on each other till I was going out of my mind with pleasure. We came together riotously and afterwards we were both drained and happy.

'I'll talk to Sax about a part for you,' he said as he was zipping himself up.

I was so delighted that I tried to kiss him, but he fended me off. 'Don't start that again,' he pleaded. 'I've got to re-do my make-up as it is.'

As he was about to leave he paused and said, 'I'm sure you won't mind doing one more little favour for me, will you?'

'Of course,' I assured him. 'What is it?'

'We-ell, let's just say that you'll know it when it happens,' he said mysteriously.

I didn't see him for a couple of days because I had a big modelling shoot, but I did a lot of thinking. Randy had been at his absolute all-time best in the trailer, and I thought I knew why. At other times he was trying to prolong our love-making because he knew I expected great things of him, and as he felt his energy flagging he got tense and worried. Result – disaster. But with a quickie he could relax. Result – wow! I decided that in future I'd arrange as many quickies as possible and then we'd both be happy.

But it didn't work out like that.

I had a phone call from a man called Jordan Adams, who said he worked for the *Sunday* **** – well never mind the exact name. It was a rag that went in for lurid exposure pieces.

'How about doing a two part feature for us?' he said. 'I'll ghost write it and you just tell me the facts.'

'What facts?' I asked cautiously.

He roared with laughter. 'Randolph Berrick's girl-friend asks what facts! That's good. I like it. A touch of innocence will go down well. Here's what we do. You pose for some really sexy pictures for us. Then you talk to me for a couple of days, tell me the spicy bits, how good he is in bed. I already have a tentative headline for Part One: 'He Isn't Called "Randy" For Nothing Says Sexy Honey.' Nice, isn't it? Then you give me the low-down on what he likes doing, what turns him on. How many times a night can he manage it and for how long? Has he ever asked you to do anything really unusual? Then you collect a cheque for ten thousand pounds? How does that grab you?'

I'd listened to him in such outrage that I couldn't find the words to interrupt. Finally I managed to say, 'I think that's the most disgraceful suggestion I've ever heard. The idea that I'd betray a friend by discussing our private life in a newspaper. . .' I trailed off, fuming. What sort of person did they think I was?

'Well of course I understand that you're a nice girl with high principles, who likes to be loyal,' Jordan said easily. 'So just for you I'll make it twelve thousand.'

'You're crazy,' I spluttered. 'I just couldn't do a thing like that to Randy. He trusts me.'

'Fifteen thousand.'

'I wouldn't do it even for twenty thousand.'

'Sorry Honey, I'm not falling for that one. Fifteen thousand is my final word.'

'And my final word is to tell you that you're a disgusting worm who ought to be trodden on.'

'I don't know what sort of game you're playing – '

'No game. I won't do it. Is that clear, or would you like me to spell it out for you in sky writing?' I was breathing fire by this time.

'But I thought you – that is, I understood – oh, hell!' He rang off.

I tried to call Randy at the studio but he was on set. I left a message but it was three hours before he called me back.

'Jordan Adams has just rung me,' he began in a terse voice that didn't sound like his normal self.

'So he wanted to get his oar in first, did he? Randy, he's the most terrible man. He actually wanted me to talk about our private life for millions of people to read. And when I said no he thought I was just trying to raise the price. But I sent him off with a flea in his ear.'

'I know you did, you silly bitch,' Randy exploded. 'That's what he called me to complain about. You were supposed to say yes.'

I couldn't take in what I was hearing. 'You mean – you knew about this?'

'Don't be bloody stupid, darling!'

So much for the man who thought swearing in front of a woman was a desecration. This was the real Randy coming out.

'Of course I knew,' he snapped. 'I set it up.'

'You *wanted* me to talk about what we do together?'

Down the line I could hear him groan. Then he began to speak slowly and patiently, as if to an idiot.

'Of course I wanted it! I'm forty-eight. What do you think people say when they see me with a girl of sixteen? They envy me. They say Randolph Berrick must still be something if he can pull a young, beautiful girl. You were supposed to tell the world just how "something" I am.' His voice was rising with every word and I could hear rage and frustration throbbing through it. 'You were supposed to say it was like being screwed by a tiger. Was that too much to ask? Just one tiny little favour I expected from you in return for everything I've given you, plus you'd have got fifteen thousand smackers into the bargain. And you ballsed it up.' He was almost crying.

'So this was the favour you wanted of me,' I snapped, thoroughly indignant in my turn. 'Why didn't you just say so instead of being mysterious?'

'Because I thought you'd have the intelligence to realize it without needing to have the facts of life explained to you in words of one bloody syllable! I should have known better. You know what's the trouble with you, Honey? You're a lousy, self-centred bitch! You think of no-one but yourself.'

'I was only trying to be loyal to you,' I yelled down the phone. 'I didn't expect to find that you've been manipulating me all the time.'

'Grow up! We've been manipulating each other. How else do you think things are done?'

'It's not how I do things,' I said firmly.

'Now look, Honey, you *owe* me.'

'Oh, *do* I?'

'And I'm calling in the debts. I've told Jordan you're just a sweet old-fashioned girl who only refused because she thought I wouldn't like it. But now I've given my permission you're happy to co-operate.'

'Like hell I am!'

'Honey, you will do that interview if I have to drag you there by the scruff of your neck.'

'You might drag me there but would you like to bet on what I'd tell him?'

There was a silence.

'No interview, no film part,' he said at last.

'Mr. Berrick,' I said sweetly, 'it would give me great pleasure to tell you exactly where you can put your film part.' I slammed down the phone.

That was the end of that relationship.

I suppose I was crazy. Fifteen thousand for three days work isn't to be sneezed at, and if Randy had asked me beforehand in a straightforward way I might have done it to oblige him. But I was incensed at the way he'd tried to use me without telling me. It was dawning on me that being used was the thing I had to look out for. I didn't mind a man doing well out of me if he was open about it (after all, I was doing very nicely myself), but I hated it when they pretended it was all straight from the heart. Clive had used me as a stepping stone to Randy, and now Randy had tried it on. In future I'd be more aware.

I found myself thinking about Steve and how honourably he'd behaved, running away from temptation for my sake. He looked even better now I'd discovered what snakes other men could be, and sometimes in the early hours I'd lie awake, thinking of him, wondering where he was and if he ever thought of me.

Clive was philosophical about the break-up. His career had taken a leap and he didn't need Randy any more. In fact, Randy went right on booking Clive as if nothing had happened. I guess photographers who can take years off an actor don't grow on trees.

The boys gave me a new look and some motherly advice on how to handle men now I was broadening my sphere of interests. Clive celebrated the new 'me' with a set of pictures that were a knock-out. I told him I wanted a fair modelling fee this time or I'd find another photographer.

'You can't,' he said. 'You belong to me. Read your contract.'

'Clive darling, I was sixteen when I signed it and it's unenforceable,' I said sweetly. 'So why don't you take that contract and stuff it – '

'All right, I get your drift,' he said hastily.

'So cough up, there's a good boy. You've made a mint out of me.'

He groaned but agreed. Then, just to show him there were no hard feelings I gave him a kiss, and one thing led to another. We were friends again.

Chapter Five

I was beginning to get invitations to open things like supermarkets. The money was good and afterwards I'd receive a card that let me buy things at a discount. By that time I was thinking of getting a place of my own and was hoping to be offered an engagement at a store where they sold nice furniture, but so far I was out of luck.

Then I got a letter asking me to open the Market Dyson Agricultural Show. I wondered what you got for doing that. A free pig? I looked up Market Dyson and found that it was a country town in Hampshire 'with strong farming connections, that borders on the grounds of Dyson Hall, ancestral home of the Marquesses of Dyson since the fifteenth century'. There was a photograph of the Hall which looked grand and ancient, and a potted history of the family who'd obviously been pretty rapacious and colourful.

According to *Burke's Peerage* the present Marquess was called Portland Cedric Arnsworth Harold James Francis. . . . There were about ten more names but I gave up after that.

The show was being held in the grounds of Dyson Hall and I realized this was my chance to meet a real lord. So I called the secretary of the Agricultural Association, who'd invited me, and said I'd do it.

Deciding what to wear gave the boys and me a real headache. I now had a public who expected me to look like something out of *Dallas*. On the other hand, I felt that for meeting an aristocrat I should aim for understated elegance. We mulled it over until Donny said, 'Darling, you couldn't look understated if you tried for a fortnight.' Which was true. So we settled for *Dallas*.

Donny got me a super dress made of pinkish cream silk, very tight-waisted, with a skirt that ended six inches above my knees. I thought the front was a bit low cut for the occasion, which struck Donny as terribly funny.

'You've never objected to showing your mammary glands before,' he remarked, with perfect truth.

'Yes, but this is an Agricultural Show,' I reminded him. 'I don't want them to mistake me for one of the cows.'

'*No* chance of that,' he said, smiling. 'Show it off while you've got it, darling. You won't have it forever.'

For the journey to Hampshire I hired a chauffeur-driven white Rolls convertible. I had the top up for the journey, to protect my hair, and took it down when we reached Market Dyson. Luckily it was a beautiful summer day.

I could see people nudging each other and pointing as I passed. The wrought iron gates to the grounds were already open when I arrived and quite a lot of the public had already gone in. The driver had to go slowly because they were blocking the path and a murmur ran through the crowd when they saw me. I actually heard someone say, 'There's Honey. I've seen her picture.' And someone rushed forward to thrust an autograph book into the car. I signed it and smiled in a way that I hoped was gracious. It was like being a film star.

The association secretary came to greet me and introduce me to the committee members. I said the right things but all the time I was looking out for the Marquess. I couldn't see anyone who looked likely though.

I got up onto a dais and made my speech. I put in a few jokes which got a good laugh, declared the show officially open and everyone clapped. Several local newspapers were there and I gave them all interviews, trying to say something different to each one. That was the hardest part because they all asked the same questions. Was I heart-broken at breaking up with Randolph Berrick? What did I think about his new girl friend, etc? I gave them the line about parting the best of friends. What else was there to do? I could hardly say he was a vain, self-centred little toad who couldn't lay a carpet properly never mind a woman, could I?

The local television station had cameras there and they followed me about asking me to pose with various animals, including Buttercup who'd won the prize for 'Prettiest Cow'. I could just see what the caption writers would make of that one, and from the way Buttercup was eyeing me I don't think she fancied sharing the spotlight. But there was no way out of it, so I put my arm round her neck and whispered in her ear that it she dared to kick me I'd kick her right back. She must have understood because she was as good as gold.

At last I spotted the man who must be the Marquess. He had a coldly noble face and looked as if he had a bad smell under his nose. I approached him and said, 'Excuse me, are you Lord Dyson?'

I thought he was going to faint. 'My name is Greaves, miss,' he informed me haughtily. 'I have had the honour to be his lordship's butler for the last fourteen years.'

'Well, where is Lord Dyson?' I asked, exasperated.

'His lordship is in town, miss,' Greaves declared loftily. 'He permits the use of his grounds for charitable purposes but does not feel it incumbent on him to be present.'

So that was that. Snooty so-and-so! Who did he think he was? I went back to the show, not the animals this time but the fair where there were roundabouts and stalls with coconuts. The photographers begged me to get on the big carousel with the horses that ride up and down, and they all stood below me trying to photograph up my skirt whenever the horse rose.

After that I was dying to spend a penny and there was a queue as long as your arm outside the portable conveniences. I thought of all the loos there must be in the house. I crept round the back where a door stood open, slipped in and found myself in a small corridor with white walls and flagstones on the floor. I followed it to the end where there was another door, which I pushed open.

I was in a huge hall, a couple of storeys high. Two of the walls were hung with pikes and spears, and one bore a vast coat of arms with several mythological animals and the legend, *Non Onmis Moriar*. I'd been looking up the Dysons so I knew that this was their family motto and meant 'I shall never completely die.'

The forth wall was covered by a tapestry depicting a hunting scene with people in medieval clothes. There were six suits of armour, one at each corner of the black and white tiled floor, and two guarding the bottom steps of a broad staircase. I'd wandered into the Great Hall of Dyson House.

I tiptoed across it, pushed open one side of a pair of oak doors that were slightly ajar, and crept inside. I didn't mean to creep, but the place had that effect on me.

I discovered a room lined with leather-bound books all the way up to the high ceiling. There was a fireplace big enough for three men to stand in, lots of scattered rugs and some shabby leather furniture. Despite its size it looked cosy. A desk stood by one of the tall windows, and at it sat a young man in an old brown cardigan with mended sleeves. He had a lean aesthetic face and was as cosily shabby as the rest of the room. It was reassuring to find a librarian whose appearance was so exactly right.

I coughed and he looked up and smiled at me. He looked nice, not handsome but kind. His hair was receding and he wore steel spectacles but I guessed him to be no more than thirty.

'Can you tell me where to find the – er?' I asked awkwardly.

'I'll show you.' He got up and I found he was at least six foot. He led me to what looked like a solid wall of shelving, turned a knob and pulled the shelves out like a door. Beyond them lay a small bathroom.

'Thanks,' I said gratefully and scooted inside.

There were fresh white towels, scented soap and lovely blue and white tiles that looked like antiques. I freshened up and came out feeling better although my feet were getting tired.

'Who'd have thought there'd be a bathroom in there?' I said when I came out.

'There w-wasn't originally,' said the young man. 'The last Lord Dyson but one put it in. He spent a lot of time in here and he got fed up having to traipse miles to one of the official bathrooms. Besides, this w-way he could avoid his wife.'

I was charmed by his little stammer. He was

obviously shy and I felt very protective towards him.

'Didn't he like his wife?' I said, settling on the sofa and tucking my feet under me.

'No, he married her because she had enough money to restore the house.'

'That's not very nice.'

'It was the done thing in those days,' he said apologetically.

'By the way, I'm Honey,' I explained.

He leaned over me to shake hands which gave him a grandstand view of my breasts. He looked down appreciatively and smiled at me. Something in that smile gave me a familiar throb between my thighs. I'd never thought I could fancy a many who was losing his hair, but now I remembered reading that baldness was a sign of terrific masculinity. Apparently it's the male hormone that makes it drop out. And of course women keep their hair, so it figures, really. Anyway, I suddenly felt that I'd been wrong to dismiss the theory without personal experimentation.

'M-my name's Myles,' he said. 'I recognized you from your pictures. Everyone's very excited about your coming today.'

'Everyone except the rotten Marquess,' I grumbled. 'I was really looking forward to meeting a lord, and then he isn't here.'

Myles' lips twitched. 'You don't mean you came here just to meet him?'

'Yes, I did. But he doesn't sound any nicer than his ancestor. Just think of him making you work in the library instead of going to the fete.'

'I don't mind. I don't feel easy in crowds,' he said simply.

'It's nice of you to say that, but I'll bet your boss is a monster.'

'I'm afraid the Marquesses have all been rather

unsavoury characters,' Myles agreed. 'The one who p-put in the bathroom used to entertain his lady friends in here, which of course was another reason for wanting to have it self-contained.'

'After marrying his wife for her money he shut her out and had women in here?' I echoed, scandalized.

'Oh yes – "had" being the operative word. He had them right there on that very sofa.'

At the words the sofa seemed to come alive under me. I thought of them romping away just where I was now, and when I looked up I knew that Myles had read my thoughts. 'I don't believe it,' I said. 'There isn't room.'

'Yes there is. It's three feet wide so two people can just about squeeze on.'

'Show me.'

He came to sit on the edge of the sofa. 'You'll have to lie down,' he said. 'It doesn't work with you sitting up.'

I slithered down until I was in a lying position and the movement made my dress ride up to the tops of my thighs. Quite naturally Myles put his hand on my leg, but instead of sliding it further up he let it drift down to my feet, moving slowly, letting his fingers linger behind my knee, on my calf, my ankle, while I purred with delight. This man was clever enough to do the unexpected.

'Your feet must be hurting after a day in these shoes,' he said sympathetically. 'Here – isn't that easier?'

'Mmm,' I said as he slipped them off.

'Poor Honey. Are you very tired?'

'Exhausted,' I said. He was rubbing my feet and it was blissful. He began to massage my legs, rubbing his hands almost up to the top then down again. My cunt was tingling to have him touch it but although he brushed tantalizingly near several times he always retreated again. I arched my back, sending him a message that he was getting through to me, and immediately he slid his fingers right up to the top of my legs, letting them linger just long enough to check that I wasn't wearing panties.

Instead of lying down beside me he slid to the floor and knelt upright, drawing my hands to the zipper of his trousers. I was curious to see how things were down there. What I discovered made me feel very good indeed. Myles might be a lamb on the surface but he was a lion underneath. I cradled his giant organ in my hands, caressing it worshipfully, aching to put it to his proper use.

'D-do you think that will do?' he asked shyly.

'Oh yes,' I assured him. 'That will do nicely.'

If I lay flat on the sofa it was just the right height for me to take in my mouth. It felt huge in there, warm and pulsating with life. I caressed it with lips and tongue and teeth, nibbling very gently while it swelled to even greater proportions.

When he drew away I discovered that while I'd been preoccupied he'd opened the buttons of my dress, exposing my breasts. I thought he'd lie down beside me but I hadn't yet learned what a highly original man Myles was. To my surprise he gently swivelled me round to face the front, then placed my legs one each side of his body, easing them down until my feet touched the ground. He was still kneeling upright on the floor so this made us just the right height for each other, and when he cupped my bottom in his hands and eased me forward we fitted together so sweetly and perfectly that I wanted to squeal with excitement.

I'd never made love in this position before. It's the sort of thing you see in books and think, 'Ye gods, they must be double jointed!' but actually it was very comfortable and pleasurable. Later, when

I could think straight, I worked out I was receiving him at a different angle, and so being stimulated in different places. At the time I just knew that it was fantastic.

Myles had his hands free and could caress my breasts as he thrust into me. The feeling of being titillated in two places was fantastic. In this position I had less control than I was used to but Myles was such a shy, gentle young man that I didn't mind. I just had enough presence of mind to murmur, 'We ought to have locked the door,' before forgetting everything else as he drove his huge cock into me while his fingers teased my nipples to peaks. I came with sensational force, feeling vibrations pounding through me.

To my amazement he showed no sign of coming. How could a man remain that big and active for so long? He smiled at my look of surprise and put his hands beneath my knees, urging my legs up until I could cross my feet behind his back, then cupping my bottom again and lifting it a few inches, keeping his hands there for support. Now I could arch against him more easily and I began to do so, squeezing him between my legs and having a whale of a time while the painted eyes of the Dyson ancestors glared down at us. But of course they'd seen all this before.

At last I came again, and this time Myles came too, plunging into me with tremendous force and smiling down into my face so that I felt a lovely sense of togetherness with him. When we'd got our breath back we disentangled ourselves carefully. Myles helped me to sit up and I dropped my feet to the floor. But he stayed there between my legs and we draped our arms around each other, exhausted, laughing and happy. Now I knew about men who were losing their hair. It was all true.

Then, to my horror, I heard Greaves' voice outside the door. 'Get dressed quickly,' I hissed. 'If the Marquess finds out he'll probably fire you.

But he didn't seem bothered and my efforts to prod him into activity only made him clasp me more firmly. We were still in that position when the door opened and Greaves came in. He didn't turn a hair.

'A bottle of my best champagne, Greaves,' Myles called out.

'Certainly, my lord,' the butler said, and departed as straightfaced as when he came in.

I pushed Myles away and looked at him accusingly. *'You're . . .'*

'The rotten, snooty Marquess,' he admitted, his eyes twinkling.

I started to laugh, and Myles laughed too. 'I'm sorry,' he said. 'I should have told you earlier but I meet so many girls who only want me for the title that I couldn't resist one who thought I was the librarian. Forgive me?'

'Of course,' I said at once. I couldn't bear a grudge against a man who'd just given me such a fantastic experience. Besides, I'd laid a lord! Fancy that!

'How can your name be Myles when it's Portland?' I asked.

He made a face. 'Would *you* want to be called Portland? Myles is one of my other names – the tenth I think – and my friends always use it.'

'Why did Greaves tell me you were away.'

'Those were the orders I gave him. I get bored by these agricultural shows. I nearly went to this one in order to see you, but I d-didn't think you'd be interested in me.'

'How could you have thought that?' I murmured, kissing the base of his neck.

'Most people think I'm a pretty dull fellow except for the title,' he confessed.

'But most people don't know you as I do,' I chuckled.

We arranged ourselves rather more sedately for when Greaves came back. He bore a tray with a bottle of Krug on it, and filled two glasses for us. When he'd gone Myles and I toasted each other.

'Here's to many more happy occasions,' he said.

I sent my hired car away and stayed at Dyson Hall that night. Myles showed me the house: not all of it, because that would take ages, but the best bits. I loved the huge four-poster beds and looked forward to making love in one. 'We will, soon,' he promised. 'In fact, we'll make love in every bedroom in this house.'

'How many bedrooms are there?' I asked.

'About two hundred.'

'*How many?*'

'I wasn't thinking of going through them all tonight,' he said, his eyes twinkling. 'I thought we'd spread it out a bit.'

I was disappointed that Myles didn't live in any of the grand apartments, but in a cosy little flat in the west wing. His bedroom was small and austere like a monk's cell, but there was nothing austere about what we did in there. We both knew something really special had happened between us.

Next day I had to be back in London to work. Myles drove me to town and collected me in the evening. We had dinner in the same restaurant where Randy had taken me, and the first thing I saw was the old phoney himself, holding hands with his latest flame. He shrugged when he saw me and looked dismissively at Myles. But his girl-friend's eyes widened and she whispered something in his ear. Evidently she knew who Myles was, and Randy's jaw dropped when he heard. I liked that.

Myles' London house was closed up so we went

back to a flat he'd borrowed from a friend. There wasn't time to drive to Dyson Hall because I had to be at work early next day. We went on like this for a week. I asked Myles what he did with himself during the day but he became mysterious.

One night as we were having dinner he said, 'My friend will be back soon. He'll want his flat back.'

'Oh dear,' I said, wishing I had my own place, but London prices were prohibitive and it was still a fantasy.

'It's your birthday in a few days, isn't it?' Myles said.

'That's right. I'll be seventeen.'

He pushed an envelope across the table to me. 'Happy birthday.'

Inside the envelope was a door key with a label attached, and on the label was written, 35, Ferris Mews.

'It's yours,' Myles explained.

He'd bought me my own flat for a birthday present. I didn't know what to say. I was over the moon.

'It's only a tiny place,' he said apologetically, 'because I had to buy it with ready cash to avoid my accountant getting suspicious.

'Can we go and look at it now?'

'But it's empty and there isn't any electricity –'

'Now – *please*.'

He laughed and agreed.

He was right, it *was* a tiny place, just two rooms plus bathroom and kitchen, but I loved it because it was mine and because dear, sweet, kindly Myles had given it to me. We couldn't get any lights on but there were no curtains at the window and the street lights shone in enough to show me my new little home.

I went and leaned out of the window, gazing at the mews below. There was a party going on in the house opposite and suddenly the door opened and a very handsome young man came out into the street.

'Hallo,' he said, staring up to me. 'Who are you?'

'I'm Honey,' I called back. 'I live here now.'

He leaned against one of the parked cars and contemplated me. He was more than a bit merry. 'We're going to be neighbours,' he said. 'I live here too.'

I was about to say something else when I felt my dress being pushed up to my hips, then Myles' hand slipping between my legs from behind. I knew he wouldn't be visible from the street below, so I stayed as I was and went on chatting.

'I'm sure I've heard of you,' the young man said.

'You might have done,' I told him. Myles' fingers were teasing me gently now, making me wet. I gripped the window sill.

'Weren't you the girl who paraded naked in the House of Commons?' the man called from below.

I gasped as I felt Myles' huge cock sliding between the tops of my thighs, finding its way to where my cunt was ready for him, easing slowly into me. 'Wh-what did you say?' I called down.

The man repeated the question. I had to concentrate hard to hear it because the great, beautiful thing was sliding in and out of me with with very leisurely movements as though we could afford to spend all night standing at the window like this. I wondered what would happen if anyone could see him after all. I was past caring. I wished the man below would go away.

'Yes, that was me,' I agreed.

'And I've seen you on that celebrity game show, haven't I?'

'Yes – yes –' I'd done several of those shows. What did it matter which one he was talking about? I eased my legs further apart to give Myles greater scope and

76

he redoubled his efforts, still moving slowly but with great power and determination.

'I'd like to get to know you better, Honey. My name's Joseph Crane, by the way.'

'Really?' I was almost ready to come. The strain of holding still while waves of aching pleasure racked me was almost unbearable.

'Why don't you come down and join the party?'

'Not tonight Joseph,' I gasped.

'I'll come up and visit you then.'

'No,' I yelled as Myles drove hard into me, thrusting again and again. I felt myself being drawn back into the room. Myles slammed the window shut and we finished what we were doing in a few glorious seconds.

Afterwards, gasping, leaning against the wall, I said, 'And to think I never knew what an odd sense of humour you have.'

He kissed me. 'It wasn't entirely a joke. I know what a handsome fellow your new neighbour is, and I'm a jealous man.'

The cunning devil! Under that shy, gentle exterior Myles was as sly as a fox. He'd made sure that whenever I talked to Joseph I'd be remembering Myles. It was the nicest form of jealousy I've ever come across.

Chapter Six

I adored Myles. He was kind, charming and funny besides being dynamic in bed. Despite this I found he was terribly unsure of himself, convinced that women only wanted him for his title, and was thrilled that I'd romped with him thinking he was only a librarian. He knew I really admired his prowess as a lover, and that made him feel terrific.

I'd developed my own grading system for men, rather like hotels. Myles looked like one-star bed and breakfast until you knew him. Then you discovered he was five-star deluxe.

I soon discovered what even tiny flats in that part of London cost and I was astounded. *Ready cash!* It was my first hint of just how wealthy Myles was. I'd always thought the modern aristocracy had been impoverished by taxes. It's what they like us to think. But no way! That's just their story to stop us wanting to take it away from them. The Dysons had been stowing away wealth for centuries and there was enough left for Myles to live up to his title. And from what I saw of his aristocratic friends that was true all round.

My affair with Myles was a fairy-tale come true. He preferred a quiet life himself, but knew I was thrilled with his world so took me out in it. During that summer we went for a quick holiday in Venice. I'd always wanted to ride in a gondola, but it wasn't quite as I'd pictured it. Most gondolas were open but ours had a little cabin fixed on top. It was called a *feltz* and consisted of four metal struts clamped on to the sides of the boat, with a roof on top. The 'walls' were black velvet curtains which could be drawn back for the occupants to see outside, or joined, giving complete privacy inside. Although it was midday, when we'd drawn the curtains it was so dark that the outside world might not have existed.

Myles began to kiss and caress me and within seconds I was at fever pitch. But the low wooden seat where we were squashed was uncomfortable, and there was a practical problem. 'We can't do it here,' I hissed frantically. 'There isn't room.'

'We'll see about that,' he murmured, directing me with his hands.

I followed his lead and wriggled onto his lap so that I knelt facing him, with my thighs on either side of his. From outside we heard an anguished yelp. *'Signori – ti prego – '*

'That's the gondolier,' said Myles with a smothered laugh. 'We're rocking the boat.'

His cock was huge, pressing against me, seeking a way in. I touched it, guided it gently to the right place and bore down. Myles cupped my bottom in his hands, drawing me closer to him. We were in the middle of the Grand Canal and from outside the *feltz* we could hear the sounds of a busy city. Motorboats and water-busses chugged past, tourists called out and a police boat siren sounded alarmingly close. All that stood between us and that world were the curtains, and if a wind should happen to lift them we'd probably get arrested. The thought of our danger exhilarated me and I moved harder and faster. Myles groaned and clasped me, the boat swayed violently and from somewhere overhead came the sound of a yell, followed by a huge splash.

As we finished, gasping and clinging to each other, Myles' eyes met mine. 'I think we've lost the gondolier.'

We put our heads out and saw the poor man treading water and shaking his fist at us. A cheer went up from some passing boats, so I guess what we were doing must have been pretty obvious. Myles collected the gondolier and paid him over the odds for his trouble, and we hurried back to Danieli Hotel to finish what we'd started.

When we got back to England he took me to a dance given by the Duke and Duchess of Brainham for their daughter Lady Caroline Harvester-FitzJames. Myles said most of the guests would be young and I should dress as I pleased rather than try to be posh, so I wore gold skin tight pants and a little top made of knitted gold thread. The knitting was quite loose, so you could see I didn't have a bra on.

'Is it all right?' I asked Myles anxiously when I saw him smile. 'I'm not too much, am I?'

'Darling Honey, of course you're "too much". That's why I adore you. Heaven preserve me from girls who aren't enough.'

'Will I make them all stare?'

'With any luck.'

The Duke and Duchess really did stare when I turned up at their house on Myles' arm, but the Duchess recovered enough to welcome me. They say the Duke never recovered at all.

Lady Caroline looked down at me with glacial good breeding. When I saw 'looked down', I mean about seven inches. I wanted to meet her eyes to show I couldn't be intimidated, but I found myself staring straight between the outposts of the flattest chest I've ever seen on a woman. She was tremendously elegant in floating blue silk chiffon and diamonds everywhere, but when I considered that chest I felt good about myself again.

The Brainhams' son, the Earl of Lythal, was about twenty-five and a flashy charmer. He'd fixed his gaze on me as I moved away from the receiving line, so I gave him a little wiggle and heard him say appreciatively, 'Cheeky!'

I gasped when I saw the huge ballroom and five hundred guests. This evening must have cost more than my Dad earned in a year. I lost count of the Dukes Myles introduced me to, but there were enough to make a football team. After a while I got quite blasé about Dukes and stopped wanting to curtsey when I met one.

Most of the girls wore the sort of clothes that showed off 'Mummy's diamonds – not the good ones of course, the other ones,' as I heard one girl put it. Luckily Myles had bought me a matching set of solid gold earrings and bracelet, so I could hold my head up.

I had a great time. The women were all fit to kill me, especially Lady Seraphina Conley, who was a second cousin of Myles. She was terribly possessive about him and kept trying to talk about people they knew but I didn't, but he wouldn't play that game, which was nice of him.

'It's all right, Myles,' I said at last. 'I'm sure you want to talk to your old friends.' And if I did empha- size 'old' just the tiniest little bit, can you blame me? I ignored Seraphina's murderous glance and allowed Lord Lythal to put his arm round my waist. We started to dance energetically together, and I guess my gold pants must have been rather revealing because soon a little crowd was watching. All men.

The music slowed and Lythal pulled me close. It wasn't a great success because, like Myles, he was over six foot, but he leaned down to murmur romantically in my ear, 'Five hundred.'

'Yes I know, it's a big party,' I said, trying not to wrinkle my nose at his horrible aftershave. It probably cost a thousand pounds an ounce, but it was still horrible.

He flashed me his grin. 'No, you know what I mean. It's a lot of money but I reckon you're worth it.'

'Pardon?'

'Five hundred pounds – with an option on a second night at a cut rate.'

The next minute he was hopping about the floor on one leg, clutching his wounded ankle and cursing. My heels were very sharp.

Myles appeared. 'Did he say what I think he said?' he grinned.

'Damned cheek!' I fumed. 'As though I would!'

Myles roared with laughter at Lythal's discomfiture, and we danced the rest of the night away together.

The following month the dance was written up in a society magazine, with me named as 'the belle of the ball'. I heard that Lady Caroline Harvester-FitzJames hurled the magazine out of the window.

I bought a huge bed that filled up the bedroom of my little flat completely. The wardrobes and dressing table had to go in the other room. It was called the living room, but my real living was done in the bedroom. Now I think about it I realize that there was nothing in that flat that was about the kind of person I was inside. There were no discs or cassettes to listen to and my only reading matter was fashion magazines. Everything was connected with how I looked for the cameras and how I interacted with Myles. I couldn't live that way now, but in those days it was enough. I was seventeen and the world was at my feet.

When I could get away from London we retreated to Dyson Hall, and as he'd promised he set about introducing me to all the bedrooms in his own way. There was one called the Queen's Apartment because Queen Elizabeth I had slept there in 1575. We gave that one a miss. After all, she *was* the Virgin Queen. We made up for it by using the Henry VIII Suite six times over!

Myles taught me to ride. I was a bit nervous of horses but it was a good excuse to buy some riding gear, and those tight-fitting breeches really suited me.

The photographers thought so too. We caught some hiding in the bushes, snapping away at us. Myles had them thrown off the estate but it was too late. Next day we were in the tabloids with a story about how we spent every spare moment together and 'wedding bells were in the air'. I was afraid Myles would think I'd set it up to promote my career. I'd have hated that, because although it didn't do me any harm to be hobnobbing with a Marquess it wasn't a career move in the way that going with Randy had been. But Myles only chuckled and said, 'That'll set the cat among the pigeons.'

The only time we ever really disagreed was when he bought me a mink coat and I refused to accept it because I was still 'anti-fur'. He was cross when he couldn't make me change my mind, but he forgave me in the end and bought me a little car instead.

I was thrilled when I learned that Dyson Hall had its own ghost. That just made everything perfect – as long as I didn't meet it.

'But there's nothing to be afraid of,' Myles told me. 'She's a dear old lady who sits by a window doing her embroidery. Nobody's scared of her.'

We were snuggled up together in the ten foot wide bed in the Jacobean Room, planning what we were going to wear for a fancy dress ball the Earl of Ellesmere was giving in London the following month. I toyed with the idea of going as Lady Godiva, but he vetoed that.

I hopped off the bed and headed for the bathroom down the corridor. There wouldn't be anyone about because the servants had orders to stay away from us, so I didn't bother to put anything on.

As soon as I came out of the bathroom I had a feeling of being disorientated. When I opened the door of what I thought was the Jacobean Room I stopped on the threshold. Myles and the huge bed had vanished. In their place was a little old lady sitting in the window, doing her embroidery.

She smiled, and I realized she wasn't scary at all. 'Do come in,' she said. 'I've heard so much about you.'

'I don't usually go about like this,' I said, feeling awkward about being starkers. Still, I thought, perhaps a ghost didn't mind.

'But you have a lovely figure,' she said kindly. 'No wonder Myles is wild about you. I'm Lady Dyson, by the way.'

I knew Myles' mother was dead, so this had to be the ghost. 'Do you mind my asking which one you are?' I said.

'The last but one. You've probably seen my picture in the hall. I was very beautiful, you know,' she added mournfully.

'Do you mean your husband was the rotten one who built the bathroom in the library?' I asked indignantly.

'Yes, that's the one.' She sighed. 'He was a very bad man, but of course, that doesn't bother me now.'

I'd have liked to talk to her some more, but I was getting cold. 'I don't know how it works,' I said, 'but could you send me back where I came from?'

'Where's that?'

'The Jacobean Room. I went to the bathroom but when I came out everything had changed.'

She smiled. 'Go back into the bathroom and you'll see another door. Try that.'

I thanked her and hurried back. Sure enough there was another door, and when I went through it I was in the original corridor again. This time I found the Jacobean Room all right.

'I've seen your ghost,' I told Myles excitedly. 'She's sweet.'

'She thinks you're lovely too.'

'You mean she's appeared to you as well.'

He laughed. 'Darling, that's not a ghost. That's my grandmother. She lives on the corridor parallel to this. She never meets anyone. She's too old and frail. But she was charmed by you.'

'But how do you know that? Mental telepathy?'

'No, a little invention called the telephone. She has one in her room and she called me as soon as you'd gone. She said she thought you had the wrong idea about her. I should have warned you there are two doors to that bathroom.'

'Good grief!' I exclaimed, appalled. 'And she saw me like this.'

'Don't worry. She was a very sporty lady in her day.'

Old Lady Dyson invited me to tea. This time I wore something more appropriate, and her eyes twinkled.

We got on really well and I found myself telling her about the calender Clive was shooting, with a different picture of me in the nude on every page.

'How enterprising,' she said, nodding. 'If you have a beautiful body, you should make the most of it while you're young.'

Which, when you come to think of it, was exactly what Phil and Donny were always telling me.

She also warned me about Lady Seraphina, who'd convinced herself that she and Myles had been engaged in their cradles and it was only a matter of time before he accepted his 'responsibilities' and tied the knot. It was plain Lady Dyson disliked her and was glad to see me occupying all Myles' attention.

'But be warned,' Lady Dyson said. 'She's got her knife into you.'

'I shouldn't think we'll meet again,' I said. 'High Society won't be inviting me into their midst very often.'

Lady Dyson shook her head. 'You're wrong. You'll get a lot of invitations. You're so lovely that they'll see you as a way of scoring off each other. Every girl who's trying to capture Myles will breathe a sigh of relief that you're warding off the competition.'

And I discovered she was right. When Lady Allenbrook was getting up a select little party for Royal Ascot she invited Myles and me, naming me by name. She wasn't angling for Myles, having snared herself an earl the previous year, but she couldn't stand Lady Caroline, whose nose I'd put out of joint at the ball.

Lady Dyson helped me choose a dress because I didn't want to look like *Dallas* this time. We settled on a simple white silk with a longer skirt and a higher neck than I was used to, topped off by a wide-brimmed hat. I was a bit nervous of trying the 'virginal' look. I didn't want to appear as mutton dressed as lamb. But when I saw myself in the mirror I knew there was no fear of that. There was nothing virginal about my face, which seemed to have ripened. It was still young but it was experienced too, and the contrast with the white dress was outrageous.

For Ascot I actually put on underwear. After all, the Queen was going to be there. It seemed only polite to wear knickers.

So that was how I ended up in a private box, sipping champagne and watching the royal family drive along the course. Seraphina was in a box nearby, looking daggers at me and from the satisfied look on Lady Allenbrook's face I could see she felt the invitation to me had been worthwhile. The air crackled with malice. It was all great fun.

Seraphina dropped in to announce that she was going into the Royal Enclosure to say hallo to some friends. She beamed from Myles to me. 'Why don't we all go together?'

That was pure spite because she must have known I didn't have a voucher. Myles had tried to get me one but the lists were closed for years ahead. But as at the ball, Myles loyally refused to leave me, and Seraphina flounced away, evidently having notched up another black mark against my name.

I had a wonderful time that day, actually backing a winner, and receiving another invitation. Lady Mendel was arranging a charity do at the Dorchester. It was to be a fashion parade with her aristocratic friends acting as models. I promised to be one of the models and a few days later found myself dressing and undressing in company with a load of ladyships. Most of them looked like the backs of buses, which perhaps explained why I'd been invited, and made me wonder what personal scores Lady Mendel was settling.

It was in all the papers next day, with captions like, 'Honey in High Society', and speculation about just how far I could go. I'd started to wonder about that too.

For the Ellesmere Ball I'd been to a theatrical hire shop and booked an eighteenth-century dress in white satin. I'd hoped Myles would match me, but he said he wasn't going to look like a 'a damned principal boy', even for me. He wasn't keen on fancy dress at all and said he wanted something that would swathe him like a tent to hide his blushes.

With the dress I wore a gleaming white wig with two ringlets that fell forward over my shoulder. I'd been doubtful about this, feeling that my own hair was better, but when I saw myself in the wig I loved the different look it gave me. Besides, the bodice was very low cut so my other assets were well displayed.

To my surprise the dress had gaps in the skirt, front and back. When I mentioned it the girl at the costumiers said, 'They're called plackets. At one time all the grand ladies had them, so that they could be ready for their lovers at any time.' She laughed and added, 'If you're going to the Ellesmere Midsummer Ball, you'll need them.'

'You mean it's that sort of do?' I asked.

'It's always "that sort of do" with them,' she said cynically.

Myles finally found something that swathed him like a tent. It was a Venetian costume that consisted of a floor-length black cloak with a half cloak over it. On his head he wore a black three-cornered hat with a length of black material hanging from the inner brim, making a sort of curtain all round his head. There were gaps for the eyes, nose and mouth, but the upper part of his face was covered in a white mask with a beaky nose. It looked terribly hot and uncomfortable to me, but Myles loved it because, he said, 'I'll be able to wear jeans and shirtsleeves underneath.' And I had to admit that with his height and those flowing black robes he looked mysterious and sinister and fantastically sexy. I made up my mind that I would have him while he was dressed like that.

It took the gilt off the gingerbread a little when I discovered that the costume had been Seraphina's idea. She worried me more when she was being friendly than when she was being openly nasty.

On the night Myles collected me in a convertible Rolls with the top down. As we drove to Ellesmere House he filled me in about our hosts, although I already knew a certain amount about them from gossip I'd heard.

The Earl and Countess of Ellesmere were in their twenties and belonged to the 'new' breed of aristocrats, which meant that he'd already been convicted of drug peddling and all the influence of his family had been exerted behind scenes to get him a suspended sentence. His father had been trying to disinherit him when he died. Now the new Earl was having a whale of a time, giving wild parties and getting through his fortune at an alarming rate. The Countess's contribution to their lifestyle was a couple of children from past liaisons. They didn't share the same father.

The Ellesmere Midsummer Ball had always been noted as a larky occasion but under the present incumbents it was becoming notorious. The press was out in force and the photographers snapped like mad as we approached. There were calls of 'Who's the lucky feller, Honey? Let's see his face. Is it the Marquess?' But I just smiled and refused to give anything away.

I'd thought I was becoming blasé about society but I have to admit I gawped when I saw the great ballroom. It was hung from floor to ceiling with silk curtains so that it resembled the inside of a luxurious tent. Through white pillars I could see another room, almost as large, which had been arranged for eating. Round tables had been piled high with food styled into exotic arrangements that looked as if you could do anything with them except eat them.

It was like a gigantic theatrical set, got up in a combination of Greek and Roman by someone who hadn't really known the difference, or hadn't cared. Myles had told me that the catering staff were really 'entertainers' hired for their looks and their skills in making people feel at home, and I could see why. They were all in tiny little tunics that barely came down to the tops of their thighs and were slit down the sides. Couches were strewn around on which people lounged to eat or otherwise amuse themselves and the whole thing was permeated by an atmosphere of delicious decadence. This wasn't just a ball, this was an orgy.

Everybody was in fancy dress and many were masked. Several of the girls wore Roman draperies which were lower in the bosom even than mine.

'It used to be the custom for unmarried girls to go round like that,' Myles said.

'How convenient,' I murmured. There was a Regency gentleman, two cavaliers and a wizard who were finding it *very* convenient.

I spotted a tiger, with a *papier mâché* head, stretched out on a sofa being ministered to by Mary Queen of Scots.

'That's clever,' I said to Myles. 'With that head on, no-one has a clue who he is.'

'Always assuming that it's a he?' Myles murmured through his mask.

'But – but Myles – look what Queen Mary is doing to him!'

'Or her?' Myles said wickedly.

It hadn't shocked me with Phil and Donny so why should it shock me between women? But it's different when it's your own sex – more threatening somehow.

Each of the tables had a solid silver sweet dish containing a white powder that the guests were passing round between them. I knew it was cocaine and didn't need Myles' warning to keep away. I was living by my wits and I couldn't afford to have them addled.

Soon after we arrived the lights dimmed and the disco got going. At first I felt a bit odd disco dancing in eighteenth-century get-up, but it didn't appear to bother the Emperor Nero or Puss In Boots. Myles seemed even more mysterious and fascinating in his black robes with the sinister white mask, and I began to wonder if I could hold out till the end of the evening.

'I really fancy you like that,' I murmured to him.

'I fancy you any time,' he whispered back.

My 'mystery man' attracted a lot of attention and girls fell over themselves to grab him from me. While he was otherwise occupied I danced with Henry VIII and Richard III, only Richard danced awkwardly because his hump kept slipping. After that I gave royalty a miss and partnered Abraham Lincoln and Napoleon.

At last, to my relief, I saw my black-swathed Venetian cavalier making his way through the crush towards me. We began to dance and he slowly leaned forward, sliding his hand down till he found the placket and entered. His fingers were cold, which was unusual for Myles, but he teased me skilfully and I arched against him. I looked round to see if anyone was watching us but all the other dancers were occupied in their own way.

'This isn't very satisfactory,' he whispered. 'Let's find somewhere more private.'

He guided me towards a door and through it to a little ante-room. There was a table with the paraphernalia for making coffee and another piled with fruit, but I only saw them for a moment before he dimmed the lights almost to nothing.

He tore open his robe at the front and I reached inside, ready to start undressing him. But there was no need. He was naked.

'So that's what you were doing while you were away,' I said.

He gave a low chuckle and pushed my hands down below. He was already huge and erect and I began to guide him towards the placket.

And then my nostrils caught a faint whiff of something that shouldn't have been there. It was a really horrible shaving lotion. I hadn't noticed it before because it was so faint, like yesterday's that hadn't been properly washed off, but at this distance I could smell it. It was one Myles never used because I wouldn't let him. But I knew who did use it.

Lord Lythal.

In one instant the whole plan became clear to me: Seraphina suggesting Myles' costume, a costume so anonymous that even I wouldn't notice the substitution until too late. Lythal was Lady Caroline's brother and had a score of his own to settle with me. Seraphina was probably on her way here with Myles right now.

'What have you stopped for?' he grunted, and now I wondered how I could ever have mistaken his voice for Myles'.

'You know I like to take any time,' I whispered back. 'Come here.'

As I spoke I stepped back, and then back again, and Lythal followed me. Mind you, he didn't have a lot of choice since I was still holding him. Inch by inch I neared the coffee table and with my free hand I felt frantically behind me. My luck held. The implement I needed was right there. I took hold of it and slowly brought my hand forward under the cloak.

'I've got a surprise for you, Lord Lythal,' I murmured.

He hesitated as he realized the game was up and that gave me just enough time to fit the sugar tongs in place and squeeze. The next moment he was giving a yell to wake the dead.

'You bitch!' he wailed. 'You double-dealing bitch!'

I turned up the lights. He was clutching himself and dancing about the room. I took advantage of his preoccupation to rip off his hat and mask. For one ghastly moment I was afraid I'd made a mistake and it was Myles after all, but it was Lythal all right, looking at me with murder in his eyes and swearing fit to bust.

'Save your breath calling me names,' I said. 'I could call you a few.'

He tried to lunge at me but had to stop and stagger. His tottery condition gave me the chance to push him over. He lay splayed out on the carpet holding his bruised organ. I could hear voices from outside the door and was sure I recognized Myles and Seraphina. I had only a moment to complete my revenge. I snatched up an apple and leaned over him.

'Open wide,' I said, and he was so demoralised that he obeyed me without thinking. I stuffed the apple in his mouth just as the door opened.

'You don't believe me now but you will,' Seraphina was saying to someone behind her. 'It's for your own good, Myles.'

Then she stopped in her tracks to take in the sight of Lythal splayed out on his back, naked, with an apple in his mouth like a boar's head, his hands clutched protectively in front of him.

She had an instamatic camera in her hand. Quick as a flash I snatched it from her, pointed it at Lythal and clicked. Everything happened so fast that she didn't have a chance to stop me. By the time she'd lunged for the camera I'd whipped out the picture and stuffed it down my dress.

'Will somebody please tell me what's happening?' Myles asked politely.

'With pleasure,' I said. I stopped at the door and spoke to Lythal who was getting up off the floor. 'If I ever have any more trouble from you I'll send this picture to the newspapers. *All* of them.'

Then I took Myles' hand. 'Come on,' I said. 'The party's over.'

In the car on the way home I told him what had happened and we surveyed the picture together. It had come out beautifully. I'd have liked to include it in this book, but Lythal has kept his distance since then and I'm a woman of my word. But it you're reading this, Lythal, I still have it.

'So that's why Seraphina said she had to talk to me,' Myles said. 'She kept dropping hints about what you'd be up to in my absence, then insisted that I follow her. She had it all planned, including the costume.'

'How could even Seraphina do a thing like that?' I fumed.

'She's afraid I'm going to ask you to marry me,' said Myles.

'That's ridiculous!'

'Why is it ridiculous, Honey?'

'Well – of course it is,' I said, feeling awkward because something in his voice told me we were moving into uncharted territory.

'Do you mean that if I *did* ask you, you'd laugh at me?'

'No but – '

'What would you say?'

He had his arm round me, and my head was resting on his shoulder. It was cosy and natural and I thought how pleasant it would be to stay with Myles always.

'I think I'd say yes,' I whispered.

'But you're not sure?'

'Ask me again tomorrow,' I said, 'when I've got used to the idea.'

He dropped me at home but didn't ask to stay the night. He had enough tact to know that I needed to be alone to think. But although I lay awake in bed I found I didn't need to think very hard. Myles and I were good together, and I was sure I could make him happy. By morning I was determined to say yes.

The next day was Sunday. I settled down with my coffee to browse through the supplements. Then I grew very still as I came across an article about an 'eminent archaeologist working in the east'. There, looking out at me from the page, was Steve.

It was a colour picture, clearly showing how bronzed he'd become. There was a new strength in his face too, and my heart turned over. It was nearly two years since I'd last seen him, but now I knew that nothing had changed. He was still the only man for me. It might seem unreasonable to turn down my chance of becoming a Marchioness because of a man I'd probably never see again, but I couldn't help it.

I told Myles that day that I couldn't marry him. He was sad but didn't seem surprised. 'I guess I was never going to be that lucky,' he said.

We stayed together for another couple of months but we both knew our relationship was drifting to an end. I kept seeing Steve's face when I was making love to Myles and I think he began to suspect something. He was very sensitive.

We said our goodbyes over a romantic dinner at Dyson Hall. And then, just for old times sake, we enjoyed a final romp on the sofa in the library where we'd first discovered each other. In some ways it was the best ever. Myles was a tiger, driving himself and me on to new heights, bringing me undreamed of pleasure.

And yet . . . and yet . . . Steve's face was there in my heart, haunting me. He was somewhere out there in the world. And one day, if I didn't lose faith, I knew I'd find him again.

Chapter Seven

W hen we parted Myles said to me, 'Honey, about the flat–' I thought he was going to ask for it back, but he went on, 'I wish you'd sell it and buy another. I don't want to think of your sharing it with anyone else.'

I promised, and put it on the market right away. I didn't want to take another man there either. As there was no mortgage to pay off I used the price as a deposit on the next one. I chose an apartment right in the heart of Sloane Ranger country and only a short distance from Harrods, where I did most of my shopping now. The mortgage extended me a bit, even though my earnings were pretty good, but I leaned over the desk at the man in the building society and he gulped and said he was sure something could be arranged.

In a month I was installed in my new home, with its 'two bedrooms and a huge reception room'. That's how the estate agent described it. Actually there was one bedroom and a cupboard. The reception room wasn't huge, but a decent size. But I'd learned about London prices by then and I knew I was lucky.

I went a bit mad and bought new carpets and furniture, which cleaned out almost the last penny I had. Luckily the work was pouring in. On the day everything was in place I toasted myself in champagne, and then thought how strange it was that I should be alone. I could have been Lady Dyson. But then I looked at Steve's picture, which I'd cut out of the magazine and framed, and I knew that I could *never* have been Lady Dyson.

Just as I was pouring another glass the doorbell rang, and when I opened it, there was my brother Ricky. We flung ourselves into each other's arms. I was so thrilled to see him that I forgot what a pain in the whatsit he could be. He was twenty-two now, and terribly handsome.

'Hey Mel, this is a bit of all right,' he said as I showed him over my new home. 'So these are the wages of sin. Perhaps I ought to have a go at being sinful.'

'You haven't got the attributes,' I told him, pouring him some champagne. 'What brings you to London?'

'I got tired of listening to Dad moaning about how shocked and ashamed he is that a daughter of his, etc. etc.'

'The hypocritical old scroat!' I exclaimed. 'He's not too shocked and ashamed to take the money I send. Who paid the gas bill? Who paid for Mum's new coat.'

'You did, but you don't send money to him, you send it to Mum,' Ricky pointed out.

'Of course,' I said. 'She'd never see a penny of it otherwise. I'm no fool.'

'Not if you can buy a place like this,' Ricky agreed, looking around him. 'Dad and I agreed it was time I came to London to cast a brotherly eye over you, plus he wants to know if you could let him have a few hundred quid. He lost a bit at the dogs.'

'He can have what he likes as long as he keeps out of my hair,' I said.

'And perhaps I ought to stay to watch over your welfare,' Ricky hinted.

'You can stay for a while if you want to, but if you cause me any trouble you'll be out,' I told him firmly.

He stared at me. 'Blimey, you've changed. I hardly know you, Mel.'

'Good. And my name is Honey. Don't forget it.' I left him gawping after me. That was another small turning point, the moment I forced someone who'd known me all my life to recognize me as Honey. Ricky never tried to call me Mel again.

It was his first trip to London and he plunged into its pleasures with gusto. Although he was older than me I was far more worldly-wise by now, and I had to work hard keeping him out of trouble. It didn't leave much time for a love-life of my own, which was just as well because Ricky's was colourful. I'd come home sometimes to hear grunts and groans coming from behind his bedroom door. I'd leave them to it while I made myself a chaste cup of cocoa. Funny, that!

Not that Ricky was entirely selfish. He noticed me looking glum the day I read about Myles' engagement to Seraphina, and suggested we go to a rock concert that night. I agreed gladly. Then it transpired that he hadn't actually got tickets. He was counting on me to use my charm to get us in! Luckily the manager of the theatre was someone I knew and it wasn't too difficult. The evening was called "Butcher – In Concert".

If Butcher's records were incomprehensible his live efforts were worse. I sat amid a solid jelly of noise and picked up the words by reading his lips. They seemed to go:

'I'm a killer . . . you're a killer . . . let's kill this rotten world together . . . let's smash it and slash it . . . let's make the blood run . . . I'm a killer . . . .'

I could hardly keep a straight face, but all round me people were closing their eyes in ecstasy, so I supposed it couldn't be as silly as it sounded. Butcher wore his usual gear of nuts and bolts and in the lurid red and green lighting he looked really evil, especially when he snarled.

In the break the manager came round to say Butcher had noticed me in the audience and wanted me to go backstage. He didn't mention Ricky but my pushy brother came anyway.

We found Butcher in his dressing room. He still wore his black leather trousers but he'd taken his jacket off and his chest heaved and glistened from his exertions. His long black locks fell theatrically over his face and he glared at me through narrowed eyelids.

'Why were you laughing at me?' he demanded.

'Laughing at you?' I was puzzled.

'The first time we met, at the première of *Crashing Out*. What was so funny?'

'You still remember that?' I asked in amazement. 'It was a year ago.'

'Yeah, but people don't usually laugh at me,' he said, sounding not so much aggressive as bewildered.

'Well, you were a bit over the top,' I said. 'The chains or the hacksaw – but not both! Look, I didn't mean to be rude.'

Unexpectedly he grinned. 'I had a row with my manager about chains and hacksaw. Having both was his idea. Now I can tell him you agree with me.'

I liked him when he grinned. He had nice teeth. Somehow I'd expected Dracula fangs.

'How would you like a better seat for the second half?' Butcher asked me. 'Come on.'

He took my hand and led me out of his dressing room. In the crowded corridor I had to squeeze past Ricky who was pressed up against a girl with black-ringed eyes and pink hair. She was part of an all-girl trio called 'Evil Eyes', who'd done a spot in the first half.

'Stop cradle snatching, Bebe,' Butcher said, and it was only then that I realized Ricky was standing there inside her. She was smoking something and seemed supremely bored. Her partners, who looked exactly the same except that one had green hair and the other blue, stood by, watching and waiting their turn with Ricky.

Butcher took me right to the edge of the stage. It was reached by three steps, which meant that the stage was just the right height for sitting on.

'You'll see OK here,' he said, and vanished.

The group returned. Butcher reappeared with his full gear on again and all the girls in the audience screamed. He snarled at them and they screamed louder. He started to play and suddenly I was engulfed in the most tremendous cacophony. I was sitting near the amplifiers and the sound that blared from them seemed to pulse straight through me. It was pure noise with an undercurrent of deafening beat, and I closed my eyes and let myself become one with it.

I became aware that it wasn't just the amplifiers that were affecting me. I was near the drummer, and his powerful rhythm was going down into the stage and up again through my body. I could feel the floor moving under my behind, against my cunt, trembling and vibrating, pounding, thundering. It was a glori-ous feeling and I began to rock with it. I couldn't help myself.

The song ended (if it *was* a song, I couldn't tell). I opened my eyes and discovered that I was looking straight at the drummer and he was looking at me. He grinned. He'd understood what was happening to me.

I knew his name was Jak because he was almost as famous as Butcher. They were deadly rivals, practically enemies, and sometimes their hatred spilled out onstage. Butcher would hurl his menacing songs at Jak and Jak would attack the drums as if trying to crush Butcher's skull. The audiences loved it.

Jak had a heavy-featured, sensual face with a generous mouth. As he played his lips were drawn back in a way that might have been a grin or a sneer. He gave me a wink and launched himself violently at the drums, making the floor tremble even more, all the time watching to see what he was doing to me. I gasped at the vibration and clasped my arms round my body, swaying in ecstatic torment. I was in a fever. It felt like ages since I'd had a man and now I wanted it, but it had to be *like this*.

I fixed my eyes on Butcher. His leather pants were very tight and his gyrations emphasized his neat but well-formed buttocks. The lurid light shifted constantly over their curved surfaces and I wanted to reach out and run my hands over them. Jak saw me watching Butcher and increased his pressure on the drums to get me back to him.

Butcher swung round and saw what was happening with us. He snarled and screamed something at Jak, who reacted by drumming even more ferociously. Butcher leapt in the air and landed hard with both feet together. I felt that too and it increased my excitement. They were howling at each other, blasting their hatred into the wall of deafening sound. I was afraid they'd kill each other in a moment.

I wanted them both. I wanted the noise and the hot, musky smell of them, and their cocks in me, and their fingers in me and their bodies covering mine. I wanted this savage, sensual beauty to last forever, but I also wanted it to end quickly so that we could get away from here and my body could have what it was craving for.

It seemed an age before the performance ended and by then I was a limp rag. I got up slowly and went to find Ricky, but there was no sign of him. I looked into Butcher's dressing room and to my surprise he was downing a large glass of milk.

He grinned at my expression. 'Come in.'

The mirror showed me how bedraggled I looked. I opened my bag to repair the damage and discovered a piece of paper. It was a note from Ricky.

I'm taking Bebe and Roxy and Sandra home. We'll have to use your bed because mine is too small for four, so I've taken your key. That way you won't disturb us. I know you won't mind.

'Damned cheek!' I fumed, showing the note to Butcher.

He considered it. 'I'd carve him up for you, but I haven't got the hacksaw with me,' he said apologetically.

'Ha ha!' I said bitterly.

'With a brother like that you shouldn't leave your bag lying around,' he said, sounding like a Dutch uncle.

'I didn't. The dirty little toe-rag must have crept up and nicked it while I was sitting on the stage.'

'And you didn't notice him.'

I looked at Butcher. 'I didn't notice anything except what was happening on stage,' I said significantly.

He met my eyes. 'Well, if you're short of a bed for the night, how about coming to my place?'

'I'd like that,' I said.

We slipped out of a side door. I could hear Butcher's fans baying for him in the front, but I wondered if he also wanted to avoid being intercepted by Jak.

I'd expected Butcher's car to reflect his rebellious image, but it was a brand new Rolls Royce that would have put Randy's to shame. The chauffeur started up as we settled into the back, and Butcher pulled out the drinks cabinet revealing some more bottles of milk.

'I've got some sherry if you prefer it,' he said, noticing my startled expression, 'but after a night of screaming I need something that will soothe my throat.'

He poured me a sherry, switched on the CD and the car was flooded by soft music. There was a piano playing an achingly sweet melody against an orchestra. I was sure I'd heard it somewhere before.

'I know,' I said at last. 'That's the *Elvira Madigan* music.'

Butcher scowled. It lacked the snarling ferocity of his earlier contortions, yet somehow it was more real. 'That is not the *Elvira Madigan* music,' he said crossly.

'But it is. They showed the film on television the other night – all about this cavalry officer who fell in love with a tightrope walker, and they had one last perfect day before committing suicide. This was played throughout the love scenes.'

'So it may have been, but that doesn't make this the *Elvira Madigan* music,' Butcher said firmly. 'This is Mozart's Piano Concerto no. 21 in C Major. The fact that some film maker, who knew he was on to a good thing, used it as background music in a film called *Elvira Madigan* does *not* make it the *Elvira Madigan* music.'

'All right, if you say so,' I said. 'Don't get your hacksaw out with me.'

He grinned. 'Stuff it! I get enough hacksaws onstage. I didn't mean to bite your head off but it's a thing that makes me mad. I don't like hearing *real* music devalued.'

'Real music?' I queried, wondering if I was going mad.

'Well you don't call that rubbish you heard tonight music, do you?'

'Then you don't do it because it's "a brilliant exposition of anguished anarchy, tearing at the vitals of a brutalist society"?' I asked, quoting one of the more pretentious rock mags.

'I do it because it delivers the bread,' Butcher said simply.

In a few minutes we arrived at his Belgravia mansion, full of wall to wall carpeting, except in his bedroom where there was simply a bed, a grand piano and a wooden floor.

'Wood is better for the acoustics,' he explained. He switched on another CD player and it started to play the same music. 'It's my current favourite, so I have it everywhere,' he said.

I was beginning to feel cheated. I'd fancied the evil, darkly glamorous rock star, but he was slipping away. Butcher pulled off his leather jacket. He was very tall and his torso was lean and muscular. I looked at the tight, leather pants, my fingers itching to strip them off him. There was a huge bulge in the front that told its own story. It was bigger than any I'd ever seen. I wanted it and I wanted it now. The tops of my thighs were hot and moist with thinking about what was inside his trousers, and I was breathing hard.

Butcher came close and began to run his hands over me. His breathing was hard too. He smelled of heat and clean sweat and it made my blood pound pleasantly. I touched him in front and felt the bulge fill my hands. I couldn't wait any longer. I began to pull on his zipper – it descended – I slid my hand inside, feeling anxiously for the huge prick I wanted.

Then I froze.

'What the hell is that?' I demanded indignantly, pulling something out.

Lying in my hand was a sock.

Butcher let out a roar of laughter. 'We all stuff those down our pants before a performance. The fans expect to see something spectacular.'

'Very funny,' I said witheringly. 'I'm glad it gave you a good laugh.'

'No, I just forgot it was there. I wasn't making fun of you, honest.'

'Tell that to the birds,' I said crossly.

'Oh come on. I didn't mean it to happen. I'm sorry.'

But I was in no mood to be reasonable. I felt I'd made a complete fool of myself and I couldn't wait to get out of there. I snatched up my bag and headed for the door.

'Wait a minute,' Butcher yelled, grabbing me. 'I've apologized.'

'To hell with your apologies,' I told him. 'And to hell with you and – and to hell with Mozart.'

Butcher moved incredibly fast, whipping one arm round my waist and lifting me off the ground, pressed tightly against him. 'You can say what you like about me,' he said, 'but nobody bad-mouths Mozart in this house.'

'*Put me down!*'

'Not until you say you're sorry.'

'In a pig's eye I'm sorry,' I said breathlessly.

The way he was holding me was making my dress ride right up over my hips. He slipped his other hand behind me and began to feel my bottom, drawing one long finger down the cleft between my buttocks. I was still furious and struggling, but there was nothing I could do to stop him.

106

'Going to say sorry?' he asked me.

I kicked him, but the movement of my leg made it possible for him to slide his fingers the rest of the way under until they were touching my cunt. To my indignation shivers of pleasure went through me. We were eyeball to eyeball and I glared at him, trying to let him know how unspeakable I thought his behaviour. But he only moved his fingers again and I found myself clutching him and moaning. I meant to kick him again, but instead I found my legs curving round him.

He eased me down a little. His fingers vanished and instead I felt something round and wet pressing against me. It was so easy to slide down it and let it find its natural home inside me. I crossed my legs behind his back, squeezing them so that he came deeply into me.

He managed to make his way to the bed with us still locked in this position, and dropped down on it, driving and driving into me while my desire rose to glorious heights.

At the last moment he grunted, 'Gonna say sorry?'

And I gasped, 'If you like. Sorry, Mozart.'

He thrust again and this time made me come splendidly. He came himself, and when it was over we lay looking at each other a little warily.

'I hope the real thing didn't disappoint you,' he grinned.

'It was great – when I finally got to it,' I said. I tried to sound cross but I was still throbbing deliciously from what we'd just done. 'Honestly,' I added, 'fancy making all that fuss about Mozart.'

Butcher shrugged. 'He happens to be my god.'

I noticed now that his voice was different. The husky snarl and rough accent was gone, replaced by an accent that was smooth and educated. 'You're a fraud,' I told him.

'Sure I am.' He began to slip off my dress. 'I was born in the Home Counties and my Dad's a retired Colonel.'

'No kidding?' I said, easing his leather pants right off.

'No kidding.' He propped himself on one elbow and talked to me seriously. 'I was going to be a concert pianist, went to the Royal Academy of Music and all that. My father wouldn't help me out because he thought classical musicians were all pansies, so I was always short of money. A couple of us tried to make a bit by playing in the underground, him on guitar and me on electric organ. I took over the singing when his voice ran out. And that was how I got "discovered". Just one record, the company said. So I did, and that was the end of a classical career. I do all the screaming and snarling because that's what people want. I'm bored with heavy rock but it's become a treadmill that I can't get off. If I could just branch out into some other kind of pop – like a really emotional ballad or something – '

'But that wouldn't be "Butcher",' I objected.

'I know. I'm beginning to hate Butcher.'

'What does your father say now?' I asked curiously.

Butcher gave a short laugh. 'He's dead proud of me now I'm acting evil. He thinks that makes me a real man. My mother started out by being shocked, but stopped when she realised I could pay all her bridge debts and no questions asked. My brother makes out he despises me but that's because he's a banker and he's as jealous as hell of what I make.'

'But you've got the money now,' I said. 'Can't you go back to the Academy.'

'I always meant to, but of course I can't. I'm caught up in this life, booked solid for the next two years. Besides, who'd take me seriously now? But I was a good pianist, I really was.'

As though I'd disputed the point he pointed some remote control terminals at the CD player. The music, which had finished, re-started, and he got up and went to sit at the piano. He began performing the concerto against the background of the orchestra on the disc, playing just loud enough to drown out the other piano. It was a fast movement now, full of twiddly bits and he knocked them off so easily that even I could tell he was brilliant. I came up and stood behind him, with my hands on his shoulders.

The fast movement ended and the *Elvira Madigan* music (sorry, Mozart) started again. This time I could feel all its melancholy. I hadn't known that any music could be so sad, but the sadness was really Butcher's. His long, sensitive fingers touched the keys softly, evoking an aching feeling of unfulfilled yearning that brought tears to my eyes.

I slipped my arms about his neck and kissed him softly, wanting to console him. He went on playing but I felt the electric tension in his body and knew he was aware of me with every inch of him. His back was long and lean and I could just make out the bumps of his spine. I began to work my way slowly downwards, flickering my tongue against his spine because some people are very sensitive there. I am myself.

He must have been too because his hands crashed on the keyboard and his playing became more forceful. The music had speeded up and he was playing all the difficult twiddly bits with great concentration, yet without ever losing his awareness of me. As I eased downwards I let my hands slide round to the front, caressing him lower and lower, until I found what I wanted, and it was red hot. He was all ready for me, but he wasn't going to stop the music, and I had a brilliant idea.

The piano stool was well back from the keyboard so I had plenty of room. I dropped to the floor, wriggled until my head came up between his legs and there was that beautiful thing, swollen and standing stark at an angle. I formed my mouth into an O and guided him towards it – then inside – flexing my lips against his cock to give an extra thrill. A violent tremor went through him. I could tell his control was being strained to the utmost but he didn't stop playing, just pounded the keyboard harder.

I rested my head against his inner thigh and gave all my attention to what I was doing. The hot, dark smell of male loins, unbearably aroused, permeated the air and increased my own excitement. But I wasn't going to think of myself just now. I wanted to make it good for him.

I pleasured him until he gave a great sigh and came. We returned to the bed and lay together again and when he came into me it was so gentle, and so unlike 'Butcher' that I knew I'd touched his real self. Afterwards I lay with my head against his chest, hearing his heart beat, wondering about the fact that I'd found tenderness in such an unlikely man.

'Thank you,' he said softly. 'I needed someone to love me like that.'

'You were right,' I murmured contentedly. 'The music made it just perfect.'

'We should try it with the Jupiter Symphony. That's really something.'

I tensed. I'd heard a noise downstairs and realized that someone had come into the house.

'It's all right,' said Butcher. 'It's just a friend who's staying with me at the moment.

He went out onto the landing and I wrapped a towel round me and crept after him to get a look at his friend. What I saw nearly made me drop the towel.

It was Jak.

'This is Honey,' Butcher said, indicating me.

'She *sure* is,' Jak agreed, regarding me with the same look he'd been giving me during the performance.

'I thought you two hated each other,' I said.

'That's just for the audience,' said Jak. 'Off-stage we find we often like exactly the same things.'

His eyes and his tone left no doubt about his meaning, and suddenly all the desire I'd thought was slaked with Butcher flared up inside me. I smiled in blissful anticipation and Jak smiled back.

'I'm just longing to hear the Jupiter Symphony,' I murmured.

'Be my guest,' said Butcher, waving us to the bed. He went off to put on the music and I leaned against the wall, letting the towel fall to my feet. My body was glowing from the fulfilment of my desire, yet tingling anew with the need to explore Jak and discover how he was different from Butcher. He was shorter and built on sturdy lines with a powerful neck, broad shoulders and torso, and thighs that were heavy with muscles. When I thought of the strength in those thighs I had to fight to keep myself under control.

Jak came towards me slowly, his eyes caressing my skin, bringing my nipples to hard peaks without even touching them. He stripped off his shirt and I saw that his chest was covered with thick, curly hair. It was matted at the top, becoming fine lower down until it vanished into the belt confining his jeans. Beneath that belt there was a most enticing bulge, but I was wary now.

'Before I go any further,' I said, pointing, 'I want to know what's in there.'

That stopped Jak in his tracks. 'Only the usual thing,' he said warily. 'What were you expecting, a Tornado missile?'

'Just as long as it isn't a sock,' I said firmly.

111

He grinned, understanding. 'I don't bother with socks,' he said. Then raising his voice for Butcher's benefit he added, 'Some of us don't need to.'

'Up yours, buster,' Butcher's amiable voice floated back.

Now I was getting really interested. If that bulge was for real I was onto a good thing. I tried it tentatively and it felt nice and solid.

'You don't trust me, do you?' Jak said. 'Well I don't blame you if you've been wasting your time on that good for nothing Butcher.'

'She didn't have any complaints,' Butcher called back from inside the room.

'That's before she met a real man. Let me show you the difference, Honey.' As he spoke Jak laid his hand on my neck and let it drift down over my skin, leaving trails of fire behind it. For a man with such a big hand he had an incredibly delicate touch. His caresses of my nipples were feather light, the merest whisper, but I felt as though jolts of electricity were going through me.

'I'm waiting for you to do just that,' I assured him.

He led me into the bedroom, made me sit on the bed, and pushed me gently backwards so that my legs were left hanging over the edge. Then he dropped to his knees between them and buried his face in me. After a moment I felt his tongue working on my cunt, teasing it with little movements that were almost a tickle. It felt delicious, so soft and gentle.

My eyes were closed but even so I sensed a shadow over me and when I looked it was Butcher, sitting on the bed just behind my head. Without a word he leaned over and began to kiss my breasts. I gasped with pleasure at the double stimulation. I'd never been made love to by two men before and it was an experience I was ready for. They were both serving me with their lips and tongues and hands, working

112

for my pleasure. It gave me an enjoyable feeling of power.

Jak lifted my legs and slipped his hands under my bottom, raising me off the bed and drawing his head back. A moment later I felt his tongue again, sliding between my buttocks, and then into me. I'd never been penetrated there before but his tongue was such a clever instrument that I soon lost any sense of strangeness and began to enjoy it.

Butcher had moved downwards to put his head between my legs, taking up where Jak had left off, his tongue thrusting in and out where his prick had been only a short time before. I took it between my hands and slipped it into my mouth while the two tongues worked on me together and I came repeatedly.

When they'd finished Jak leaned his head against my thigh and said, 'I'm feeling a bit left out.'

I laughed and drew him between my legs. I'd thought that the regular thing might be an anticlimax after what I'd just had but that was doing an injustice to Jak. He was full of energy and there was an edge on his performance that I appreciated very much. I'd been getting tired but his vigour inspired me to new efforts.

We slept for a few hours, the three of us entwined together, and then we all took a shower. Butcher stood in front of me and Jak behind, both of them lathering me thoroughly, sliding their soapy hands everywhere. I put my arms round Butcher's neck while he came inside me, and a few seconds later I felt Jak's prick sliding between my buttocks, then slowly and carefully into me. I was glad he'd done it with his tongue first because now I was more ready to enjoy the new experience.

Jak slid his hands round between Butcher and me, caressing my breasts as he fucked me. I thought I'd go out of my mind from the stimulation coming from so many different places at once, and when I came it was like the explosion of the universe, incredible, earth-shattering, glorious.

I was in a mood to experiment now, so when we returned to bed I made Jak lie on his back while I straddled him and sucked his prick. Then Butcher straddled me and inserted his tongue where Jak's prick had been a few moments before. It might have been uncomfortable being the meat in the sandwich but they were both such gentlemen that we managed easily, and for some reason we finished up by collapsing in giggles. Finally we slept again.

I woke to the sound of music. Butcher was sitting at his piano, softly picking out the notes of a tune. He smiled when he saw me.

'I've got an idea for a new song,' he said. 'It's going to be called, "We Three".'

He began to sing snatches of the words. 'Three of us – always we three – never alone with you – he's always there – never two – always three –'

It was about a man who sensed that his girl was secretly thinking of a past lover even when they were in bed together, but if you read between the lines there was no doubt where Butcher had found his inspiration. It was an unusual kind of song for Butcher, not heavy rock but soulful and full of feeling.

'I've found it,' he said. 'I'm off the treadmill. *You* gave me that, Honey.'

Over the next few weeks I spent lots of time with Butcher and Jak. I was there in the studio when they recorded "We Three". We all said goodbye when they left for a foreign tour. They wouldn't be back for six months and although we all loved each other in a triangular sort of way, we knew none of us was going to keep anything on ice for that long.

The fans fell over themselves to buy 'We Three'. The pop mags raved over Butcher's 'new maturity' and his 'courage in refusing to be confined by the parameters of his fame'. It was at number one for ten weeks and made him a fortune. Jak was featured prominently on the record and got a special cut of the royalties.

Guess who was the only one who never made so much as a broad bean out of that record.

That's right.

Muggins!

Chapter Eight

A few weeks after Butcher and Jak left for their tour I slung my sponging brother out on his ear. It wasn't just the way he'd left me stranded at the concert. After all, I had good cause to be grateful for that night. It wasn't entirely the fact that I had to support him, although that was part of it. And not being able to get into my own bed because he was using it wasn't too funny either.

But we really hit rock bottom when he took my car without permission and crashed it. It wasn't insured for him to drive and it was too badly damaged to be worth repairing so I ended up without a car. Naturally I waited to see if he was hurt, but when I knew that he'd survive undamaged to be obnoxious for a few years yet I gave him the push. He took it quite well. I think he'd got away with more than he'd dared to hope.

So I was on my own again with a dwindling bank balance. Then, to my relief I got a call from Sax, the director of Randy's film who'd thought I had possibilities.

'How would you like to do a commercial?' he asked.

'But I thought you were a film director?'

'I am, but a lot of us do commercials these days. The trick is to make it into a little work of art. This one's going to be a beauty. It's for Mata Hari Creations.'

I knew the firm. It made very glamorous, *very* pricey underwear. In fact it was a joke in the trade that once you'd bought Mata Hari you were the wrong shape to wear it, because it had cost you an arm and a leg.

'It's to publicize their new range,' Sax was saying. 'We're shooting it in Kamar.'

'You mean that Arab kingdom that's the size of Cornwall and produces almost as much oil as the rest of the Gulf put together?' I asked quickly.

Sax whistled. 'I'm impressed. Most people have never heard of Kamar.'

'I studied geography very keenly,' I said. In fact I'd read up about that part of the world because it was where Steve had gone.

'Perhaps you've also heard of Sultan Abdul Kamar Hassamid,' Sax said. 'He's the absolute ruler, a real despot, and we had to get his personal permission before we were allowed in. We'll be staying in the Kamar Hilton, and you'll get ten thousand pounds. What do you say?'

'I say when do we start?' I said excitedly.

'Next week. Get yourself some clothes that cover your arms and legs, and a hat that shields your face. They're for wearing when we arrive. Women have to dress modestly in public over there and, what's more important, your skin has to stay all one colour. Don't you *dare* get a tan before I've finished filming you.'

I promised. When I'd put the phone down I looked up Kamar. Although it was so small it was what politicians called 'strategically important', because it had

117

borders with two other countries, a stretch of shore and a port. The book gave a lot of facts and figures about its exports and the fact that the Sultan was fast modernizing the country with the help of Western experts, while striving to maintain the traditional ways. It also mentioned an ancient civilization, relics of which were still being discovered. I closed my eyes and thought of Steve, which was a treat I rarely allowed myself. I was going to be close to him again. Perhaps . . . just perhaps . . . .

The following week I flew to Kamar with Sax, the camera crew and a woman called Janice who looked like a prison wardress and worked for Mata Hari Creations. I went crazy when she showed me all those lovely scanties made of minute amounts of satin and lace with lots of delicate hand sewing. They were designed to make a man want to remove them as quickly as possible.

At the airport there was a welcome committee, ten soldiers of the Kamari National Guard, all very straight and upright. The officer in charge looked me over. I had on a white silk travelling suit, cut very loose, and a big white hat and after a moment he grunted which I supposed meant approval. When he came to Janice she scowled at him and he backed off.

His name was complicated but sounded like William so that's what I called him. Not to his face, of course. He was a villainous looking character in his forties who looked as if he ought to have a knife between his teeth.

Sax and I were shown to an air-conditioned stretch limousine, while Janice and the others were herded into a second. William indicated the drinks cabinet and invited us to be 'His Majesty's guests'. The soldiers got into two jeeps, one ahead and one behind us, and rode with their machine guns at the ready as though they were expecting an attack, and we roared off through the desert at a hundred miles an hour.

At the Kamar Hilton I had a suite of rooms decorated in black and gold. The bathroom was pure luxury with taps of solid gold. The huge bed had black silk sheets, and over it was hung a picture of a very fat elderly man in a uniform that was too tight for him, standing in front of a cloth drape, and saluting. The caption underneath said, 'His Majesty, Sultan Abdul Kamar Hassamid III'. I was disappointed. He didn't look at all like I thought a Sultan should.

That night Sax and I had dinner on my balcony, watching the sunset turn the sea to ruby red. Sax was an entertaining companion, and a very attractive one, and I was toying with the idea of taking him up on the interesting suggestions he was making. But not tonight. I was tired and wanted to try those silk sheets on my own. I gave him a lingering kiss as a promise of things to come and bid him goodnight.

Next day we started work on a part of the beach that had been kept private for us, with the soldiers to see off intruders. A circular tent was set up and inside it I stripped off and put on the peach satin teddy Janice handed me. As soon as I stepped out William bawled out some orders and the soldiers turned their backs. All except William. He kept a shocked expression on his face, but his eyes were on stalks.

I lay down in the white sand under a colourful umbrella, and turned this way and that to Sax's directions. Then I changed into camiknickers of brilliant cerise satin, with a tight bodice that nipped my waist in and pushed my breasts right up. When I emerged I got the shock of my life. Sax was waiting for me, holding the reins of a large white stallion.

'His name's Snowflake,' he told me.

'What am I supposed to do with him?'

'Ride him of course,' Sax told me, all innocence.

'You're off your nut.'

'I thought Lord Dyson taught you how.'

'I just about learned how to stay on. I can't ride bareback,' I protested.

'Of course you can. It's easy.'

'You ride him then.'

Sax started coaxing. 'Darling, don't be unreasonable. Just mount him for a moment to get the feel of it. I'll hold him.'

Why ever did I fall for it? I let Sax help me up on to Snowflake's back. As soon as I was up Sax let him go. At once the stallion shot forward at a gallop, and I shrieked and held on for dear life. There was no saddle or stirrups. I had to grip him with my knees as best I could.

We galloped for a quarter of a mile along the edge of the shore then someone headed us off. The horse turned and galloped back in the other direction and there were Sax's cameramen dotted all over, filming me like mad. As I swept past Sax yelled, 'Smile! Look as if you're enjoying it!'

And I yelled back. 'Fuck you, buster!' as I flew away from him.

But now I was becoming aware of a change. I could feel the animal's back directly against my bare thighs, beneath my cunt, the muscles rippling as he pounded the ground in his swift flight. The vibration pulsed up through me deliciously just like the night I'd been possessed by Jak's drumming. I'd heard it said that this was why some women liked to ride: the feel of the beast's controlled power between their legs, the tremors that went through them with every thundering stride. They were magnificent sensations. I began to smile with delight, and out of the corner of my eye I could see Sax leaping about exultantly.

120

At last we stopped and Sax practically hauled me off Snowflake, throwing a sheet over me to protect me from the sun. It was time to halt for lunch. We had a champagne picnic in the tent while Sax explained that we'd resume work when the worst of the day's heat was over. The final shots would be taken in the sunset, with me wearing black.

I was supposed to take a nap, but couldn't. The morning had left me excited and if Sax had made his move then he'd have got the benefit. But he spent siesta time fussing around looking for good shots. I lay in the tent having feverish dreams. I think I knew even then that I was on the verge of one of the most extraordinary erotic adventures of my entire life.

My final costume for the day was a bra so tiny that it consisted of two black satin triangles held together with lace and hope, and a pair of matching panties, although the panties were little more than a G-string.

'You can hardly see I'm wearing them,' I said.

Sax nodded. 'I've thought of that. You need something to draw attention to them, so I want you to use this.' He produced a large piece of multicoloured cloth. 'I sent my assistant into the bazaar at lunchtime and he brought this back. I don't know what all those signs represent, but they look good.'

'I think I've seen them before,' I said. 'I wonder where?'

Sax shrugged. 'Apparently there are lots of these in the bazaar. They probably use them as shawls. I want you to lie back on the sand and draw it slowly through your legs.'

'OK,' I said. 'No problem.'

I walked out into the beautiful golden light and stretched out on the sand. Sax switched on his portable CD player and a stream of languorous music poured out. This was how I liked it. I made myself one with the music, letting its sweet throbbing rhythm pulse through me until I was alive with erotic tension. I imagined the shawl was my lover, twined seductively around me, lying softly against my skin. I rubbed my cheek against it and pouted at the camera. Then, slowly, savouring every movement, I let it slide between my legs, feeling the faint friction against my crotch which was already heated from the day's excitements.

And then all hell broke loose.

One minute I was writhing to the insinuating beat of the music. The next the air had been rent by the most ear-splitting yell I'd ever heard. Cameras flew in all directions as William came charging across the sand to hurl himself on top of me. He grabbed the shawl and held it up, skrieking something in a language I didn't recognize.

But I suddenly remembered where I'd seen a cloth like this one: it had been hanging behind the Sultan in the picture and I had a horrible feeling I knew what it was.

The soldiers had converged around us and were laying rough hands on Sax and the cameramen. 'You are under arrest,' William screamed. 'You have insulted the honour of my country.' He waved the cloth at Sax.

'But it's only a bit of material,' said Sax, bewildered.

'This is the national flag of Kamar,' William yelled, red in the face. 'To insult it is punishable by death. Take them away.'

'Wait a minute. . .' I began. But before I could say any more William grabbed my wrists and fixed a pair of handcuffs on them.

'You've got no right to do that,' I yelled.

William didn't seem to have heard. He picked up the sheet I'd worn to keep the sun off and wound it round me. Then he removed his own leather belt and tightened it about my waist so that the sheet couldn't come undone. My wrists were pressed right against my breasts, so I couldn't even move my arms. To my horror William tossed me over his shoulder, holding me with his arm across the back of my knees, and strode away.

I yelled the place down but nobody seemed to hear me. William took me to a military jeep, dumped me on to the back seat, bound my ankles with rope, then got into the front and began to drive. I struggled as best I could but there was very little room and I couldn't get my hands free to reach the belt.

I think we drove for an hour. As far as I could tell we were going into the desert, but it was getting dark quickly. 'Just where do you think you're taking me?' I demanded, trying to sound braver than I felt.

'To His Majesty, to be sentenced for your crime,' he said over his shoulder. 'You will learn that Kamari national honour cannot be insulted.'

The thought of appearing before that fat old man wasn't appealing. He looked as if he was long past appreciating any of the weapons in my armoury.

From time to time William spoke into a radio, and I suppose he was arranging to be met, because when the jeep stopped and he hauled me out there were several men waiting there with horses. The road had come to an end and sand stretched ahead of us. William vaulted on to a horse and two of the others handed me up. The next thing I knew he was galloping across the desert with me lying face down over the horse in front of him.

At last he pulled up. I couldn't see much except sand but I could tell there were lights and when I twisted my head I saw a huge tent with armed guards standing at the entrance. William pulled me down from the horse and stood holding me while he yelled orders and someone went into the tent. All around us stood men with flaming torches, and I thought I could make out palm trees and camels. I wondered which century I was in.

Suddenly I felt myself being hoisted over William's shoulder again and he strode into the tent. After a few steps he halted, dropped to one knee and tossed me on to the ground so that I rolled over and over, helplessly, until I came to rest at the edge of a kind of dais. I was lying on my stomach and my hair was all over my face, but I could just see the red velvet of the dais, a huge pile of satin cushions on top, and a bare, masculine foot.

It was brown and very elegant, and it led to a long, firm calf. I tried to raise myself to see higher but the foot shot out and settled on my bottom, pushing me firmly back to earth with irresistible force. There was steel in those lean muscles.

'Let me out of here,' I yelled.

The man on the dais, whom I couldn't see, said something sharply to William who dropped down and hissed in my ear. 'It is forbidden to speak to the Sultan unless first spoken to. Be silent or you will have us both executed.'

'I don't care if he is some little tin-pot Sultan,' I snapped. 'He has no right to do this to me.'

From the frozen silence that fell I guessed the Sultan understood English. I was too furious to be scared. I started kicking and struggling again, although I knew it was useless and the only result was to make the Sultan withdraw his foot and use it to flip me over on to my back.

Raising my eyes, I saw a young man with a bronzed, handsome face. He was dressed in a flowing white cloak with the traditional Arab headdress, also white and held in place by golden ropes. But he bore no resemblance to the fat old man in the picture I'd seen.

'Who the hell are you?' I raged. 'The Grand Vizier or something?'

124

This time the silence was more than frozen. It was terrified. At last the man spoke. 'I am Sultan Abdul Kamar Hassamid.'

'Liar,' I flung at him. 'The Sultan's a fat old man. I've seen his picture.'

A cold smile disturbed his beautifully formed lips. 'Ah yes, my grandfather was very popular with my people. Some of them still display his picture rather than mine.'

Suddenly I could see that he bore a slight resemblance to the old man. His face was marked by centuries of pride in kingship and autocratic power. There was something slightly cruel about his features, as though he was used to being ruthless in pursuit of his own will. I gulped. Oh boy, was I in big trouble!

In that long, silent moment I realized that there were several other people in the tent. There were four of them, standing round the sides, swathed completely in black, with their heads covered, so that they were no more than formless shapes. I looked at the Sultan again and found he was looking at me. His eyes were fixed on my breasts which were heaving after my struggles, and there was an interested look there that I thought I recognized. Perhaps if I played my cards right he wouldn't execute me after all.

Abruptly he stood up and as he did so his long white cloak fell apart, showing that he was completely naked underneath it. His body was marvellous, bronzed and lean and taut. He was smooth all over except for the jet black curly hair between his legs. I looked at those curls, struck with wonder at the splendid organ that arose from them. At the thought of having that toy to play with I felt the familiar twitch between my thighs. My blood was already pounding from the hectic ride and now I felt excitement surge through me. If only he'd get rid of everyone else.

125

'I will deal with his matter personally,' he announced, snapping his fingers. At once William bowed and began to walk backwards out of the tent. When the flaps had closed after him I began to struggle up to my knees, but the Sultan turned a cold look on me and pressed me back with his foot.

'You will wait until I am ready to give you my attention,' he declared. 'First I must finish the important business that you interrupted.'

He clapped his hands and immediately the creatures at the sides of the tent turned round and threw off their black covering, revealing four young girls. They were all beautiful except for being too plump, and all naked. Laughing, they ran to the Sultan and took hold of him. One removed his cloak, another his head-dress, while the others pulled him gently back and urged him down until he reclined against the cushions. He took no initiative. He simply lay there and let them minister to him.

One slipped between his legs and took him in her mouth, closing her eyes in ecstasy. When she tired another took her place, while his cock swelled into a hard weapon that showed no signs of flagging. I wanted to wail aloud at the sight of it. That beautiful thing should be in me, and instead I had to lie there in an agony of frustration while they pleasured him and he seemed to have forgotten my existence.

What astounded me was that he appeared perfectly calm under their attentions. His breath came smoothly and he made no effort to touch them. That huge cock was the only sign of excitement. I groaned inwardly at the thought of the superhuman control he must have, and what a man like that could do for a woman.

Suddenly, at a signal from him the girl 'on duty' moved back and they all stood submissively before him while he considered them, finally pointing to

126

one. She knelt and touched her head to the floor before taking her place between his legs, working hard with her lips until he gave a faint sigh and arched his body, coming into her mouth for what seemed like an age.

I could hardly believe my eyes. He'd looked them over and calmly selected who was to have the honour of making him come. Can you believe such outrageous arrogance? And the one he'd chosen was humbly grateful. I wanted to spit. Instead I kicked furiously against my bonds.

As soon as it was over they all averted their eyes. They dressed him quickly, managing to keep their gaze away from his loins until he was covered. Evidently no woman was allowed to see the Sultan's prick in its small, defenceless condition. He stood immobile while they put a long, white tunic on him, and tied the sash. When he snapped his fingers they vanished.

At last he deigned to notice me on the floor, and knelt beside me to unbuckle the belt. He yanked the sheet so that I rolled over and over until he could see me. Leisurely he rose to his feet, walked over to where I'd stopped and stood astride my legs, surveying me. When he'd seen enough he flipped me over to get the rear view. I twisted my head, trying to see him over my shoulder.

'Turn your head,' he commanded. 'I have not given you permission to look at me.'

I was furious at this high-handedness but hardly in a position to argue so I looked away again. He dropped down to one knee and began to run his hand over my back, my hips, my buttocks. At last he rolled me on to my back again, sliced through my ankle bonds with a knife, and said, 'Get up.'

When I'd got to my feet he said, 'Raise your arms so that I can see you better.'

'I'll do no such thing,' I said, getting my courage back. 'You've no right to do this and I want to see the British Consul.'

How he laughed at that. His laugh was rich and attractive, almost diverting my thoughts from the danger I was in, but my temper was rising again.

'I want to see the British Consul,' I said emphatically. 'That is my right as a British Citizen.'

His laughter died. 'What you have to understand is that I am an absolute ruler. In Kamar, *I am the law*. Your only rights are those I give you, and I have given you none. Therefore you have no rights. How can you have? You are a criminal.'

'Only by accident,' I said. 'I didn't know it was your flag.'

'Ignorance of the law is no defence. I learned that excellent maxim when I was at Oxford University in England. You should have made yourself aware of this country's customs before you came here. You are guilty of treason.'

'But I haven't had a trial,' I said, outraged.

'This is your trial. You have been found guilty. The only question is what am I to do with you?' He stood back and regarded me as impersonally as if I was a head of cattle he was considering buying. 'I understand that in your country you are considered a great beauty,' he mused. 'But I do not find you so.'

'What's wrong with me?' I demanded, too indignant to be afraid.

'Too thin. To be beautiful a woman should be well rounded.'

'Hah! You mean like those heifers I saw working on you,' I snorted. 'They wouldn't get far where I come from.'

'And where do you come from?' he asked languidly.

'Great Britain,' I said, emphasising the "great" defiantly. But it was a failure.

'Great Britain?' he mused. 'I'm not sure that I've heard of it.'

'And you an all-powerful ruler,' I said sarcastically. 'Yet you haven't heard of a country that does two billion pounds worth of trade with Kamar every year.'

That froze him. He glared at me out of black eyes. 'Women do not discuss such matters,' he said curtly.

'That's too bad because I just did.'

'That is impossible. Women do not discuss such matters, therefore you did not.'

'Are you deficient in hearing, or something?' I yelled. 'Last year you sold twenty billion barrels of oil to America and used the dollars to buy missiles and wheat. You have thirty British technicians here this minute helping to build a hydro-electric damm. *I discuss what I damned well please!'*

There was total silence. The Sultan's face was a mask. He reached out and rested a hand on my breast, letting it drift down to my waist and over my hips. I resisted the shudders of pleasure that threatened to possess me I wasn't going to give him that satisfaction.

'Too thin and too pale,' he said, continuing our previous conversation as though he hadn't heard a word I'd said. 'I am seeking gifts to reward men who have served me well, but I couldn't offer you to them. They would take it as an insult.'

'*I* would take it as an insult,' I snapped.

He shrugged and didn't bother to reply. He released my handcuffs then, settling himself back on the cushions, he indicated a table that stood nearby. 'Wine,' he said curtly.

The wine jug was solid gold encrusted with rubies and emeralds. The goblet was also gold, polished to a mirror surface. As I poured the smell of the wine assailed my nostrils and I turned faint. I was exhausted with everything that had happened to me.

I managed to keep steady as I approached him, but at the last moment my head swam and I tottered as I held out the goblet. I saw the dark red stain on his white tunic and my last thought was, 'Now I've done it.'

I came round to find my head cradled against his chest and the goblet pressed to my lips. Looking up into his face I saw an expression of almost kindly good humour, as if he was another man.

'Drink,' he said. 'I don't want you dying of malnutrition before I decide what to do with you.'

'What *are* you going to do with me?' I whispered.

'That will take much thought. You are like no woman I have ever known and I am a connoisseur of rarities.'

He made me drink some more, then helped me to my feet. While I stood there, still dazed, he picked up the sheet and wound it round me himself. 'No other man must see you as I have done,' he explained.

He drew a two-way radio out from under a cushion and spoke into it in a language I didn't understand. In a moment two guards appeared carrying something that looked like the *feltz* I'd seen in Venice, except that the curtains were gold satin. It was supported on two long poles that ran underneath. The Sultan lifted me into it and drew the curtains tightly. I heard him say something in the foreign language. The next moment the palanquin was lifted and I felt myself carried away.

Chapter Nine

*A*fter a few moments I felt the palanquin being set down. The curtains were swept aside by a young girl who bowed low to me and proceeded to unwind me from the sheet.

'I am Sufia,' she said. 'I am here to serve you.'

'Where am I?' I demanded.

'You are His Majesty's prisoner and this is your cell.'

It was like no cell I'd ever seen before. I was in a silk-hung tent, half of which was taken up by a large bed with its own silk curtains. Yet I could just make out the silhouettes of armed guards standing outside the entrance.

A table stood there, laden with meats, fruit and bread. Sufia produced a flowing robe in peacock blue and I put it on gladly. It's cold in the desert at night and I was beginning to feel the need of something more substantial than Mata Hari creations. She ushered me to a chair and poured a goblet of wine.

I ate heartily and while I did so more women came in carrying a bathtub and large brass pitchers filled with water. When I'd finished eating they removed the table and conducted me to the bath. I let them do all the work because I was too tired to help. They soaped, rinsed and dried me, and Sufia led me to the bed, waited while I lay down, and drew the curtains.

I'd expected to sleep at once as I was so tired, but as soon as I was alone I found myself alert. It was only a tent, and this might be my chance to escape. I slid quietly to the ground and began to examine the base of the tent wall. It could be lifted by an inch and I squinted down to see what was outside. I saw two pairs of very military looking boots. Moving along a few feet I tried again, only to find more boots. When it happened a third time I realized that there were guards not just at the entrance, but all the way round the perimeter. The Sultan was taking no chances. I was completely trapped.

I went back to bed and lay wondering what had happened to the others. I was still worrying about that as my eyes closed. I slept deeply, my rest disturbed only by a dream. I dreamed that Sultan Abdul came to the side of the bed and stood looking down on my naked body, and there was something in his eyes that I had never seen before in any man's.

I dreamed he ran his hands over me, touching me everywhere, and his touch had a magical softness that contrasted with his arrogance. He knew how to inflame a woman, enchanting her with his fingers, teasing her nipples to peaks of desire, caressing the secret heart of her passion until it was moist and hot for him. In my dream I grew tense with wild physical longing, waiting for him, yearning for him. But he went away without claiming me, and my body ached with deprivation.

When I woke it was daylight and the noises of the camp stirring reached me through the tent walls.

I could hear camels braying and horses stamping their feet and jingling their harness.

I lay still, wondering at a strange tension in my body, the awakening of troublesome yearnings, inspired by memories of my dream. It was almost as if – but surely that was impossible. He'd said he didn't find me attractive.

Sufia came in. As before she bowed deeply and I said, 'Why do you do that?'

'It is His Majesty's command that you be shown all respect,' she replied.

'But you said I was a prisoner.'

'That is true. There are many guards outside your cell. And yet you are to be to be shown respect.'

As I ate the women poured water into the bath-tub. After I'd been bathed they made me lie down while they massaged scented oils into my body. It was nice to be tended, but I couldn't help feeling a bit like a horse having its mane plaited for exhibition. Finally Sufia rubbed me down to wipe off the excess oil and leave me smooth and glowing.

The table and bathtub were replaced by the palanquin. By now I was so used to being pampered that I'd half forgotten I was a prisoner and was taken by surprise when two of the woman tied my hands behind me.

'You don't need to do that,' I protested. 'Where could I escape to?'

'A prisoner who is to be alone with the Sultan must be bound,' Sufia told me. 'Otherwise you might try to assassinate him.'

'How could I?'

She shrugged. 'Those are His Majesty's orders. We are all his humble servants.'

'You may be humble,' I said firmly. 'But I'm not.'

Her eyes widened with horror. 'Do not say that to the Sultan or you will force him to humble you. His wrath is very terrible.'

Furious, I got into the palanquin, and the women made sure the curtains were completely closed lest any other man's eyes but the Sultan's should happen to glimpse me. Once more I was lifted and carried away. Now I could tell that I was outside my tent, being transported through the camp, then inside again and I could hear the Sultan's voice. A slight bump and I'd landed.

The words were foreign but from the inflections I could make out that one of the guards had drawn the Sultan's attention to the palanquin and he had acknowledged it. There were several other voices. A discussion was going on. I waited for the Sultan to dismiss his companions and attend to me.

And waited.

And waited.

I knew there'd be hell to pay if he caught me looking out but at last I couldn't contain my curiosity any longer. I put my eye to a crack in the curtains.

Damned cheek! He was sitting round with a group of men examining papers and talking in an absorbed manner, as if there was all the time in the world. I could have exploded with indignation. This man had reduced me to just another item on his schedule, to be attended to when it suited him. From behind the curtains I could hear the occasional rumble of laughter. Food was served, courtesies exchanged. And all the time I lay there, naked, bound, helpless and furious.

After what seemed like an age I heard everyone move to go. There was a silence, and then the Sultan drew back the curtains of the palanquin. He stood looking at me and I glared back at him. I was too cross to put on a good act.

'You might have thought of me stuck in here all this time,' I snapped.

He smiled. Something in that smile reminded me of my dream the night before and I felt myself growing moist again. But I fought it.

'I did think of you,' he said. 'My thoughts this last hour have been very pleasant, almost enough to distract me from the affairs of state that I was forced to discuss with my councillors.'

'Then why bring me here before you were ready?' I fumed.

He looked surprised. 'So that I had you immediately to hand, of course. Do I have to remind you again that you have no rights?'

'Not even to consideration, evidently.'

'That is correct. I'm glad you begin to understand your position. It will make our association so much pleasanter.'

'Are we going to have an association?' I asked ironically.

'Perhaps. It depends how much you please me.'

'I understood that I *didn't* please you.'

'You have – shall we say – possibilities.' He let his fingertips brush across my nipples. I was still furious and determined not to respond to him. I'd always been glad that I was highly sexed, but now I cursed it because it was the thing that might make me truly his slave in a way that had nothing to do with the bonds about my wrists.

It took an almighty effort but I managed to suppress the tremor in flesh. My lips wanted to part so that the shuddering breath could come through but I wouldn't let them. I stood like stone and saw his eyes darken, at first puzzled and then angry. This man wasn't used to women who had the temerity to stand lifeless while he touched them.

'Do you dare to resist me?' he murmured.

'I can't stop you,' I told him coldly, 'but I don't have to pretend to like your touch.'

'But you do like my touch,' he declared simply.

'You delude yourself. I endure you. Nothing more.'

He gave me a slow smile that turned my loins to water. 'And these,' he said, touching my nipples again, 'do they not speak the truth?'

They were hard and pointed, telling him clearly of the response I'd have liked to deny.

'It is *you* who are lying,' he said softly. 'You burn at my caresses and I will make you admit it.'

He slipped an arm round my waist, drawing me against him, looking down into my face. I was glad now that my wrists were bound for if they'd been free it would have been a struggle not to embrace him, and I was determined not to give him an easy victory.

With his free hand he began to caress one breast, working with soft, subtle strokes of his fingers until my flesh burnt with the sweet torment. He had a sensual mastery that was unlike anything I'd met before in a man. He'd mastered the art of teasing a woman lightly, patiently, until she yielded herself to him despite her own resolve. I gasped, knowing that my shuddering breaths were telling him all he needed to know, but unable to stop myself.

At once he dropped his head and covered my mouth with his own. His lips were firm and demanding, giving me no chance to deny him entry. His tongue was in my mouth, taking possession as though I belonged to him. I felt my resolve slip away. He was a ruler, a man of inflexible will and all that will was now bent on making me surrender. He had formidable weapons. His tongue was full of witchery as it teased and explored the inside of my mouth, starting trails of excitement that streamed down inside me to my belly, my cunt, gathering

136

there, building up to a frantic craving to feel him in that place.

I arched against him, willing him to drop his hand and touch me between my legs, but he wouldn't do it. I tried to tell him silently what I wanted. My tongue met and challenged his, seeking the inside of his mouth, trying to drive him to similar heights. He responded forcefully, thrusting his tongue down my throat fast and hard in a way that echoed another thrusting. With every plunge my pleasure spiralled to new and more dangerous heights. I moaned, wanting him, agonisingly frustrated.

Suddenly my body was wracked with shudders. I was coming, but coming in a way that left me unsatisfied and still in need. He drew back and looked down at my head thrown back against his shoulder. My face with its swollen lips and blurred eyes must have told him a tale.

'Well?' he demanded softly. 'Is my touch abhorrent to you?'

'No,' I whispered.

A smile of satisfaction touched his cruel, beautiful mouth. 'Good. Now you tell the truth.'

Even in my extremity I thought, 'Arrogant bastard!' I wanted to cry out that he couldn't leave me in this state, but I had enough pride left to bear it rather than let him know how he'd made suffer from the lack of him. But of course, he knew anyway. He was used to being supremely desirable to women. It would have been nice to be able to take him down a peg, but the throbbing between my thighs was a reminder that sexually he could do whatever he liked with me. And I knew I wouldn't rest until I'd had him.

He tried to let me go but my legs were shaky. He led me to the dais where he'd lounged among cushions the night before and dropped down among them, making me kneel before him.

137

'Now we can talk about your sentence,' he said. 'A grave crime has been committed, by you and by your companions, who are also under arrest.'

'All of them?' I asked in horror.

'Of course.'

'Even the camera crew?'

'They stood by and photographed your crime. Naturally those pictures have been confiscated and destroyed.'

So there's no proof that any crime was ever committed,' I pointed out.

He raised one eyebrow. 'For a woman you have a quick brain.'

'It isn't fair to arrest everyone,' I said. 'The camera crew just do as they're told. You *must* release them.'

I reckoned that was a mistake as soon as the words were out of my mouth. Now I'd get another lecture about who was the boss round here. But instead he learned back and surveyed me ironically.

'I might consider it. It would depend what you have to offer in exchange.'

'If you'll untie my hands I shall show you what I have to offer.'

He took a gleaming knife and cut my bonds, then surveyed me expectantly. I drew his tunic apart. As I'd hoped he was naked beneath it. The black, curly hair grew luxuriantly between his legs, a soft bed for the heavy balls and powerful cock that lay there. He was already big from our earlier encounter and when I touched him I found a hard rod. I enclosed him in my hand revelling in the thickness, thinking of it in me, *belonging* to me.

I dropped my head between his legs and inhaled the scent of his loins. It was a scent full of darkness and spice, musk and heat and barely leashed power. It rushed to my brain like rich wine, filling me with intoxicating thoughts and inexpressible desires. Dark

138

longings coursed through my blood and I fell on the great phallus like a hungry animal, caressing the tip with my tongue till it was well moist, then taking it between my lips and letting them play with it. How easily they shaped themselves to its roundness and how they loved teasing it.

I remembered last night when the four women had worked on him and he'd accepted their ministrations with unnatural calm. I swore he wouldn't get away with that now. He might feel it was beneath his dignity to respond too easily but he'd discover that he'd never met anyone like me before.

I removed it from my mouth and began running my tongue up and down its length with little skittering movements. I felt the faintest tremor go through him, followed by an instant effort to suppress it. I renewed my assault, flicking my tongue against his balls and from above my head heard an unmistakable sigh that he'd been unable to bite back. I smiled to myself.

I returned to the penis, swirling my tongue about its head first one way then the other, occasionally darting the very tip in and out of the little slit at the end. While I did this I gently squeezed his balls in one hand, while the other slid between his legs, between his buttocks, exploring and teasing. A growl of pleasure broke from him and I felt his hands in my hair, the fingers twining among the strands.

'Witch!' he said hoarsely.

He was swelling . . . swelling, hot and throbbing in my mouth. I opened the back of my throat and took him in deeply. It was a trick I'd learned with Randy and I knew it could drive a man crazy.

'Witch – devil – this is black magic,' he cried.

By the changes in his breathing and a sudden tension in his muscles I knew he was ready to come. Then I gathered all my courage, let his penis out of my mouth and squeezed the end gently between my finger and thumb so that he was forced to hold back.

'You dare!' he said with soft fury.

I glanced up at him provocatively. 'What I do, I do for Your Majesty's greater pleasure,' I told him.

'You take great risks, do you know that?'

I laughed up at him and enclosed him in my mouth again, sucking him deeply into my throat, bringing him to the edge of orgasm but again choking him off at the last second. It is safe to say that no woman had ever dared flout his will in such a way before. Looking at his face I saw that he was totally astounded.

I repeated the process a third time, lashing him to greater heights of excitement. But this time he was ready for me. In one swift movement he slipped out of my mouth, pushed me down to the floor and covered me. His knee parted my legs, urgently pushing them apart and moving between them so that his frantic desire could find relief. My cunt was aching, clamouring for him, and then his cock surged thunderously into me, seeking its home in the hot sweet place that enclosed it with joyous welcome. I came as soon as he entered me, and then again, thrusting against him as hard as I could while he poured himself into me with total abandon.

And then we lay very still together. I knew I had done something very dangerous. I'd made him lose control which was something he tried never to do, even in the moment of desire, but it was a risk I'd had to take. Also my pride was involved. How dare he say I didn't please him! Well, I'd shown him. It remained to be seen whether I'd pay for my temerity with my life.

He rose and looked down at me. I was still lying on the rich carpet, my hair spread about me. A little smile played about his beautiful mouth.

'Are you ready to hear your sentence now?'

'I am ready.'

'Here then is the Sultan's justice. Your companions are free to return to their country. But I sentence you – ' he laid a hand on my throat, drawing it lazily down across my breasts, my belly, until it slid between my legs to where I still pulsed with the memory of his possession – 'to remain with me for ever.'

I smiled back at him. 'If that is His Majesty's will – what can I do but obey?'

'Nothing.' He smiled again. 'I am the law. And if it were otherwise, if I had no legal right to own you, then I would find some trick to force you to stay with me.' His voice vibrated with passion. 'I am an honest man, but there is no lie or deceit to which I would not descend to keep your beauty in my bed, in my heart. Stay with me always. Be the star that shines forever on my life.'

I heard the unusual note in his voice, almost a plea. From this all-powerful man this was tribute indeed. It prompted me to tease him.

'Why do you say that when you have already said that I have no choice?'

'Ah, there is the paradox that curses my life. The Sultan is all-powerful but the man needs to believe in his beloved's desire. Tell me, Light of my Heaven, that our being together is your will as much as mine.'

'It is my will,' I promised him.

He rose, drawing me to my feet. Keeping hold of my hands he led me to a small table inlaid with a rich mosaic pattern. On it stood a wide goblet made of gold, studded with emeralds and containing a heap of snowy white pearls of incredible size and perfection. He looked over them, selected the best.

'Here is my pledge,' he said, putting it into my hands. 'We shall be together until the last star has ceased to shine.'

'Until the last star has ceased to shine,' I echoed, revelling in the words.

Then he lifted me in his arms and bore me back towards the satin cushions, laying me among them with a gentleness that was almost reverent.

'We have much to discover about each other, my Bright Star. Let us begin in this moment.'

He drew me into his arms and laid his lips on mine. It was as though our previous loving had happened so long ago that our desire had regained its sharpness. And yet we had learned from that loving. We knew each other a little better, knew that we could surprise each other and were eager to learn more. Our mating was tumultuous, exhausting and yet infinitely sweet and tender. As I lay in his arms afterwards, my head against his heart, I felt my old life slip away and a new one – unknown but thrilling – begin for me.

Chapter Ten

I became the Sultan's favourite, or, as I was officially
known, the Chosen One of His Heart, and my
life was a wonderland of lavish wealth and exotic
customs.

Abdul, as he wished me to call him, explained that
he didn't normally live in the desert. He was having a
kind of holiday, playing at living as his ancestors had
done. Of course the oil revenues had enabled him to
add a few luxuries that his ancestors didn't have, like
silk hangings for the tent and all mod cons. He had
a battery of cellular telephones by which he kept in
touch with his capital city and the international stock
markets, and if he grew bored with desert life there
was a helicopter standing by to whisk him away. He
had the modern day equivalent of a magic wand:
incalculable wealth.

On the day we discovered each other we loved
and slept the hours away until evening. Then he
told me to prepare for the evening meal which we
would take together. The palanquin conveyed me to
my tent, where I found my suitcases which I'd last

seen in the Hilton. I took out my vanity case and, with a sigh of relief, discovered that my make-up was intact.

Abdul had ordered the costume he wanted me to wear that night and it was already laid out for me. It consisted of a floor length skirt that began over my hips, and a top that ended immediately under my breasts, so that my midriff was left bare. It was made of cloth of gold.

As I prepared for the night ahead I reflected on where Abdul would fit into my grading system. The trouble was that he was so extravagantly gorgeous that he fitted in nowhere unless you could imagine the Hilton, the Dorchester and the Ritz put together.

Perhaps the 'growl factor' would be better. This had become my second method of assessment, and was more flexible. A really gorgeous man could make a growl of pleasurable anticipation start deep inside me. If he was less gorgeous, but still attractive, it was more of a purr. On a scale of 1–10 Clive was a 7, Randy a 5 (I'd have rated him higher at the time but I'd learned a lot since then), Myles was an 8, Butcher and Jak were both 7. I'd only known Abdul a few hours but already I'd discovered his growl factor was so high it was right off the Richter scale.

When I'd finished my make-up and put on the clothes Abdul had sent, Sufia placed a cloak about my shoulders. It too was made of cloth of gold and fixed with a clip of solid gold studded with diamonds. Fully dressed, I seated myself in the palanquin, but this time the curtains were left drawn back. I reclined in splendour on white satin cushions as I was carried from the tent.

Outside the darkness had already fallen. Men with flaming torches held high led our way to a place at the far side of the camp from which I could hear the sound of reed music accompanied by the insistent

144

beat of drums. It seemed Abdul and I were not to dine alone.

At last the festivities came in sight. People were crowded into a large circle, watching dancers who whirled and leaped in the centre. I could see Abdul seated on a dais, wearing a white burnous, held in place with gold ropes. He rose to his feet as the palanquin approached and was set down before him. As he did so the music fell silent and the dancers became still. Everyone in that gathering had their eyes on us as he walked down to meet me, offering me his hand to help me out.

'You are more beautiful than ever, bright Star of my Existence,' he said. 'Come, take your place with me.'

He led me on to the dais and indicated for me to take a vacant seat at his side. As soon as I did so everyone bowed low. I couldn't believe this was happening to me.

A small procession of women, each carrying a black box, approached us. The first knelt at my feet and at a signal from Abdul opened the box, revealing a heavy necklace of diamonds and sapphires lying on black velvet.

'It is yours,' he said.

I gasped and reached out to lift it, but he stopped me. 'Look later,' he said, 'or there won't be time for you to see everything?'

'Everything?'

He waved a hand at the rest of the procession. 'They each bear a gift for you.'

He snapped his fingers and the woman rose. As she moved away her place was taken by another woman, who also opened her box. Inside was a diamond tiara and diamond ear-rings. The next woman offered me an aigrette of pearls, and after that came rubies, emeralds, gold, silver. They were all for me.

'I can't believe this,' I said weakly as the procession finally came to an end.

Abdul laughed and produced another box from behind him. Inside were two matching bracelets and ear-rings in gold, studded with diamonds. These Abdul lifted out and fitted on to me himself.

'And now I have one final gift for you,' he announced, 'the officer who first brought you to me in such a disrespectful fashion.' He snapped his fingers and to my amazement a squad of soldiers appeared escorting a prisoner, his hands tied in front of him. It was William.

They came to a halt and gave William a shove so that he fell to his knees before me. He was shivering.

'You have insulted my favourite,' Abdul informed him coldly. 'For that the punishment is death.'

William burst out into lamentations. I didn't understand the language but he was probably pointing out that it wasn't fair to punish him for not knowing I was going to become the favourite. I knew I had a problem. I didn't want him to die (although I wasn't sorry to see the smug look wiped off his face) but to question the Sultan's decree in public was going to be tricky.

I leaned over and whispered to Abdul, 'I bear him no ill-will. He thought I was just another criminal.'

'He should have known better,' Abdul declared imperturbably.

'But I don't want to start our love with bloodshed,' I pleaded. 'You've given me so many gifts. Now I'm daring to ask for one more.'

'You want me to commute his sentence to life imprisonment?'

'I want you to free him.'

Abdul frowned. Then he seemed to find inspiration. A curved, jewelled scabbard was fixed at his waist. He pulled out the short, gleaming knife and handed it to me.

'Cut his bonds or his throat, as you will. I leave the choice to you.'

I took the knife and went down to where William was kneeling. He held up his wrists in supplication and I slashed through the rope that bound them. As I did so I met his eyes and was startled by the hatred in them. How he loathed being beholden to me! Then the expression passed so quickly I might have imagined it and he began gabbling his thanks.

As I reseated myself Abdul sheathed his knife and said grimly, 'You have made a mistake for which you may be sorry. My people do not understand forgiveness.'

'But what should I fear when I have you to defend me?'

'Nothing, my Bright Star. You are right.'

William was still talking fast, resisting the efforts of the soldiers to drag him away. Abdul said, 'He is offering you his own daughter, Mumtaz, as your attendant.'

'I shall be delighted to take her,' I said firmly.

William burst out with more gratitude, but this time an exasperated look from Abdul made the other soldiers carry him off bodily, still swearing eternal loyalty at the top of his voice.

Abdul clapped his hands and the music and dancing resumed. Trays bearing sweetmeats were carried to our feet and Abdul guided my choice, sometimes popping a morsel into my mouth himself. They were stronger flavours than I was used to, either intensely spicy or very sweet, soaked in a local syrup known as sugar gum.

All around I could see people giving me curious looks, trying to assess the impact that the stranger was going to have, but none of them passed before

147

us without bowing to me. At last the feast was ended and I was carried to Abdul's tent, escorted by almost everyone who had been present, some of them dancing alongside the palanquin and taking the chance to stare at me. Many of the women threw flowers that landed in my lap. I was like a queen that night.

When we were alone Abdul took me in his arms, but before he could do more we heard the sound of a telephone ringing. Exasperated, he pulled it out from under the cushions and barked, 'I hope it's an emergency.'

He listened for a moment, then groaned and said, 'All right. Put him on.' He held out the phone to me. 'Your friends are refusing to leave without you. Please talk to them before there's a diplomatic incident.'

I found myself talking to Sax. 'Are you all right, Honey?' he demanded.

'Sax, I'm fine. Honestly I am.'

While I talked Abdul was unclasping my top at the back. When it was loose he slipped his hands round the front and cupped my breasts. The things he was doing to my nipples with his fingers and thumbs made it hard to think straight, but also clarified the one point that mattered. I wanted to stay with him.

'Have they hurt you?' Sax was demanding.

'N-no. Everything's fine,' I insisted as shudders of pleasure ran through me. Oh yes, everything was very fine.

'We're at the airport with a load of guns trained on us – '

Abdul had got my skirt loose and was slipping it over my hips, down my legs, until it was off and I was naked. He rose and stripped off his own clothes, standing over me with his legs apart so that I could see his gigantic organ, held aloft at a proud angle, waiting for me, demanding my attention, almost seeming to threaten me.

My mouth watered. I couldn't take my eyes off it.

'Well, you get right on the next plane,' I told Sax, hardly knowing what I said. Abdul knelt and flipped me over on to my stomach, raising my hips and sliding a cushion beneath them. 'D-don't take any risks,' I burbled into the phone.

'That's sweet of you, Honey, but I hope you know me better – '

Oh, please Sax get off the phone. Abdul's fingers are between my legs, touching my cunt which is wet and slippery for him.

'– than to think I'd just go off and abandon you – '

He's kneeling between my legs, inserting that marvellous member into me . . . oh so slowly . . .

'– in a strange country. I've demanded to see the British Consul – '

Slowly . . . slowly . . . again and again . . . thrust and retreat . . . thrust and retreat . . . I like it so much in this position because it stimulates me in new places and Abdul is an expert.

'– but it seems there's no way. But when I get back to England – '

Just get back there, Sax, as quick as you like, leave me to enjoy Abdul, his fingers parting my buttocks, sliding inside me there . . . while his cock still possesses me in front and I'm totally, deliciously full as I was with Butcher and Jak, but Abdul is only one man and I could never need another.

'– I'm going to make sure that this disgraceful business – '

Now his other hand in front, touching me . . . teasing me . . . stimulation from all directions . . . glorious . . . wonderful . . . agonisingly beautiful . . .

'– is made known – '

My loins are overwhelmed with pleasure, my body is burning.

'– and there'll be a scandal – '

I can bear it no longer. I'm coming and coming, convulsively. Pure physical pleasure is washing over me like a waterfall, leaving me gasping.

'Sax, please don't do that,' I managed to gasp. 'No scandal. Don't tell anyone. I'm staying here of my own free will.'

'I can't believe that.'

'Its true, I promise you.'

Abdul is kneeling beside me so that his still huge cock is close to my mouth, tempting me.

'Honey, do you expect me to believe that you want to stay?'

'Yes, Sax. I swear it. I want to stay. I want to stay more than anything in the world.'

The tip pressed against my lips. Wildly I tossed away the phone, opening my mouth to take him in, and it all began again.

William's daughter Mumtaz arrived and I took an instant dislike to her. She was about my age with spiteful eyes, gross, sensual features and a figure that looked as if she spent too much time eating sugar gum. Not that that detracted from her charms in the eyes of her admirers. Kamari men like plump women. I guessed that they all thought I was on the skinny side and were baffled at Abdul's preference for me.

The wonderland holiday in the desert continued. Abdul provided me with a gleaming white mare and we went riding alone together among the sand dunes, always sooner or later coming across an oasis that had been warned to expect us. There was a cool tent in which to rest, fruit and coffee to refresh us, and blessed privacy in which to slake our passion. Hot and stimulated after our ride, we'd face each other like two frantic tigers and these sexual encounters were the most lusty and unsubtle that we ever had.

We always wanted each other. At any moment of the day or night we would be ready to make love. Abdul casually confided that he'd had his first woman when he was twelve years old, and thereafter he'd been attended by experts. Now in his late thirties, he'd had years of practice and experimentation and there were few aspects of the art of love he hadn't personally experienced. He could hold off his climax almost indefinitely, making me come repeatedly while he controlled his own pleasure in a way that seemed superhuman.

None of the men I'd previously enjoyed sex with had been imaginative or adventurous, except perhaps Myles, and even his knowledge paled beside Abdul's endless inventiveness. He disliked making love in the same position twice running and introduced me to a whole variety of new positions and sensations, sometimes without warning.

It was a favourite joke of his to uncover me while I slept and slip his head between my legs, kissing and teasing me so that I woke up to find myself already coming. One morning, when he was sure I was properly awake, he gently pushed my legs up and back, till my feet were almost level with my ears.

'Not every woman is supple enough for this,' he said. 'Shall I stop?'

'No, I'm fine,' I murmured. 'I want to see what happens next.'

'This,' he said, entering me and lying on top of me, while his fingers gently massaged my feet. It was a fantastic feeling, especially as I found I could rock my hips in a new way, and when he rocked with me the stimulation was thrilling.

I'd thought that such a proud man might be reluctant ever to let me on top, but he was too secure in his dominance to be worried by that, and it was his pleasure to have me sit astride him, controlling his penetration by the movement of my hips, sometimes leaning down so that he could caress my breasts, and sometimes drawing back to tease and tantalise him.

But he loved it most when I used the inner muscles that I'd made strong over a short but energetic love life. When he was deep inside me I would squeeze him softly, gently and he would groan with unbearable pleasure, calling on me to do it again and again. At such moments I knew a feeling of triumph that I could make him as much my sexual slave as I was his, and when we had loved each other to exhaustion I would lie in the crook of his arm, my head over his beating heart, and hear him murmur above my head, 'Till the last star has ceased to shine . . .'

The day came to return to the capital. I'd only seen a small part of the city, by the shore, but Abdul's palace faced inland on the far side. At my first view of it I thought it was one of the seven wonders of the world. It was huge, stretching apparently for miles, built of gleaming white marble with a roof of beaten gold. I had to cover my eyes against its dazzling light, which pleased Abdul.

We entered its great portals riding side by side on horseback, but almost at once we separated. Abdul said I would be conducted to the Rose Apartment while he had affairs of state to attend to.

The apartment was palatial. It consisted of five enormous rooms, one of which was a bathroom with a bath like a small swimming pool sunk into the mosaic floor. Next door was the bedroom, with a bed that must have been ten feet wide, hung with drapes of rose brocade. One room was entirely given over to wardrobes and strong boxes to contain clothes and the vast fortune in jewels Abdul had given me, and the room in which I was supposed to live and dine was big enough to give a banquet in. At one end were a pair of curtains that pulled back to reveal a screen, twelve foot by eight, and a huge cupboard nearby housed shelves for videos. Any film I wanted could be ordered and obtained within twenty-four hours.

There was also a garden where I could relax beneath the trees or wander among exotic plants, listening to the cry of peacocks. My privacy was protected by high walls topped with savage spikes which curved outwards.

My ladies were awaiting to welcome me to the Rose Apartment, including Mumtaz. I was trying hard to warm to her but it was uphill work. She was a sly girl, given to eavesdropping, and her manner to me always managed to be subtly insolent, even while outwardly respectful. She clearly blamed me for her father's disgrace, for although he was still free he'd been demoted in rank.

That night they prepared me for Abdul with especial care, bathing me in water scented with patchouli and orange blossom. Then Mumtaz dusted me down with sandalwood powder. Suddenly I winced as I felt a scratch on my shoulder and when I looked up I saw her looking at me with a malicious smile. The scratch was a sharp one, too sharp for a finger nail, but the huge powder-puff she was holding might hide any number of pins.

That night, as we made love, Abdul noticed the scratch and demanded to know how it had come about. I described what had happened and he immediately rose, put on his robe and ordered Mumtaz brought before him. She stood with eyes cast down, occasionally raising them slyly to his face. Abdul lectured her sternly about her carelessness, but when she'd gone he refused my request that she be dismissed.

153

'After the way she came into your service it would create too much awkwardness,' he said thoughtfully. 'I have seen to it that she will be more careful in future. Now, my Star, to more pleasant matters.'

I had little time to think further of Mumtaz. Despite Abdul's remarks about affairs of state the kingdom seemed to run itself with the minimum of interference from him. Only a week after we arrived he sent a message telling me to get ready to leave at once, and a few minutes later a helicopter whisked us away to the airport where his private jet stood on the tarmac with its engines running. That evening we were in the Casino at Monte Carlo.

For once Abdul was in western clothes, looking handsomer than ever in a black dress suit and bow tie. He lost heavily but hardly even seemed to notice. For him it was the bet that mattered. He stuffed wads of money into my hands and told me to enjoy myself. Then he seemed to forget me. I discovered that night that gambling was the one thing that could take his mind off physical pleasure. Once I tried to attract his attention but he looked right through me with cold, hard eyes.

We left in the early hours. Abdul never spoke a word all the way back to our hotel. He'd thrown away two million pounds and seemed to be in a kind of trance, although I knew the amount was nothing to him. When we reached our suite he threw himself on to the bed and lay staring at the ceiling. I began to undress him, pulling open his bow tie and undoing the buttons half buried in frills on his dress shirt. I kissed the smooth brown chest beneath and he stared at me blankly as if wondering what I was doing, and why.

He lay unresisting while I removed the rest of his clothes, occasionally shifting to make my job easier, but never seeming involved, even when I threw off my own clothes. His penis was quiet, uninspired, and for once Abdul didn't seem troubled by it. I urged him over on to his stomach and began the massage his body as impersonally as if I was a masseuse. I rubbed his back in firm circles until I could sense him relaxing and only then did I sit astride him so that he could feel my inner thighs against his buttocks. From here I could work on the back of his neck and shoulders, leaning forwards and sometimes back so that he could feel the soft contact repeatedly against his behind. He'd closed his eyes but now he opened them and I sensed a new alertness in him.

I moved off him and began to work on the small of his back easing down slowly to the top of his thighs so that I could knead them, letting my fingers drift casually inwards as he moved them further apart. Now I definitely had his attention and it was the moment to drop my head between his thighs, flickering my tongue against the skin. I heard him laugh and then rolled over, revealing something that made me smile with pleasure.

His organ reared up straight and proud, a tribute to my efforts. I took it between my hands and began to kiss it as I'd done that first day, putting all my art into inflaming him with flickering movements of my tongue, and when I felt him harden even more I sat astride him again, easing down on to that great rod and feeling it come up inside me. I sighed with satisfaction and completeness. I enjoyed this position because of the control it gave me. I could be penetrated deeply or lightly as I pleased, and by moving my hips I could increase my own pleasure.

I felt myself ready to come and tried to hold back, but Abdul sensed what I was doing and his brow darkened. He drew me down so that I lay full length on him and then with one quick movement turned so that he was on top again, moving fast and hard, making me come whether I wished to or not. He'd taken control back from me and now I understood his frown. Tonight he hadn't been quite himself and my dominant position had seemed to threaten him in a way that usually it didn't. I was content to let it go at that. At least he'd returned from the icy place where I couldn't reach him, and I was glad. I told myself that nothing else mattered.

But when it was over and I looked into his face I found him gazing at me with a look in his eyes that I didn't understand. The next day we flew back to Kamar. We'd been in Monte Carlo less than twenty-four hours.

One evening Abdul came to the Rose Apartment a little earlier than usual. I was still damp from my bath, but I hurried when I heard his voice.

Just before I went into the bedroom I heard him ask someone, 'Why have you done this?'

Then the voice of Mumtaz saying, 'Because Your Majesty should not be deceived by this woman.'

I felt an angry satisfaction that the question of Mumtaz had come to a head at last. She'd taken to gloating over my jewels with a greedy look in her eyes, and twice I'd caught her trying on the sapphires which, in the teeth of the evidence, she persisted in believing suited her.

When I went in I saw a great many newspapers and magazines lying about on the bed. They were western publications and all contained pictures of me in various stages of undress, plus lurid stories about my relationships with Randy, Myles and Butcher. I drew in my breath. Abdul had never asked me about other men in my life. What would he say now?

'See how she has lived in the past,' Mumtaz sneered.

But she'd said the wrong thing. Abdul looked at her coldly. 'You are mistaken. My Chosen One had *no* existence before becoming mine. Her past life is as something that never was. Now remove yourself from my sight.'

Mumtaz scurried away looking frightened.

'She cannot remain with me,' I said angrily.

Abdul shrugged. 'It would appear not. These quarrels become boring. She can go and serve my elderly mother. Mama is a tyrant and will keep that one in her place.'

'I want her sent right out of the palace,' I snapped, exasperated by his lack of understanding.

'Come Star of My Heaven, the matter is over. We should concern ourselves with more pleasant things.'

He refused to speak of it again, and soon I was swamped in our mutual passion. Mumtaz disappeared next day and I gradually forgot about her. Abdul's devotion to me continued unabated. He lavished jewels on me, more than I could ever wear, but my favourite was the perfect pearl he'd given me the first day. It had more meaning than the shower of gems that sometimes seemed almost impersonal.

And then a strange thing began to happen, one that was almost shocking in the circumstances. I began to dream about Steve, remembering his kindness and the unselfish way he'd left me to get on with my life. Once I woke from a dream of him, weeping, to find Abdul shaking me and looking concerned.

When he asked me what I'd been dreaming of I said the first thing that came into my head. 'I was remembering something – a long time ago – '

'How can that be when you had no life before me?' he asked, and I might have imagined it but I thought I heard a warning in his voice. I wondered if I'd spoken Steve's name in my sleep.

I thought of him by day, too, wondering how things would have been if he'd stayed in England and waited for me. And sometimes my life in Kamar seemed terrifyingly unreal. I lived like a hothouse plant with nothing to do but keep myself perfect for Abdul and the fantastic sex that we enjoyed.

Oh yes, it was still fantastic, but it had become my whole life, and I was realizing that it wasn't enough. Weeks had turned into months and it seemed a long time since I'd needed to use my mind for anything. Increasingly this felt like a drugged dream from which I struggled to awake.

My bored, sleepy mind began to wander even when I was making love with Abdul, and being sensitive to impressions he soon realized that he was losing my attention. Perhaps that was why one night his energy faded sooner than usual, and instead of falling asleep in my arms he rose, bade me a coldly courteous goodnight, and left me. And I discovered that I was actually glad to see him go. It meant I needn't fear to dream of Steve.

Chapter Eleven

*E*very night I tried to think of something new to divert Abdul so that our love-making never became routine. Or perhaps I was trying to divert myself. I was fascinated and intrigued by him and his vast sexual skills held me in thrall. Yet I was never in love with him. Steve's image was always there to prevent it.

I'd seen the belly dancers gyrating with jewels in their navels and thought I'd try it. I took the snowy pearl that had been his first gift to me and lodged it in my navel. At first it fell out whenever I moved but at last I thought of fixing it with sugar gum, and that held it in place perfectly.

That evening I dressed in cloth of silver adorned with sapphires. But instead of coming to the Rose Apartment he summoned me, which he'd rarely done before. I left the pearl where it was, thinking I might entertain him with a dance and then he could lick the sugar gum away and we'd take it from there. I covered my navel with a silk sash, the better to surprise him, and hurried to answer his summons.

159

I found him in his study. He looked up from his papers as I came in and smiled briefly, but as though his thoughts were elsewhere. Then he seemed to recall himself and drew me into his arms for a long kiss. I kissed him back fervently, feeling my passion rise. When he drew away he was smiling.

'Delicious Honey,' he murmured. 'How I shall miss you.'

'Miss me? Are we going to be apart?' I asked.

He released me. 'Alas yes. I have to go to America and may be away for some time. When I return . . .' he shrugged '. . . time will have passed. We shall both be changed. It is better if we say our farewells now and treasure only happy memories of each other.' He caressed my cheek. 'You have meant so much to me. Already my heart is breaking because this is the last time we shall ever meet.'

He didn't look like a man whose heart was breaking. He looked like a man who'd found himself a new playmate and wanted to rid himself of the old one quickly. I didn't mind too much. I was restless and the thought of going home again thrilled me.

'It breaks my heart too,' I told him. 'I shall think of you always. But I must admit it will be nice to return to my own country.'

He looked at me quizzically. 'Return to your country? You're not serious?'

'Of course. It's my home.'

'But my dear girl, how could you have ever imagined that I would let you return to England? You belong to me.'

'But you don't want me any more.'

'That makes no difference. You have known me intimately. You are aware of – ' he paused uneasily '– those very few weaknesses that I have. Such knowledge makes you dangerous. Besides, a woman

160

who has belonged to the Sultan cannot belong to any other man. It would be a desecration.'

I couldn't believe what I was hearing. 'You've changed your tune a bit, haven't you?' I said indignantly. 'What happened to being together until the last star has ceased to shine?'

He shrugged. 'Of course, such speeches are expected.'

How cold his eyes were, cold and indifferent. Why had I never noticed before? Or had I? Wasn't I now seeing something brought to the fore that I'd instinctively recognized long ago, something from which I'd chosen to avert my eyes?

'Well, I hope you have your pretty words all polished up for your new favourite,' I said sarcastically.

'She will receive every honour, as you did. Already she is being moved into the Rose Apartment. You will have no further use for it. Your prison will be comfortable, as befits an ex-favourite, but you must resign yourself to living in it forever.'

'You must be quite mad . . .,' I began.

'Please do not waste my time with protests.' He glanced at his watch. 'You have had your allotted time. You may take consolation in the thought that I have honoured you by telling you of your fate myself. In the past, other women have been informed by minor officials. The guards will take you to your new apartment.'

'The hell they will,' I snapped, striding to the door. 'I'm getting out of here.'

But I opened it to find two enormous guards barring my path. I tried to dodge them and they seized me.

'Wait,' called Abdul.

They held me as he walked towards me and unclipped the sapphire earrings I was wearing. 'You will not be needing jewels now, and my new beloved has a taste for sapphires.'

161

Suddenly the truth hit me. 'Mumtaz!' I spat.

'It is not permitted that you speak her name,' he said coldly. 'You no longer hold any place in my esteem.' He took the sapphire tiara from my head. 'Remove her.'

There was no point in struggling with those two great hulks but I did so for the sake of it. I was taken far away from Abdul's apartment, down long passages. The decoration became less lavish and I knew I was being taken to the rear of the palace where only humble persons lived.

At last we reached my prison, which was in a tower at the far end of the building. I was thrust into a large room and the door was locked behind me. I didn't waste time beating on it or yelling because I knew it would be useless. Instead I took stock of my surroundings.

Abdul had said my prison would be comfortable but after the luxury I was used to it looked very austere. Instead of the lavish mosaics of the royal apartments the floor was covered in black and white tiles and the walls were white. The room was divided into three by two arches and the far section contained a bed. There were curtains that pulled across the arches, giving some sort of privacy for sleeping.

The main room contained a table and chair and a few orange and blue cushions scattered over the floor. These and the red cover on the bed gave the rooms their their only colour. A door, covered by a beaded curtain, led out on to a small balcony from which I could look down into the yard filled with scurrying servants. Immediately beyond that was a wall which marked the palace boundary. By craning my neck I could see a road on the other side. That road led to freedom, if only I could get to it. In the meantime I was trapped here, a prisoner of the overweening vanity of the Sultan who couldn't bear to set free any woman who knew of his 'few weaknesses'. I might be here for the rest of my life. I shivered although the evening air was still warm.

Bitterly I recalled Abdul's warning that it was a mistake to forgive William, and the hatred in his eyes. He'd planned to take his revenge by putting his daughter in my place. And now they were triumphant. Tonight, doubtless, there'd be a feast at which a procession of women would lay jewels at Mumtaz' feet – those same jewels that I'd foolishly thought Abdul had given to me. And they'd remain hers until his eye lighted on another female, at which time they'd be snatched away again and presented to the new favourite, who would be allowed to enjoy her delusions for a little time. What baffled me was how I could have been so stupid.

While I was musing, the door opened and a tall woman entered. She bowed to me in the way I was used to. Evidently even an ex-favourite was allowed some respect, but this was no cause for hope, merely another aspect of Abdul's arrogance. Once a woman had been honoured by him she was permanently marked out from other women.

She had come to give me my suitcases and to tell me that the clothes I was wearing must be returned. I was about to tear them off and say I hoped Mumtaz would have fun fighting her way into them, when a sudden thought stopped me in my tracks.

'His Majesty's will is law,' I said humbly, 'but I should prefer to undress alone.'

I shooed her out of the bedroom section and pulled the curtains firmly across. I undressed quickly and grabbed the first thing I found from the cases, which happened to be the white pants suit I'd worn when I arrived. Then I summoned her back and handed over my silver Kamari costume. She bowed low

163

and retired. I stayed quite still as she left, but as the door closed I couldn't resist running my fingertips over my navel where the pearl was still in place.

It was the one thing I still had and I was determined to hang on to it. If ever I got out of here that little jewel was worth enough to restore my fortunes. The problem was, getting out.

I searched the cases but as I had feared everything valuable had 'disappeared'. My passport, my money, the few pieces of personal jewellery I'd brought with me, had gone. All that was left were my make-up and clothes.

My jailer returned with a meal. She was a heavily built young woman with a face that might have been attractive if she'd made the best of it. She saw me examining the make-up and a look of longing came into her eyes. In that moment I knew how I might escape.

'What's your name?' I asked in a friendly tone.

She told me her name was Lea and she was the daughter of the Sultan's chief jailer.

'Are you often set to guard women prisoners?'

'I asked to have this job,' she said shyly.

'Why?'

'Because – you can teach me things – about men.'

Then it all came out, how her father had arranged a marriage for her with Ali, one of the young guards. Ali was a worthless good-for-nothing but she loved him with all her heart, and she spent every night crying because he paid attention to other women and none to her.

'You made the Sultan love you. You can show me how,' she pleaded.

'The Sultan's "love" didn't amount to much in the end,' I observed wryly.

She looked surprised. 'No man's love ever does,' she said. 'A woman must be content with what she has at the start. But I have nothing.'

'Come here,' I told her.

She obeyed, and when she was close I dabbed a little Chanel No. 5 behind each ear. 'Now we'll have to wait and see,' I said.

Later that night I heard the sound of giggling and scuffling from behind the outer door, and when I peeped through a crack I saw Lea making an unconvincing pretence of pushing Ali away. At last the noises stopped and there was a long silence.

Next morning Lea was radiant and begged for some more perfume. I gave her another little dab and bided my time. Soon she was my slave, willing to do anything for a trifle of cosmetics, which I'd taken the precaution of hiding away. At last I told her what I wanted her to do for me. She shook her head in fear, but I said, 'When I escape I shall leave behind all I have, and it will be yours.'

She wavered, but the lure was too great and at last she consented. I gave her a strip of material that I had earlier torn off one of my slips, and on which I had written in eyebrow pencil, *I am an English woman, held captive in the Sultan's palace. Tell the British Consul.*

Lea promised that next day, when she went shopping in the bazaar for her father, she would find someone suitable to give it to. That night I couldn't sleep for hope.

But when I saw her the following evening she was in tears. She'd been followed into the bazaar by palace guards who'd watched her suspiciously. In desperation she'd thrust the message down the neck of an earthenware jar that stood outside a shop. She knew her pursuers hadn't seen that because on her return to the palace she'd been searched. But although nothing was found she was still under suspicion and a new jailer had been appointed for me. This was the last time we would meet.

I thanked her and gave her the rest of the Chanel, plus the advice to make Ali marry her before it ran out. Then I lay down and for the first time I cried. I had no hope unless someone bought the pot, found the message and knew what to do with it. But it would need a miracle. I tried not to give in, but that night I was very close to despair.

For a week everything went on as before except that a new woman was put in charge of me, not nearly so agreeable as Lea. She'd heard of the make-up and demanded I hand it over to her. I did so because otherwise I knew she'd go through my cases. Besides, what did I need with make-up now? My life as Honey was over. No man would ever think me beautiful again.

One night as I lay staring into the darkness I thought I heard a faint sound. I sat up in bed, straining my ears, and it came again – the scratch of metal on stone. I got quietly out of bed and went into the main room. Through the beaded curtain I could just make out the gleam of a three-pronged hook that had come over the edge of the balcony and clung there. My heart beating, I leaned tentatively over the balcony and could just make out a rope swaying in the darkness, and a man climbing up it. All I could see of him was that he wore an Arab burnous. It could be anybody, but my heart prayed that it was a rescuer.

I hurried back to the bedroom and put on a slip, for I was naked. A moment later a booted foot appeared over the balcony and the man hauled himself up.

'Is anyone there?' he whispered. 'Don't be frightened. I'm English too and I've come to get you out of here.'

I bit back a cry of joy, for I knew that voice. It was the voice I loved but had thought I'd never hear again.

'Steve,' I whispered in frantic joy.

'How do you know my – *who is that?*'

'It's me – Honey. *Steve.*'

The next moment we were in each other's arms and his mouth was on mine for the first time in three years. Time stopped as that blissful kiss went on and on. My heart was full to overflowing with joy. I'd always known Steve and I would find each other again, and now he'd come to me in my darkest hour.

'Honey,' he said hoarsely, kissing me repeatedly, 'Honey. . . Honey. . .'

When we drew apart he laid his finger against his mouth and crept to the door, listening. He came back and drew me into the bedroom, pulling the curtains quietly across.

'How did you get here?' I asked, dazed.

'My excavation is only about ten miles away. One of the servants went into the market to get supplies and bought a wine pot. We found your message in it and decided to come for you.'

'We?'

'There's three of us. Hamen is an Arab and he dressed up as a peasant and mingled with the palace servants. He got the information about where you were, bribed two of the guards to look the other way while I shinned up, and another one to open the gate for us. Johnson is the leader of the 'dig' I'm on and he provided the money for the bribes. When we get out he and Hamen are waiting for us.'

167

'Hurry, let's go,' I pleaded, longing to be out of there.

'Hush, we have to wait. The guard who's going to open the gate won't come on duty for another two hours. It's safer if we stay quietly here.'

I touched his face. 'I can't believe that I'm seeing you again after all this time,' I said. 'It's like a miracle.'

He seized my hands and kissed them. 'Love is a miracle, my darling. It's the miracle that's reunited us against all the odds.'

'Oh Steve, you should never have left me.'

'Darling, it broke my heart to go like that, but I had to, for your sake. And you see how right I was. I get the English newspapers, although they're several weeks late. I've read about your glittering career.'

'I never wanted anything but you. I never stopped loving you and wanting you to love me.' I kissed him softly. 'Love me now,' I pleaded.

'I mustn't,' he said in agony.

'But why? We have two hours.'

'I'm here to save you. I should spend the time on guard at that door. We're not safe yet.'

'I know, and maybe we never will be. Perhaps they'll catch us and kill us. If that happens, I want to have had one night in your arms,' I pleaded.

With a groan he seized me and held me close to him. 'I can't resist you. I was strong once but I can't be strong again.'

'You must never be strong enough to resist me,' I told him. 'I won't let you be. You belong to me. You always have. Just as I belong to you. Oh, Steve, haven't you always known that this would happen?'

'Yes . . . yes . . .' he was kissing me urgently between the words.

Last time he'd held me in his arms I'd been a child. Now I was a child no longer but an experienced woman who knew what she wanted. Steve had inspired my first innocent passion, and since then there had been many passions, not all of them innocent. If desire had been all that united us I would have forgotten him by now. But as I looked up into his beloved face, so handsome, so much firmer for his rough life, I knew why I'd been unable to make a rich marriage, why Steve had haunted me through the past months when my every whim had been law. He was the man I loved, the man I would always love. It was as simple as that.

We claimed each other like boy and girl discovering the joy of the flesh for the first time. And perhaps that was true, for that night I felt as though we and only we had created passion and given it to the world, blessing it with our miracle. It might sound foolish now, but it was in our hearts that night, as it is in the hearts of all true lovers when they make love for the first time.

We lay naked together, exploring each other's bodies in the darkness, discovering things we couldn't see. He had scars from injuries sustained during his dig, and I kissed them tenderly. He was thin from heat and hard work. I could feel his ribs and the individual outline of every bone in his spine. Yet he was full of wiry strength that I could sense as I ran my hands lovingly over him.

His hands on me traced my curves and he murmured, 'You're as beautiful as I once told you you'd be. Remember?'

'I remember everything about you,' I whispered.

He kissed my eyes, my mouth, my breasts. I burned to have his kisses all over my body, to feel his tongue and lips invading every place where his hands now explored. He touched me gently between my legs where the moist heat welcomed him, and when he knew I wanted us to become one he moved his body over mine. I felt the firm tip of his cock probing me, then sliding easily inside, filling and fulfilling me as my heart had always known he could do. I wept for joy. It was for this I had been made a woman.

He thrust slowly like a man savouring every moment of a dream, long held, hoped for, longed for, and now only half believed. I understood this instinctively because it was the same with me. Our hearts were even more one than our bodies and I knew that my feelings were mirrored in him. Such beauty was impossible, and yet it had been granted to us. All around lay danger. Perhaps neither of us would survive this night but that knowledge made this affirmation of life all the sweeter. In that narrow little bed, surrounded by our enemies, I found the man I loved, gave myself to him body and soul, and felt my life begin.

We lay together quietly, listening to the beat of each other's hearts. At last Steve said, 'We should go now.'

We dressed and went to look out from the balcony. It was still dark but there was enough starlight to show us the way down. In a few minutes we might be on our way to freedom, or it might all be over. We kissed each other one last time before he fixed the hook over the balcony. After testing it he whispered, 'Can you manage alone or do you want to hold onto me?'

'I can manage,' I said.

'Then I'll go first. If you feel it becoming too much, slide down a little and I'll take you on my shoulders.'

He swung himself over and down a few feet, then called softly, 'Now.'

I took hold of the rope and launched myself into space, trying not to think what a long way it was down to the ground. At first I managed well but it grew harder, my wrists and hands ached until suddenly I found I couldn't grip any more. My hands seemed to let go of the rope of their own accord and I felt myself falling through space.

But not for long. An arm like a steel hawser snaked out and clamped me hard to a wiry male body, and Steve was murmuring in my ear, 'That was a near thing. Not much further now.'

A few moments later we were on the ground. Mercifully the yard seemed deserted. We ran along the base of the wall until we were in sight of the gate, guarded by one man. He raised a hand when he saw us and began to draw back the heavy bolts slowly. By the time we'd reached him the gate was open. Steve gave him a brief word of thanks and we were through.

The first cracks of light were just appearing and I could make out an ox-cart by the side of the road, the driver slumped as though he'd fallen asleep over the reins. But when he heard our footsteps he became alert at once and pulled back a blanket on the cart. Steve helped me up, then climbed in after me and drew the blanket over us. The cart began to move forward. My heart was thundering, and all the time I expected to hear the cry of pursuers. But nothing happened and the cart trundled slowly on. Steve put his arm round me and held me close, and I knew that as long as he was with me I was safe.

Chapter Twelve

*A*fter what seemed like an eternity we came to a halt. We were on the outskirts of a small village. A plump middle-aged man helped us out of the cart and pointed to a Range Rover parked nearby.

'Quick,' he said.

We got into the back and I hid on the floor, covered by a blanket. We roared off, and when I was allowed to look out all I could see was barren landscape, divided by a stony road. In the front seats were the man I now knew was Hamen and the plump man who'd been waiting for us.

'I'm Johnson,' he called over his shoulder. 'I'd have brought the car nearer but motor vehicles aren't allowed on that road in case they disturb the Sultan.'

I told him how grateful to him I was for paying the bribes and asked where they were taking me.

'To the dig,' Johnson said. 'You can lie low there until we can think of a way of getting you out.'

The route lay through some huge sand coloured stones, and when we were well hidden among these

Johnson stopped near a cave. Steve helped me out of the Range Rover.

'We've got some clothes for you to change into,' he said. 'Here's a good place.'

It was deliciously cool inside the cave and I thought I could make out the sound of running water.

'It's a small underground stream,' Steve explained. 'There.' He pointed.

There was a break in the rock above us, with a natural tunnel leading up into the daylight, and down through it poured a shaft of light that illuminated the stream and the little pool it ran into. I longed to bathe in it and feel the freshness of cool, clear water, unscented by orange blossom or ylang-ylang, or any of the perfumed stimulants that had seemed so natural in the world I'd left behind. Quickly I stripped off and plunged in, gasping at the cold. It was wonderful.

Steve followed me. I opened my arms to him and we embraced under the gleaming light from the world far above. Down below I could feel his cock probing me and wondered how it could be so big in that chilly water. But my own passion too was at fever pitch, reinvigorated by the joy of being free at last. I curved my legs round his lean body, guided him into me and bore down.

How good it felt to have the man I loved inside me. Steve put his hands under my buttocks and with that support it was easier for me to tighten my legs, drawing him deeper into me for the searing moment of our mutual coming.

He carried me out of the pool in his arms and set me down. 'We must hurry,' he murmured. 'This isn't fair to the others. But tonight –?'

'Yes,' I whispered. 'Tonight.'

I put on the shabby old shirt and trousers that they'd brought for me. Everything was much too large and concealed my shape, which was perhaps just as well. My hair was pulled back and hidden under a wide-brimmed hat. We returned to Johnson and Hamen. Johnson looked at his watch,

'There was no need for you to hurry,' he observed ironically.

It was night before we reached the dig. By the starlight I could just make out some tents and some trenches in the ground where they were excavating. Steve took my hand and led me down a slope into one of the trenches. Since no-one else in the camp must know I was here they were going to hide me in a chamber of the actual tomb they were working on.

There was a mattress in the corner, something to eat and drink and a lamp by which I could make out that this was a large room whose sandstone walls were covered with paintings.

Johnson made sure I was all right and left us alone. Steve and I looked at each other in the dim, flickering light. For a long moment neither of us moved, then, almost tentatively he touched my face

'I don't believe this is actually happening,' he said. 'I've wanted you so much . . . you can't be real.'

'I'm real and I'm here,' I promised him. 'And I want you too.'

I took his face between my hands and kissed him as tenderly as I knew how. Now we had time to love each other properly and neither of us wanted to rush it. Our loving in my prison cell had been spiced with danger, our union in the pool had been a celebration. But this would be more. This would be an affirmation of what we were to each other, what we would always be.

We kissed for a long time, exploring each other's mouths with our tongues. I used the tip of mine to trace the outline of his beautifully shaped lips, something I'd always wanted to do, even in school.

174

He tasted of heat and sand, clean sweat and eager, roused male.

He began to undo the buttons of my shirt, slipping a hand lovingly inside to feel the softness of my skin against the rough material. How many other men had done that? My answer is – none. Steve was the first man to make real love to me. There was a sense in which that was true. His touch was unique and special, and the shudders that went through me as he brushed my nipples were more intense, more beautiful than I had believed anything could possibly be. I sighed his name longingly.

'Yes,' he whispered. 'What is it my love?'

'Steve, I want you . . . I love you . . . .'

He removed my shirt, drew me down to the mattress and finished undressing me there. When I was naked he threw off his own clothes and lay beside me, stroking me with reverent gentleness. The flickering oil lamp revealed the pictures on the walls, pictures of love and union. They represented the passion of three thousand years ago, looking down on our passion tonight. I felt at one with them, for some things never change, and our loving was part of every loving there had ever been since the world began.

His arms were strong and there was tenderness in his gaze as he looked down at me. When he entered my body we became one flesh, one heart and one soul. He thrust slowly, waiting for my smile, joyful when it came. My eager response to him wasn't merely the fulfilling of desire, the slaking of an appetite, but a whole-hearted acceptance of the man for himself, everything he was and might be. I was his woman. It was what I'd been born for.

This wasn't Abdul who had to vary his sex to hide its emptiness, who contorted himself to avoid looking a woman in the face. This was a man for whom love-making was an expression of emotion, and to whom the face was everything. He made love to me with his eyes as well as his loins, and my own eyes told him that he had shown me a new world. I knew that we would climax together and we did. We were one in that as in everything else.

I fell asleep in his arms, dreaming of the days to come when we would be together many times.

But even that little time was denied us. The very next day a detachment of Kamari guards came to the camp seeking me. I was quickly hidden in the secret chamber. I could hear everything that was said above and stood listening with my heart thumping.

It soon became clear that the guards had no specific information. They had headed for the dig because it was run by Englishmen. Johnson was magnificent. Inside that plump, comic exterior beat the heart of a lion. He berated the guards up hill and down dale, demanding whether they realized that this dig had the personal interest of the Sultan. Search? By all means they could search. But if they disturbed so much as one bone of the royal ancestors they would answer for it to His Majesty personally.

Actually none of them was Abdul's direct ancestor because his family had usurped the throne seven hundred years ago and this was a three thousand year old tomb, but it was a safe bet that none of the guards was going to point that out. Besides, it sounded good, and as Abdul was in America by now none of them was quite sure how far to go. They made a lot of noise but departed without a search.

'But they'll be back,' Johnson said later. 'You've got to go tonight. Hamen has a cousin in the Kamari Air Force who is eminently bribable. I'd hoped not to have to use this method because it's very risky, but we can't wait. Here's what's going to happen. . .'

That night Steve and Hamen took me in the Range Rover to an airfield twenty miles away. Dawn was just breaking when Hamen went off to find his cousin and stuff his hands with Johnson's money. I'd given Johnson a specially big kiss as a thank you, and he'd gone red and muttered, 'Steady on – don't want Steve gunning for me.' But I think he was pleased.

Steve and I were alone for a brief, precious minute.

'I wish you could come with me,' I said.

'But I can't. If I vanished now, poor old Johnson would be in the soup when they come back. And he's been so good to us.'

'Oh yes, I know you're right. It's just that I don't know when we'll meet again.'

'Neither do I, my darling. It might be a long time. I can't renege on my contract with Johnson, and it might be a couple more years.'

'Oh no!' I threw myself, weeping, into his arms, and we clung together.

'Darling,' he said huskily, 'listen to me. Whatever happens, you'll always be the woman I love, and I know you'll always love me. That's all that counts. People do what they must. If we should meet again – the past won't exist any more.'

Dear, generous, understanding Steve. He knew that however much I loved him I was sexually voracious, and also that I had to survive. He was telling me that he'd never blame me for the way I lived.

Hamen was returning. He signalled us to follow him. Steve took my hand and we hurried along in the shadows until we came to a helicopter, and there was Hamen's cousin, ready to fly.

Steve seized me in his arms for one last kiss. Then I was being helped into the helicopter. I pressed my face to the window, trying to see him through a blur of tears as we lifted off in the early morning light.

'Where are we going?' I asked of a second man who was sitting quietly in the helicopter.

'Not far,' he said. 'Then we're going to winch you down.'

'Onto what?'

He grinned. 'You'll see. Let me help you into the gear.'

He fitted me into the winch and when I looked out of the window we were over brilliant, sparkling water. Before I could ask any questions the man had opened a trapdoor in the floor and was easing me out. And suddenly there was nothing around me but air and wind, and I was going lower and lower. . . .

Until I landed on the deck of *HMS* ****.

But that's an official secret.

Unfortunately I can't go into the details of how the Royal Navy got me back to England, because I promised the Home Secretary that I wouldn't, but all the nice things they say about sailors are true.

And so at last I found myself back in my own flat. I'd been gone for five months and felt as if I'd lived a thousand lifetimes. And you might think that, apart from experience, I had nothing to show for it.

But you'd be wrong. The first thing I did when I got home was to retrieve my pearl from where I'd been hiding it right through the journey, in a very private place.

After so long away I was bound to have money problems. Sax had sent my ten thousand pound fee for the advertisement to Clive, who'd banked it for me, and some overdue fees had come in while I was away. But although the mortgage payments had been kept up the other bills hadn't. I needed to make some money fast.

I considered selling my pearl, but I really wanted to keep it for a rainy day. I was rescued by the *Daily Cobblers*, offering very big money for my story of eastern lust. It was virtually written and all I had to do was add some details and pocket the cash. Once I would have refused, but I was older and tougher now. I agreed but made them triple their price.

The three part series was entitled "*A Love-Slave In The Desert*", with sub-titles like 'My months of sexual bondage' and 'Desire among the sand dunes', and some pictures of me wearing chains and little else. The paper's circulation went up half a million overnight. I got together with Clive, Phil and Donny for a private party to celebrate my home-coming and we all roared with laughter over the lurid stories. I didn't tell them that the reality had been ten times as lurid. If I'd put everything in they'd have had to close the paper down.

Phil and Donny nearly had nervous breakdowns over what the desert had done to my hair and skin. I couldn't see any difference but they made me feel I was falling to pieces, so I put myself in their hands to stop them committing hara-kiri, and I had to admit they made me look better.

I had dinner with Sax who told me an unbelievable story.

'We were released only on condition that every last foot of film was handed over to the Sultan,' he said. 'So I did. There was no choice. What nobody realized was that the early reels had been given to the "gofer" before it all went wrong, and he'd simply taken them back to the hotel. So he wasn't there when we got arrested and they missed him. As soon as he heard what had happened he got the first plane out of there, taking the film. When I got back I made the ads with the early shots. They're peachy. Everyone loves them. In fact, I want to talk to you about making some more.'

'As long as it doesn't mean going back to Kamar,' I said firmly.

'Paris,' he said enticingly.

'You're on.'

We flew to Paris and I posed in a black satin teddy on the Eiffel Tower. Would you believe I nearly got arrested again? I thought the French understood these things, but this young policeman got terribly agitated and carried on about a national monument. Luckily he was extremely handsome so we soon reached an understanding and. . . .

But that's another story. He was a nice boy and I promised that his fiancée with the three six foot brothers would never find out.

When we returned I did some television appearances, TV-am, Wogan, that sort of thing. I'd been away too long and I wanted everyone to know I was back.

There was a nice letter from Myles saying how glad he was to hear of my escape. He enclosed a picture of his ten day old son, 'The new Lord Portland – poor little sod,' as he put it.

Then, out of the blue, I heard from Leonard Hawkburn, saying that he would be coming to see me.

It was the same Leonard Hawkburn whose speech I'd ruined. He'd been moved to the Foreign Office now. The very day I got his letter he was in the news because of a visit he'd made to Kamar. He flew back full of praise for Kamari women who were apparently devoted to their homes and their husbands.

'Juvenile crime is non-existent,' he said in a television interview, 'because young people have the full-time attention of their mothers. Nothing is more damaging to society than a generation of children raised without standards because their mothers. . .'

He went on to talk about his own mother who'd apparently been utterly content at home, raising her son and deferring to her husband. 'She loved and trusted my father,' he said. 'She gave us all her attention, and because of her I had a bedrock of security that supports me to this day.'

The sisterhood reacted by marching down Whitehall with banners saying, 'Come out of the ark, Hawkburn'. There were shots of him striding past them into the Foreign Office, looking purposeful and radiating masculine strength. The annoying thing was that he could just about make you believe it would be worth giving up everything else as long you had him in bed every night.

I prepared for our meeting very carefully, and I was all ready for Leonard when he arrived at my flat next day. In his dark suit and carrying a black leather briefcase he looked extremely official and correct. He refused my offer of a drink but accepted a cup of tea with lemon. I began to wonder if I'd miscalculated.

'I've just returned from Kamar,' he said, 'where I've had talks with the Sultan. He claims that you are a fugitive from his country's justice and that you escaped from prison. He asks that you be extradited.'

'The rotten so-and-so!' I exploded. 'Tell him to get knotted!'

'It isn't quite as simple as that,' Leonard said. 'We have good diplomatic relations with Kamar which we are anxious to maintain.'

'But you can't extradite me because of a flag!' I said. 'Anyway, if you've read my story in the *Daily Cobblers* you know how it came about.'

He seemed to choke on his lemon. 'You surely don't think that *I* – scandal rag – serious man – grave responsibilities – '

'I'd have thought it was part of your responsibilities to discover the facts before coming to bully me,' I pointed out.

'Not bully you – misunderstanding – may have glanced at it – probably did – '

I was wrong. It wasn't lemon that was choking him, it was embarrassment. 'Then perhaps I'd better tell you everything?' I suggested.

'Yes – good idea.'

'I went to Kamar to model underwear for Mata Hari Creations,' I explained. 'Perhaps you've heard of them?'

He gave me his best dominant male frown. 'May I remind you that I am a Minister of State?'

'Well, anyway, they make underwear, and I was modelling something like this.' Quick as lightning I unbuttoned my dress and threw it aside to reveal a tiny bra and panties. I'd bought them from Mata Hari and they were exact duplicates of what I'd been wearing when the custard hit the fan. Some instinct had warned me that they might be useful at this interview.

Leonard was sitting very still, looking at me. 'I have to show you *exactly* how it was,' I explained. 'You see how skimpy this underwear is?'

Leonard swallowed. 'I see.'

'We all felt I needed something else to cover me, and there was this piece of cloth from the bazaar.' I flourished a silk scarf I'd left handy. 'There was some music,' I had a CD player by now and I switched it on to something soft and sensuous, 'and I had to move about while they filmed me.'

I suited the action to the words, gyrating so that my hips swivelled close to him. He looked as if he were being strangled. 'Do you see what I mean?' I asked innocently.

'Yes,' he whispered.

'And I played with the scarf like this. . .' I swung the scarf behind me, holding a corner in each hand and drew it against my hips, moving them back and forth against the material. I began to think how awkward it would be if he had a fit in my home. He was becoming a funny colour.

I raised a corner of the scarf to behind my shoulder and began to draw it forward down my body, between my breasts. I turned my back on Leonard so that he had a grandstand view of my bottom as it moved to the music, and from behind me I thought I heard faint choking noises.

I turned to face him again. 'And then,' I murmured, 'I did this. . . .'

On the words I began to draw the scarf through my legs, letting it brush against my cunt . . . slowly . . . slowly . . .

. The music stopped. Leonard was a complete wreck.

'And that was all,' I said. I looked at him, wide-eyed. 'Is that really an extraditable offence?'

'I'm – I'm sure it isn't,' he said, running a hand round the inside of his collar.

'I have made everything perfectly clear, haven't I?'

'Perfectly,' he said in agony.

'Is there anything else you want?' I purred.

'Yes,' he said hoarsely, wrenching his buttons open.

I helped him undress because in his haste he was fumbling about all over the place. We tumbled on to the carpet together and in a moment he was on top and inside me. Two thrusts and it was over.

I lay there, unable to believe what had happened. I'd hardly felt anything. His prick was so small heaven knows how he'd got it up that far. Talk about Wham, Bam, Thank you Ma'm! This hadn't even lasted as long as the 'Thank you.' What had happened to the dominant bull of my fantasies?

Now I could see he had a wonderful body, heavy and muscular with broad shoulders and torso.

Despite his bulk there was no fat on him. His flesh was firm and attractive and his whole frame seemed full of power. Yet it was all a con. He was a great empty balloon. Prick him and he'd go off pop.

'Well,' he was saying heartily, 'well, well – I don't know what – I'm uncontrollable sometimes – ha ha!'

Was I supposed to tell him that he was the demon lover who'd swept me off my feet with his flaming passion? While I was deciding what to do he gave a pathetic little groan and collapsed on the sofa with his head in his hands.

'I'm sorry,' he moaned. 'I'm so sorry. Oh, I wish I was dead.'

'Hey, it's all right,' I said, thinking I understood. 'You didn't force me or anything like that. If I hadn't wanted to do it I could have dealt with you, no problem.'

'I know you could,' he groaned. 'You could deal with me or any man because you're such a strong woman.' He seized my hand. 'You're not afraid of men, are you, Honey?'

'Well no, but – '

'I know you're not. You take them on your own terms and make them do whatever you want. I've admired you ever since I first saw you in the House of Commons.'

'Admired –?'

'Your courage. You sat up there, bold as brass, and you weren't intimidated by that big place. You were doing what you wanted, just as you always do.'

He was gabbling now, words tumbling out over each other as he clutched my hand feverishly. 'And then there was that Marquess. You could have married him but you spurned him.'

'I didn't exactly – '

'Because you're big enough, powerful enough, to do without titles. I've followed your career. I know how you dealt with Lythal, too. That's what I mean, you see. Strong. Of course Dyson wanted to marry you. The aristocracy have a weakness for dominant women. It's what's kept England great.'

'Here, who are you calling dominant?' I demanded indignantly.

'Oh but you *are*, my sweet Honey, you are! That's what's so wonderful about you, why I adore you so madly. Look how you managed in Kamar. Trapped in the hands of some tinpot little foreign despot, but you wrapped him round your little finger, didn't you? You weren't really in bondage to him. You were just playing him along, making a fool of him until you could escape, because you're strong enough to do anything.'

I didn't understand what he was on about, but one thing stood out loud and clear. All that 'keep the little woman in her place' stuff was so much window dressing. The real Leonard Hawkburn felt very differently. And once I knew that I knew how to handle him.

'Well, I don't let any man mess me around, that's true,' I mused.

He nodded. 'Woe betide the man who tries. You'd make him regret it.' He seemed to relish the thought of my unknown victim's repentance.

'But this doesn't explain why you wish you were dead,' I pointed out.

He became a quivering heap of misery again. 'Because I disappointed you. I know I did. Don't try to deny it.'

'Well – '

'You see, everything has to be just right before I – that is – under the right conditions – '

'You become a lion?' I offered.

'I can do better than I did today. I could – ' he gulped – 'I could do anything that you told me to.'

'But I have to tell you?' I hazarded.

'You have such wonderful authority.'

So that was it. Now I knew how to play it.

'Well the first thing I'm going to tell you is to stop weeping and wailing,' I said in a firm voice. 'Stop it *at once.*'

Ye gods, I'll swear his prick jumped six inches just from the tone I'd used.

'How dare you come here talking nonsense,' I scolded him. 'You should be ashamed of yourself.'

'I am,' he admitted humbly. 'I know I've behaved badly. I deserve anything you do.' His prick was swelling in direct proportion to his humility and becoming a very interesting size.

'All I'm going to do is throw you out of here and order you never to come back,' I told him sternly.

'Oh please don't do that,' he begged. 'I promise to be good. Say you'll forgive me.'

'It won't be easy. I'm very angry with you.'

That did it. With a growl he pulled me down onto the sofa. I opened my legs, eager to receive that huge throbbing thing that was rioting out of control, and felt it plunge into me. Now it was just like I'd imagined it would be with him, forceful and vigorous, all power and no subtlety. He wasn't an imaginative lover but once he'd got going he had great stamina. I could feel the strength of his arms holding me and the steel of his loins thrusting into me. His cock was thick and heavy and gave me a feeling of blissfully satisfying fullness.

When we'd finished we were both happy and absolutely knackered. Leonard got up, looking self-conscious. He seemed reluctant to meet my eye and I guessed that now his need was slaked he felt ashamed of what he'd revealed. But I liked him a lot better since I'd discovered that he was human and it was easy for me to be kind and say, 'You're the absolute best. D'you know that?'

Poor Leonard. He blushed.

When he was about to leave he said, 'I may need to call again. Your case is going to need some complicated paperwork.' Before my eyes his chest swelled and he became 'Leonard Hawkburn, Minister of State' again. 'But there's nothing to worry about. You can leave me to deal with the Sultan.'

'It's such a relief to know that I've got you on my side,' I said worshipfully.

Leonard returned in a few days with some papers for me to sign. He said they'd clear the matter up and he must have known what he was doing because there wasn't another peep out of Abdul. (Although Clive's theory was that he'd read about himself in the *Daily Cobblers* and gone to hide in the desert to die quietly of embarrassment.)

For our second meeting I'd gone in for some power dressing and had on an elegant suit with padded shoulders. My hair was tied back in a style that, for me, was very severe, and I was actually wearing black stockings. I was playing up to his view of me as a dominant lady and I wanted to see how it affected him. I knew I was on the right track as soon as he arrived. His eyes lit up, but he kept up his official manner until we'd dealt with the papers. He could have sent them just as easily so I knew why he'd come.

We had a drink and then he reached over and kissed me. 'You look different,' he said.

'If my public could only see me now,' I murmured. 'They wouldn't recognise me.'

'Oh, but I like you like that. You remind me of my mother. She was a school-mistress.'

'I thought your mother sat at home deferring to her husband.'

'That's just what I say so that people won't suspect –' he broke off.

'Come along,' I said severely. 'I want the whole story and no shilly-shallying.'

He nodded eagerly. 'Oh, you're so like her. She didn't stand for any nonsense either. My father was terrified of her. In fact we were *all* terrified of her.'

It was quite a story. His mother had been head-mistress of a mixed school and a strict disciplinarian who believed the cane was the answer to everything. Leonard had attended the school and since his mother had been determined not to show favouritism he'd been caned more often than the others. I'm not sure he realized what he was revealing, but I think he'd adored her and he'd played her up to get her attention.

Now I knew why he couldn't keep his eyes off my black stockings. As he talked his hand was creeping closer until at last I slapped it away. 'No,' I said in my sternest voice.

'Now I've offended you,' he said submissively.

'I shall get very cross if you misbehave,' I warned him.

And of course he did misbehave, and I did get very cross. And the crosser I got the more he misbehaved, sliding his hand up my leg until he reached the top of the stocking and discovered the suspender belt but no panties. After that there was no stopping him – or me either, come to that.

This time we got into bed and enjoyed ourselves at leisure. It was rather like being made love to by a train going at a hundred miles an hour, and don't think I'm knocking it, because I like vigour in a man. Leonard was one of the very few men I know who could wear me out.

Afterwards I went to fetch us some drinks and when I came back he was lying on his stomach regarding me with a conspiratorial twinkle. I stopped a moment to savour the view of his rear. He had a delightful bum, taut and muscular with buttocks that were sort of square shaped. On impulse I gave them a playful smack.

The result was electric. Leonard grabbed me so fast that the glasses went flying across the room and before I knew it we were away again. My little gesture had brought him back to life with a vengeance and I suppose I ought to have known it would.

Afterwards he was lyrical with gratitude. 'I was trying to find ways to ask you but I was afraid you'd laugh at me,' he said. 'But you understand everything without being told.'

I stopped him there. I didn't want him carrying on again about me being all-powerful because I didn't think I could keep a straight face a second time. But I stored it up for future reference.

Chapter Thirteen

*A*fter that Leonard came to see me every week and I did for him what no other woman would. Not that any other woman had been given the chance. He'd never risked marriage and his rare courtships had all foundered on the rock of his inhibitions. For a while his parliamentary colleagues had suspected he might be gay but that rumour faded for lack of evidence and now they'd written him off as a kind of neuter. The truth, as I discovered, was that he was highly sexed and rampantly heterosexual – under the right conditions.

Now, for the first time, he'd dared reveal his deepest longings. After years of repression his sexuality was at bursting point, and he was insatiable. He was also, he said, happier than he'd been for years.

Now I knew he liked to be chastised physically I applied all my ingenuity to making it a really exciting and fulfilling experience for him. We experimented with a variety of instruments seeking one that would be both firm and flexible, that would smart like mad and leave an afterglow lasting several hours, without doing him a real injury.

I found the perfect item by chance when I was shopping and came across the biggest pair of men's slippers I'd ever seen. Whoever wore them must have been a giant. They were just the right size for Leonard.

The next night I used one of them on him till his rear was scarlet. I finished off with a brisk spanking with my open hand, which made him crow with pleasure. It was tiring work but he rewarded me with two hours of vigorous and satisfying sex that left me even more tired but feeling good.

After that the slipper became our preferred method. If he had an important speech in the House or some tough foreign negotiations to conduct he always came to me to get him into the mood. I'll never forget the Common Market summit in London. The Foreign Secretary had instructed Leonard to take a firm line in the meeting he was to chair, so he visited me early that morning to get into the mood.

The lunchtime news showed pictures of Leonard striding purposefully with other European officials, his face full of manly determination. The commentator spoke of his inflexible will and I thought of the bright red bottom that I'd warmed for him so energetically that morning. He received praise from all sides for his firm stance. 'No-nonsense Hawkburn' they called him and the P.M. spoke of his value to the country.

He sent me a bottle of champagne, a bouquet of red roses, and a gift of some shares which doubled their value within a few months.

Now Leonard was getting his oats regularly with me his confidence soared and he revealed himself to be a very nice man, generous and considerate. It was through his foreign connections that I obtained news of Steve, still in Kamar. I hadn't dared write to him in case the letter was intercepted and used as evidence against him, but Leonard told me that everything seemed quiet. Steve, Johnson and Hamen were still on the dig, and no move had ever been made against them or against Hamen's cousin in the Air Force.

I still dreamed of Steve, but the dreams were different now. Instead of making me weep they gave me happy nights, filled with memories of our brief idyll. I'd wake with the certainty that one day we'd meet again, and this time nothing would divide us.

Leonard's kindness went further. When he found me fretting about my income tax he told me to leave everything to him. My tax affairs had always been a mess because I'd made the mistake of relying on Clive, only to discover that chaos was his middle name. He was very good at making money (especially since he discovered me), it was explaining what had happened to it that gave him problems. The result was that I ended up doing what *he* did; shoving things into the back of a drawer and hoping the problem would go away. But it didn't.

A couple of days after my talk with Leonard a man called Freddie came to see me. He was a very highly placed official from the Inland Revenue, and I can't tell you his last name for reasons of discretion. He looked through all my papers and tut-tutted about my lack of method. But he tut-tutted even more when he saw the last bill they'd sent me.

'But it's your own fault if the taxman makes a high estimate,' he pointed out. 'If you don't send in figures he has to rely on what he reads in the papers.'

'But you can't trust *anything* you read in the papers,' I told him earnestly.

'I'm sure it can be sorted out,' he reassured me, smiling. 'I'll contact your Tax Office and you'll have no further problems.'

Sure enough, not only was the claim halved but I received a hefty rebate for the last two years. Freddie gave me a crash course in how to understand tax, so that I wouldn't get into a mess again. He taught me other things, too. I hadn't realized rubber could be that much fun.

I was so grateful to Leonard that I got hold of a catalogue that claimed to provide 'Everything necessary for connoisseurs of bondage and chastisement'. Some of the things were very inventive. I purchased two pairs of manacles, a cane, a paddle and some very special wearing apparel for me. I was going to give my lovely Leonard the time of his life.

When the parcel arrive I examined the contents, thinking how thrilled Leonard would be. The next time he called me I told him over the phone what I'd done and described my purchases in great detail. I could hear him breathing hard on the other end and stopped to ask, 'Are you all right, darling?'

'I'm fine – just fine – '

'Perhaps I shouldn't have told you this while you're at work. After all, running the country is a serious business – '

'To hell with the country. Don't stop now,' he groaned.

I went into some more detail and his breathing speeded up. Then, in the background, I heard a door open and a young man say in a terrified voice, 'Sir, the meeting started ten minutes ago. *She's* chewing the carpet – '

'Then I hope it's her favourite flavour,' Leonard yelled. 'Now *get out!*'

The door closed hastily.

'I'd better go before I ruin your career,' I said when I could speak through my laughter.

'Yes, perhaps you had. Oh hell, I've got this damned meeting that'll go on half the night. I've got to go to Coventry tomorrow but I'll be back by evening.'

'I'll have everything waiting for you,' I promised.

Next day Leonard was in Coventry giving a speech about 'Britain's place in the world . . . set an example of rectitude and morality . . . order and good management . . .'

It set me thinking just how many others of the great and the good who governed us were hiding similar secrets.

Late in the afternoon Leonard called me, in a bad mood. 'That fool secretary of mine has committed me to speak at a dinner tonight and forgot to write it in the diary,' he growled. 'I've only just found out. I gave him a flea in his ear that he won't forget in a hurry, but I've got to do it. It means staying here overnight.'

'Never mind. We'll fix it for another time.'

'I can't wait for another time,' he protested. 'Darling, it's only an hour and ten minutes on the train.'

'You mean – you want me to come to Coventry?'

'I'll send a car to meet you at the station.'

'You're mad,' I said. 'People will recognize me.'

'Not if you look severe. You're booked in as Miss Forrester, my researcher, bringing me vital papers. Don't fail me, darling. And bring *everything* with you.'

'The vital papers, you mean?' I couldn't resist teasing him.

'You know what I mean,' he said frantically.

I gave in because there was no way to talk Leonard out of it. But a scandal would ruin him so I worked hard at looking unlike my normal self. I wore the school-mistressy suit that he liked, a big scarf over my hair and no make-up. Even so I felt horribly conspicuous as I got off the train at Coventry that evening. Leonard's driver was there. I greeted him with my face buried in a hanky, muttering about a cold.

A young man was waiting in the hotel lobby. 'I'm George Preston, Mr. Hawkburn's secretary,' he declared. 'I'm afraid I don't know you, Miss Forrester.'

'I'm new,' I mumbled into the hanky.

'Well, I have to check the contents of your case for security reasons.'

I nearly died on the spot. Wild visions of him discovering the manacles and cane floated in front of me. Then inspiration came to my rescue. I put the case down on a table between us.

'Of course,' I said. 'There you are.'

Preston tried it and found it locked. 'I shall need the key as well,' he said patiently.

'Yes,' I said as stupidly as I knew how. 'Yes.'

There was a silence.

'Well?' he said crossly.

'Well what?'

'The *key*.'

'I haven't got the key,' I protested. 'I thought you'd have it.'

'Of course I haven't got it. You must have it.'

'Look, I'm just the messenger girl,' I told him belligerently. 'These are *confidential* papers. Mr. Hawkburn keeps the key himself. Didn't he give it to you?'

He ground his teeth. 'No, he didn't.'

Through a half open door I could see a banquet in progress. Leonard was on his feet making a speech. I smiled sweetly at the secretary. 'Well, why don't you go and ask him for it?'

He flinched. Leonard might be submissive with me but he was a terror to his employees and Preston had already been bawled out once that day.

195

'Very well,' he said at last. 'You can give the case to me.'

'I'm not allowed to give it to anyone but Mr. Hawkburn,' I said firmly, clutching tight hold of it.

A burst of applause announced that Leonard's speech had finished. 'Stay here,' Preston ordered and marched into the Banqueting Suite. I crept closer to the door and was able to see him speak to Leonard who was just sitting down. I had a clear view of Leonard's face and the blenched look of horror that appeared on it. He said something and Preston jumped back like a scalded cat. I managed to have my face straight again by the time he tottered out.

'Just a misunderstanding,' he burbled, looking ghastly. 'No problem – let me escort you to your room.'

I had a room adjoining Leonard's with a connecting door. I loftily informed Preston that he could get me a gin and tonic and he hurried to comply. I dismissed him and got down to work.

After a luxurious bath I laid everything out on the bed, surveying it to make sure nothing had been forgotten. When I was satisfied I began to dress. First there was a pair of black satin panties, so slight that they were little more than a G-string, then the leather basque that nipped my waist in tight and pushed my breasts right up. From it hung four suspenders for the black silk stockings which I slid on very slowly and carefully. It wasn't easy to breathe in that basque.

I surveyed myself in the mirror, wondering whether Leonard would like this effect or whether he'd have preferred the other version with the tassels hanging from the nipples. I completed the ensemble with some leather boots that came almost up to my knee and had heels so high that walking was difficult. I stood with my legs apart and my hands on my hips and practised curling my lip until I'd got it perfect.

I heard noises from the next room. Putting my ear to the door I could tell that Leonard had come in followed by Preston, who was maddeningly determined to be useful.

'Miss Forrester is in there,' I heard him say, coming closer to the door. I locked it just in time.

'You can go now,' Leonard insisted.

'But if the papers this woman has brought are important I should help you – '

'Look, Preston, the only way you can help me is by making yourself scarce,' Leonard growled. 'I'm going to have a shower and I'll do that better without you here. Clear out, and don't let me hear of you again this evening.'

I heard Preston leave, but didn't go in yet in case he came back. Leonard must have had the same thought. I heard him in the shower and didn't make my move until the water was turned off. Then I unlocked the connecting door and kicked it wide open. Leonard was there with a towel wrapped round his loins. I stood confronting him with my cane held horizontally across my body.

'You're late,' I snapped.

He jumped. 'I'm very sorry.'

I flexed the cane. 'Sorry isn't good enough. I don't like to be kept waiting.'

I strode into the room and walked round him, giving him plenty of chance to look at me. His eyes were bright with pleasurable anticipation but he kept his manner submissive.

'It won't happen again. I promise.'

I gave a sneering laugh. 'It certainly won't. I'm going to make very sure of that. I've been too lenient with you.' I thwacked the cane against a leather book and thought I detected some movement under the towel. 'It's time you were dealt with, 'I told him. 'By the time I've finished with you you won't even think of misbehaving again. That's *my* promise to you.'

I kept talking to him, knowing that he liked to prolong this part, building up his excitement gradually until his desire to be chastised became uncontrollable. As I talked I flicked the cane through the air several times, so that it made a swishing sound. It baffled me how any man could enjoy this but I could see Leonard was having the time of his life, and I believe in people doing whatever pleases them. So I swished away, letting him hear the threatening sound, and the towel jumped about some more.

'Are you going to beat me with that?' he asked humbly.

'I might.' I let a gloating smile play across my lips. 'Or I've got something else that I might use.'

I strode back into my own room and fetched the paddle, drumming my fingers on its smooth, wooden surface. Leonard trembled with pleasure as he looked at it.

I picked up the cane and flicked the edge of his towel. 'Take that off,' I snapped.

He dropped the towel to the floor, revealing his rampant organ. I pointed to an arm chair and he bent over it. I prolonged this moment, swishing the cane some more where he could hear it but not see it so that he tensed for the lash which didn't come. I knew I had to judge this carefully. I didn't want him getting over excited too soon. On the other hand it was important to keep up the tension. Once I'd spoilt everything by stopping when things became heated and asking worriedly, 'Darling, are you sure you want me to do this?' The sudden collapse of the illusion had caused him to shrink like a pricked balloon and it had taken a lot of work to get him going again. Taking care of Leonard's needs was a work of art.

At last I let the cane land once on his buttocks. It wasn't a heavy blow, just enough to sting. I let it sink in before I prepared for the second, and while I caned him I talked in the way he liked.

'You thought I was becoming more lenient, didn't you, my lad?'

'No,' he protested.

I gave him a stroke of the cane. 'Don't answer back.'

He gasped and before he could get his breath I administered another two strokes in quick succession. They were only light ones but he was in a state of high excitement, gripping the back of the arm chair and taking long ecstatic breaths. I began to swing the cane in a steady rhythm. Leonard's bottom was getting red and he flinched with every stroke, but he stayed where he was until I shifted position so that he could see me better. Then he pounced on me and tried to take me to the bed.

Usually it ended here and we spent the rest of the time enjoying ourselves in a more conventional way, but today I'd planned a special treat for him so I stiffened, resisting him, and snapped.

'Stop that at once!'

When he'd released me I barked, 'I didn't give you permission to get up. You move when I tell you and not before.'

'Yes, ma'am,' he said humbly.

'I thought you were learning, but it seems drastic measures are called for. All right, this time I'm going to punish you very severely indeed.'

I stalked back to my room, reached into the bag and brought out the manacles.

'Lie down.' I cracked my voice like a whiplash.

I'd never restrained Leonard before but I knew it was a fantasy of his. Not that he'd told me in so many words but he'd dropped hints and I'd developed sensitive antennae for the things he was still too embarrassed to say. He obeyed me now with a readiness that told me I'd got it right.

Luckily it was a brass bedstead with bars. I manacled his hands to the head and his feet to the bars but left the chains fairly slack to give him some freedom of movement. Then I picked up the paddle.

'Now,' I said in a threatening voice.

Leonard's eyes were shining with delight and anticipation. But as I drew my arm back for the first whack we were both appalled by the sound of a key in the door.

I dropped the paddle and was across the floor like greased lightening.

'Who is it?' I yelled, pressing my weight against the door and managing to lock it.

'I'm the housekeeper for this floor,' came a woman's voice from the other side.

'Well I'm sorry, you can't come in here,' I said firmly.

'But I have to turn down the bed – '

'It doesn't need it.'

'And put some extra towels in the bathroom.'

The key rattled again. This was obviously a determined woman. If I sent her away she'd be back eventually, rattling and disturbing us.

'Wait there,' I yelled.

I grabbed up the first thing I could find, which happened to be Leonard's bath towel, and wrapped it round myself. It covered me from my breasts down to the tops of my stockings. Then I went out, standing there very firmly between the door and the grim looking woman I found there.

'I'm really supposed to put these in place,' she said.

'Well you won't be able to now,' I said. 'Just give them to me.'

200

She gave me a funny look, as if she'd never seen a woman in a bath towel before.

'I've just had a bath,' I said defensively.

She said nothing but her eyes rested on my leather boots and black stockings. Then she thrust the towels into my hands and scuttled away.

I groaned at my own stupidity. Never mind. I'd got rid of her. I turned back to the door.

It was shut.

Frantically I rattled the handle but it was no use. The yale lock had clicked shut behind me while I was talking. I was trapped out here wearing leather brothel get-up and my poor Leonard was in there manacled to the bed. Whichever way you looked at it the situation had the makings of a first-class scandal.

I knocked on the door. 'Leonard, the door's locked,' I called softly. 'I can't get in.'

I thought I heard a moan of anguish.

'Can you reach the key and release yourself?'

'*No!* Honey for the love of heaven. . . .'

Don't worry, I'll think of something,' I promised.

'You'd better damned well think of it quick,' he called frantically.

'I'm trying. Leonard . . .'

There was a silence.

'Are you still there?' I asked before I could stop myself.

This time there was no mistaking the wail that wafted through the door.

'Of course I'm still here. Where the bloody hell do you think I can go?'

It was the first time he'd ever sworn at me but I supposed in the circumstances I should make allowances.

'I'm going for help,' I hissed.

A strangled noise was all the response I got. I think he was beyond comment by then.

I looked up and down the corridor but I was alone. I checked my own door on the off-chance that it might still be open but it was firmly shut.

I crept down the corridor looking for a maid. I could have used the internal phone to call the desk but that would have attracted attention and Preston might still be lurking. At last I found an open door through which I could hear two young voices, one male, one female. There was an argument going on and a lot of giggling. I looked in cautiously.

The boy was in the uniform of a page and the girl was obviously a maid. He was trying to indulge in what used to be known as 'a little slap and tickle' and she was fending him off. But what really caught my eye was a row of keys hanging on the wall behind his head.

Luckily the maid had her back to me. I positioned myself in the doorway, one arm leaning on the jamb and one held delicately in front of the towel in an attitude that suggested it was about to fall off. Then I made my expression as sultry as possible and pouted.

The boy gulped and let the maid go so fast she had to grab the wall. She looked round but I'd retreated out of sight by then.

'What's up?' she demanded indignantly.

'Nothing. Look, I'll see you tonight, eh? Maybe.'

'What d'you mean, "maybe". A moment ago you couldn't have enough of me.'

'Ah, but like you said, Mavis, I ought to show you some respect,' he babbled. 'Besides, we are at work. Why don't you get along before the old trout comes back and finds us together?'

He was pushing her out as he spoke, urging her down the corridor, silencing her protests. When she'd gone he came round the corner and looked behind the huge potted plant, which was the only possible hiding place.

'Can I do something for you, miss?' he asked in a voice that wasn't perfectly under control.

'I've got shut out of my room,' I told him. 'But you're just the man to help me.'

He must have been about sixteen. I don't suppose any woman called him a man before. He blushed.

'Yes, miss – um – if you'll just come in here.' He led me back into his cubby hole and picked up a pencil. 'Name and room number?'

I shook my head. 'I'm afraid I can't tell you that. It would be too – you know – awkward.'

'But I have to check that before I let you in,' he persisted. 'Otherwise you might be an international jewel thief.'

'In *Coventry?*'

'Yeah, I know.' He sighed. 'Nothing exciting ever happens here.'

'Something might,' I hinted, 'if you could slip out of here for a few minutes and leave me alone with the keys.'

While he hesitated I leaned down and brushed my lips lightly over his. He jumped.

'I'll just go and get some coffee,' he declared in a strangled voice.

As soon as he was gone I grabbed the key to my own room, fled back down the corridor, opened my door, put it on the latch and closed it again. I had the key back on its hook by the time he returned.

'That was very sweet of you,' I declared. 'And you won't tell anyone, will you? It'll be our very own secret.'

'Here, aren't you – ?'

'Ssh!' I put my finger over his mouth and let it run very lightly round his lips. Then I took his head between my hands and gave him the kind of kiss he wouldn't get from Mavis, not in a thousand years. I worked hard and fast. Leonard was horribly vulnerable with my door on the latch.

When I released the boy I could see his legs were shaking. I helped him back into his chair and vanished before he could protest. I managed to slip into my room before he recovered sufficient strength to get to his feet and look out.

Chapter Fourteen

M y poor Leonard nearly fainted with relief when I
got back. One glance showed me that his awful
experience had undone the results of all my earlier
efforts, so I immediately started work to compensate
him. After all it was really my fault for being careless.
Not that I told him that.

'I blame you entirely for that fiasco,' I told him
severely. 'Luckily for you, I know how to deal with
a crisis.'

'Yes – yes you do,' he burbled. 'Everything's all
right, isn't it?'

'If you mean, have I put the problem right, yes. But
everything isn't all right for you, my lad. I'm going to
have to deal with you very severely.'

I laid into him with the paddle and by the third
stroke he'd recovered all his lost ground. In fact his
erection was so huge that he had to lift his bottom
off the bed to make room for it, which presented me
with a very inviting target. I accepted the invitation,
applying the paddle firmly until he was bright red and
almost at bursting point.

'Honey,' he pleaded, 'let me go, quickly.'

I released his feet but not his wrists. The chains that secured his arms were slack enough for me to turn him over onto his back. His cock was so powerfully erect that it pointed towards his head at an angle of seventy degrees.

'Are you going to leave me like this?' he gasped, rattling the fetters on his wrists.

'Yes,' I said simply.

I ripped off my panties and sat astride him. I was afraid he was going to die of joy. I felt pretty joyful myself as I considered the huge cock that was soon to be inside me. Oh beautiful object, oh bliss, oh heaven, oh cock-a-doodle-do!

I advanced on him purposefully and lowered myself onto that great rod. My cunt was twitching with happy expectation and he didn't disappoint me. He came at once but he was far from spent. A second explosion followed the first almost at once, and still he was erect. I raised and lowered my hips in much the same movement I used in riding a horse, and at the same time I was supple enough to reach one hand behind me and give his balls a gentle squeeze. A long ecstatic growl burst from his throat.

I rode him harder, seeking the deepest penetration and the movement that would give me most friction, and felt delightful shudders go through me. This man was a giant of rampaging sexuality, and we each came four times before we'd finished.

When I'd untied him we lay curled up contentedly in each other's arms, and Leonard said, 'Honey, will you marry me?'

'Darling, that's a sweet offer,' I said, genuinely touched, 'but it wouldn't be a good idea.'

'It's the best idea I've ever had. With you I can climb to any heights.'

'Yes I saw that,' I murmured.

'That's not what I mean. With your help I could even become Prime Minister.'

I didn't want to hurt his feelings so I bit back my mirth at the thought of me following him round the world to summit conferences, concealing paddles and chains in the diplomatic bag, doing my bit for the nation.

I kissed him. 'Dear Leonard, I'm really terribly fond of you, and I wish I could say yes, but I can't. But I'll always remember that you asked me.'

He sighed. 'Never mind, it was worth a try.'

That night he did something that charmed me even more. He asked me to sleep in his bed till morning. I refused because the risk to him was far too great, and left the hotel at dawn before Preston was about, getting nosey.

I mention it because that's how Leonard and I were together, friendly as well as sexy. When he was his 'everyday' self he was never embarrassed about the odd things we did because he knew he could trust me. Even after we stopped seeing each other regularly we stayed friends. Our association came to a natural end when he started courting a nice woman. She was several years older than him and a motherly type so I faded into the background to give it every chance. He told me I could always go to him if I needed help, which I appreciated. Another man might have been afraid of blackmail but Leonard was very innocent in some ways. Or perhaps he just knew I'd never hurt him. In fact the only reason I feel free to tell you all this now is because – well, I'll come to that in the last chapter.

I discovered that Leonard had given me a new perspective on myself. In some ways he was right. I was a strong woman, not the domineering school-mistress of his fantasies, but a shrewd cookie who could make her way in the world.

I went in for more power dressing. It was nice to know that I wasn't confined to looking like something from *Dallas*. I could handle understated chic and I began to study the couture houses' ready-to-wear shops. I lacked the height for lofty fashion but if I stuck to clean simple lines I could look taller, and classic clothes suited me.

I knew what I was. I was a bimbo. The term didn't offend me because I'd made a very good thing out of being a bimbo, but I was heading for twenty and I needed to mellow into something more elegant because an over-aged bimbo is not a pretty sight.

I had plenty of work on hand and except for missing Steve I was fairly content that summer. A cosmetics firm hired me to launch their new line called *Success*. That was fun. I made television ads with lots of close-ups and me doing breathy voice-overs, talking about how beauty was the secret of my success (which was true, but not the whole story). I also did a few celebrity game shows. You know the kind I mean, where the celebrities are mostly people you never see except when they're on celebrity game shows. I had a horrid feeling that if I didn't watch out I was going to end up 'famous for being famous', and I aimed at something more solid than that.

One day Myles phoned me. After we'd exchanged greetings he said, 'Darling, I wonder if you'd do me a favour? A friend of mine would like to have a date with you, and he's asked me if I can fix it.'

'Who is he?'

Myles told me his name, but I'm afraid I can't tell you. I promised not to. But I was definitely impressed.

We set the date for two nights ahead. Phil and Donny gave me a real going over to make sure I looked my best. For tonight I abandoned power dressing and went back to being Honey as the public knew me, because I was pretty sure that's what my date wanted. I chose a short evening dress in flowered silk chiffon, cut low and worn with no bra. With my hair done *à la bedswept* my appearance was complete.

My date's secretary telephoned to inform me that there were 'a few points to observe', when I was with him, one of which was that he must always be addressed as Sir.

'*Always?*' I said, visions dancing before my eyes.

'Always,' he replied firmly.

I was collected by a car that had the windows blacked out. Even the glass that separated me from the driver was black. No-one could see me and I couldn't tell where I was going. I tried to work it out by the turns and the noises, but all I could tell for sure was that we didn't go far. When I got out I was in a mews. A man was waiting for me by an open door and he ushered me into a very luxurious house, where my date was waiting for me upstairs.

I tried to remember everything I'd been told but it wasn't easy because I was so nervous. Funny thing, he seemed nervous too. He offered me a drink and tried to make small talk, but he wasn't very good at it. We came from such different backgrounds that it was hard for us to find things to chat about.

I reckoned I knew why he was on edge. Him being who he was, he probably thought I expected him to be madly dashing and romantic, Rudolph Valentino, Robert Redford and Prince Charming all rolled into one. If I hadn't had to be so formal and deferential I could have set his mind at rest, but how do you say, 'Look, if you don't set the Thames on fire it's not the end of the world and I promise not to sell it to the Sunday papers – Sir'?

It's not on, is it? So we stumbled on until he decided the moment had come to put his hand on my knee. It was a pity he had to spoil it by looking at his watch first.

He was nice in bed, not earth shattering but nice. I could have done with it lasting a bit longer, but I awarded him six for effort.

Before I left he gave me a present of a silver cigarette case. I don't smoke but I didn't like to say anything because I had a feeling this was the standard gift in the circumstances. It reminded me of something I'd read recently in a book about Prince Rudolph of Austria, who used to give all his lady friends inscribed cigarette boxes. Apparently there were hundreds of them knocking around Vienna at one time.

Sir assured me that meeting me had been 'Awfully, awfully wonderful,' and hoped we could meet again. I wasn't sure. I mean, there are some things you do once so that you can tell your grandchildren that you did them, but after that you don't need to do them again.

I saw him twice more, but after that I refused. I think he was probably very nice, but it was hard going trying to talk to someone who always referred to himself as 'one' and seemed terrified of his mother.

That autumn I got an invitation to open Lander's, a new store in Knightsbridge. It was the latest in a chain owned by Sir Pierce Lander, a self-made billionaire who'd been buying up and converting stores all over the country. There was already one Lander's in Oxford St., but the new one in Knightsbridge was going to be the 'big' one. It was an open secret that it was supposed to out-Harrods Harrods.

When Clive, who was still my manager, called me up to tell me that they wanted me for the opening ceremony, I was eager to say yes.

'That's a pity,' he said. 'I told the PR office you didn't look at that sort of work any more.'

'*What?* Clive, you louse! I'm just doing up the flat. I could have bought some of their furniture at a discount. Oh, how could you?'

'Honey,' he said patiently, 'how many times have I told you to play your cards close to your chest? Never let people see you're eager. They came back to me an hour later, offering more money.'

'That's better.'

'Which I refused.'

I groaned.

'And they came back again. They've offered ten thousand pounds.'

'And?' I said in agony.

'I've accepted on your behalf.'

'Ten thousand pounds! They want me that much?'

'Someone does. *Someone* was very determined to get you for that job, Honey.'

I thanked him and hung up, feeling thoughtful. I felt I had a lot in common with Sir Pierce. Like me, he'd started from nothing. There'd been a television programme about him a few nights earlier which made a lot of his background: the son of poor Lithuanian immigrants, his early days working on his father's market stall, his ambition, his first shop, his first store, and then the runaway success that had made him a man of legendary wealth.

There was a Lady Lander but she was divorcing him. She'd brought a lot of money to the marriage at a time when he had little, but his 'shrewd' (i.e. crooked) use of her fortune had made her far wealthier. Now their mud-slinging over the division of the spoils regularly brightened up the tabloids.

The programme had contained interviews with defeated rivals all making carefully worded observations about his 'pioneering' business methods. They stayed just this side of libel but it was pretty clear he went in for sharp practice. And, according to the commentator, just what he'd done to earn a knighthood was obscure – as obscure as the precise amount of his rumoured donations to a certain political party.

He sounded a fascinating man. It wasn't so much his wealth that intrigued me as the fact that he'd made it himself. He was a survivor, and now that I'd learned to see myself as a survivor I felt a sense of kinship. I was eager to meet him, and if I'd read the situation rightly, *he* wanted to meet me.

The occasion was special for another reason. It was to be the public debut of the 'new' me. Out went the tight dresses that outlined my rear and let everything hang out in front. In came a little white silk dress with gold buttons and a pleated skirt, by Christian Dior. No, I'm not kidding. *Christian Dior!* Oh, how much it cost! And, oh, how sensational it looked on me. Even though I'm short.

Phil pulled a face at the high neck. 'Have they vanished or something?'

'No, they're still there,' I said, patting my discreetly hidden assets.

He tore his hair. 'Then what's wrong with showing them? Darling, get smart. This man wants to meet you. He set it up.'

'In that case he's probably already seen them,' I replied calmly.

'He'll expect the Honey he's used to. He won't like this.'

'*I* like it,' I said. 'If he thinks I'm going to display myself for him, he's wrong. He can take me as I am or go jump in the lake.'

I didn't tell him that this time I was wearing pantyhose because they gave my legs the sleek look that the dress needed. I added the solid gold chain and ear-rings Myles had bought me, and my outfit was complete.

The opening ceremony was at three o'clock, but Lander's PR office had called to say a car would collect me at eleven in the morning. There was no explanation, no enquiry whether this was convenient. Just – be there!

The Rolls was waiting at eleven on the dot and the chauffeur handed me in. The rear was made entirely of glass, like the cars the Queen had so that everyone can see her, and I knew, from the TV programme, that this was Sir Pierce's own car. No blushing violet, he. A lot of people got a good look at me as we swept on our way to Knightsbridge and I felt so grand that it was an effort not to wave.

I was taken into Lander's by the back way and ushered up to the PR Department. A rather agitated young man called Henry told me that Sir Pierce had planned to be here to meet me but he'd been delayed by 'urgent business'. So I sat and twiddled my thumbs for an hour, which didn't make the best start.

I was just on the verge of saying, 'That's it. I'm off and he can stuff his ten thousand pounds up his – ' when the door burst open and a man in a long leather coat stormed in. I don't mean that he was in a temper, but Sir Pierce Lander always gave the impression of storming about. He was just over medium height, about fifty, with a tanned face and crinkly hair going grey at the sides. His eyes were the deepest and sharpest blue that I've ever seen, and he exuded dynamism, enthusiasm and money. I don't just mean the coat which must have set him back a good two thousand, or the Rolex watch or the silk knitted tie and socks, or the hand-made leather shoes. If you saw this man naked (which I often did) he'd still have carried the aura of money.

He came in, crying, 'Is she here yet?'

'What do you mean, "yet"?' I demanded in outrage. 'Bloody cheek!'

It didn't really go with Christian Dior but it made him roar with laughter. He had a wonderful rich laugh that seemed to bring the whole room alive with the power of his personality, and for no reason I was delighted. He was like a great big eager kid and when he laughed he could make you feel you'd given him a present. He came towards me with his two hands outstretched, seizing both of mine and shaking them hard.

'I'm intolerable, aren't I?' he said.

'Yes,' I told him.

'But you're going to forgive me, aren't you?'

'I think I'd better before my hands drop off.'

'Honey, you're wonderful. I've thought about nothing else for weeks except meeting you.'

And he could make you believe it, even though you knew he was busy doing people down in the stock market at the same time. He believed it himself. He always believed what he said at the moment he said it.

'I invited you early because I want to show you the store myself,' he said. 'Henry, follow us with champagne.' He'd dropped my hands but now he seized them again. 'I insist that you call me Pierce.'

He obviously thought he was doing me the big favour by letting me drop his title. I didn't remind him that 'Sirs' were ten-a-penny and I'd nearly been Marchioness of Dyson, but I had to struggle not to laugh. Like a lot of self-made men who'd managed to get a teeny-weeny handle to their name he was a crashing snob about his title. It constrasted oddly with a real aristocrat like Myles who couldn't have cared less what people called him as long as it wasn't Portland.

Pierce and I toured the store from top to bottom, sipping champagne from crystal goblets that Henry kept replenished with Chateau Petrus. It was a wonderful Aladdin's cave for a very upmarket

214

Aladdin. All the couture houses had their ready-to-wear on sale here and going through the jewellery section was like walking down Bond Street.

'Look at this,' Sir Pierce said, picking up a delicate diamond watch and fitting it round my wrist. 'Isn't it beautiful?'

It was the loveliest thing I'd ever seen. The watch face was rectangular and framed by tiny diamonds, and the strap consisted of two connecting strips which were also studded with diamonds. More diamonds decorated the clasp. I lifted my arm and turned the wrist this way and that, watching the lights flash off the stones, glad that I was dressed to carry off something so elegant. It looked gorgeous and I wanted it with all my heart.

'How much is it?' I asked, holding my breath for the answer.

'Twenty-eight thousand pounds,' said the assistant, smiling. She must have read my face because she added quickly, 'Of course, for a friend of Sir Pierce there would be a discount . . .'

Even with a discount it was way beyond my means. I quickly took it off and returned it.

'Hey ho,' I said cheerfully.

He lingered a moment to say something to the assistant, then hurried to catch me up. He showed me the store with a huge, childlike pride that made it clear this was his lifelong dream, and he talked about the branches of Lander's that he was going to open up in Paris, Rome, New York. To him the whole world was just a giant market place full of coloured toys for him to play with. From the very beginning his vibrant enthusiasm affected me. I couldn't imagine him being boring or less than fascinating.

'We've just time for a quick snack before the ceremony,' he announced at last. We took his private lift up to the top floor where he had an apartment.

'I hate hotels,' he declared 'so I keep a little cubby hole of my own in each store.'

His idea of a cubby hole was breathtaking. There was a huge bedroom with a kingsized bed, a bathroom big enough to hold an orgy, and a reception room with a magnificent view over London. The furniture was antique and the pictures on the wall must have been worth a fortune. One of them was identical to a Rembrandt that had been stolen from a Dutch museum a few months earlier. He saw me staring at it and laughed.

'Don't worry, it's only a copy.'

And to this day I don't know if he was telling the truth.

We had a delicious lunch of chicken salad, sent up by the store's cordon bleu restaurant, and as we were finishing the telephone rang. Pierce grunted into the receiver, then said, 'OK, I want it now.'

He went to the door of the lift which came up directly into his living room and waited for it to arrive. When the doors opened there was a tiny package lying on the floor. He picked it up and brought it over to me.

'For you,' he said with an air of sly triumph.

I opened it and found myself holding the diamond wrist watch I'd tried on downstairs.

'It's my gift to mark our first meeting,' Pierce said.

'But – I can't take something as valuable as this,' I protested, and I really meant it.

'You can't do anything else,' he said. 'Look at the back.' I turned it over and saw engraved, 'To Honey from Pierce.'

'I ordered that done as soon as I knew you liked it,' he said. 'I can't send it back now.'

I nearly wept, it was so beautiful. Pierce fitted it on to my wrist, then drew me into his arms and kissed me deeply. I responded with a deep surge of excitement. It wasn't his money that thrilled me but his power. This man had made the world dance to his tune. The watch was only one manifestation of his success. Among lions there's competition among the females to mate with the pack leader, and I suppose humans have the same instinct. My loins throbbed with the urge to mate with this dominant male.

He quickly unbuttoned the front of my dress and slipped his hand inside. It was a large hand, implicitly powerful like the rest of him but with a sensual skill in the fingers, and I arched eagerly against him as he caressed my breasts. He made love as I imagined he did everything else, purposefully and with economy of effort. There was no fumbling. Each movement of his fingers against my skin was intended to produce a certain effect, and it did so. He'd seen something in me that he liked, and he'd come bounding after it like the king of the jungle he was. It was his style to be direct with no time-wasting preliminaries, and once I was in his apartment he simply reached for what he wanted in that spirit. But it was a generous spirit, as the diamonds on my wrists proved, and I was delighted to be able to respond to it generously.

'We both knew this was going to happen, didn't we?' he murmured against my lips.

'I guess we did,' I gasped.

Still with his mouth against mine he drew me up out of the chair and we began to move towards the bedroom. We'd reached the bed and fallen onto it, feverishly undressing each other, when the phone rang.

'Hell!' Pierce said savagely. He reached across to his bedside extension and growled into it, 'What is it?' Uhuh. All right, put him on.' He glanced briefly at me, 'Sorry sweetie, this is important.'

And evidently *I* wasn't. It was a quarter to three already. By the time he'd finished his call it would be time for the ceremony. I got up indignantly and stalked out.

From the bedroom I could hear him barking orders into the phone. 'I won't accept a delay – never mind that, call Tokyo – get a quote – check that with the Bundesbank – ' I closed the door and left him to it.

At quarter past three he came out, rubbing his hands and looking pleased.

'We're late,' I informed him coldly.

'So we are. Never mind. They'll just have to wait. Sorry about that, but we can take up where we left off tonight, can't we?'

'I'm afraid I have an engagement tonight,' I said frostily.

He grinned. 'No you haven't. You're just mad at me. Please don't be. I can't help the way I am. Come on, say you forgive me and we'll have dinner tonight. There, I knew you would.'

'I haven't said anything.'

'No, but you were just going to. I could tell.'

I discovered I couldn't stay annoyed with him. Against my will I began to laugh, and he laughed too. I forgave him because it suited his convenience that I should. This wasn't a man like other men.

'I almost forgot,' Pierce said, handing me some papers. 'This is your speech.'

I glanced over it and found it full of facts and figures about how Lander's was the biggest this and the first that, and had set the record for something else. I fed it into his shredder.

'What are you doing?' he yelped.

'Putting it where it belongs,' I informed him. 'I'd stuff it down the loo if I had time. Keep that stuff for the shareholders.'

'But – '

'Look, darling, if you wanted that kind of speech

you should have hired the head of the CBI. But if you'd done that you wouldn't have half the TV cameras that you've got down there waiting for *me*, not to mention that he wouldn't look so good in this dress. You hired Honey and you'll get a Honey speech. Now come on.'

I don't think anyone had treated him like that for a while and he looked a bit dazed as we got into the lift. But he didn't say anything.

The ceremony was on the ground floor. As I swept in on Pierce's arm the air was filled with flashlights, the television cameras whirred and I gave them my best professional smile, blowing teasing little kisses all round. That had them riveted, I was glad to see. One of the TV men dropped his mike on his foot, tried to pick it up without taking his eyes off me and got tangled up in his cable.

My speech was a great improvement on Pierce's, full of titillating little jokes about what a 'big' man he was, and how the store, like the man, had 'everything' a girl could want. It went down very well and I could see that Pierce was enjoying it hugely.

Afterwards I had to do some television interviews and pose for pictures with Pierce, and there was more champagne to be drunk with all the big-wigs he'd invited. I must have got through quite a bit by that time and I was beginning to feel sleepy. Pierce saw me blinking and shaking my head to clear it and looked at me inquiringly.

'I'd better go home and have a nap before I meet you this evening,' I said.

'No need. Have a nap upstairs. I have to go to my office for a few hours so I won't disturb you.'

'Fine.'

He came upstairs with me and led me into the bedroom. 'It's all yours,' he said, pointing to the huge bed. 'And let me show you this.'

He pulled open a door that I'd thought led to a cupboard but it was his own sauna.

'Nothing like it for making you feel fresh again,' he
said. 'Here are the switches. There are the towels. Be
my guest. I'll be back about seven.'

When I was alone I stripped naked and got
thankfully into bed. The sheets were smooth and
cool and I luxuriated for a while until my eyelids
grew heavy and I nodded off.

Chapter Fifteen

I woke a couple of hours later feeling much better. There was a panel of switches in the headboard and I explored them. One was labelled 'TV', but I couldn't see a television anywhere, so I touched it tentatively.

At once there was a whirring sound and a television appeared at the end of the bed, apparently having come up from the floor. It was supported by steel rods on either side, which continued to rise until the set was a comfortable height, then turned it forward at an angle so that it could be watched easily in bed. I touched the button that switched it on and lay back to enjoy the evening news and the sight of myself opening the store.

Afterwards I studied the knobs again and found one marked 'Ceiling'. I'd been a little puzzled by the ceiling which seemed lower than usual, so I tried it.

I heard a noise overhead and before my eyes the ceiling split into quarters which simply withdrew, apparently into the walls. Behind them lay a huge mirror, covering the entire ceiling. Now I knew why it was low. Two people lying in this bed would get a closer view of their own activities.

I'd never been a voyeur and it hadn't occurred to me that there'd be any thrill in watching myself make love, but I must admit I was curious to try the experiment.

The bedroom was a mass of gadgets. Another button opened a panel in the wall, revealing a coffee machine already switched on. In a few minutes there was piping hot black coffee, with sugar and cream if I wanted it. I could get to like living like this.

I decided a sauna would be just what I needed to wash the last of sleep away and leave me ready for Pierce. As I'd expected, his very own personal suana was the last word in luxury. The towels were a deep gold to blend in with the pinewood, and embroidered on each one was an elaborate monogram, showing the letters PL intertwined, topped off by a coronet. Why a coronet? I wondered. Did he think being a knight entitled him to one? I wondered what Myles would say. He bought his towels from M&S.

I folded a bath towel on one of the benches, switched the sauna to 'Low' and lay down. When I was comfortably warm I turned it to 'Medium' and then to 'High'. In a few minutes I was perspiring all over.

Soon there was another effect. Even in Kamar I'd never sizzled quite like this. My heated blood was pounding through my veins in a soft, steady rhythm that was hypnotic and extremely pleasant. I was aware of every inch of my hot, damp body, especially the place between my legs where the pounding sensation seemed to be specially concentrated.

The heat gave me a sensation of hallucinating. Visions of every prick I'd ever had inside me filled my fevered brain. I could feel them now, pressing for entrance, in my cunt, in my rear, in my mouth. Some

222

were thick and heavy, some long and elegant, every shape, size and ability, but they were all powerful and upthrust, ready for action. The air seemed to be full of the particular aroma of a sexually aroused male, the headiest, most stimulating scent in the world. I breathed it in, feeling myself become more inflamed. My heart thundered with an almost agonising desire to blend my femaleness with maleness.

Suddenly the door opened and there stood Pierce. I'd lost track of time, but he must have returned, realized where I was, and decided to join me. He was naked and already rampant, his eyes gleaming when he saw the state I was in. He advanced into the sauna, shut the door behind him, and stood looking at me as if I was a valuable new acquisition. I could stand it no longer. With a growl I pounced on him and hauled him forward so hard that he dropped to his knees on the floor. In a flash my legs were round him and I was pressing myself down on to him. . .down. . .down. . .

He came up deeply inside me. I hadn't had time to study his cock properly, beyond checking that it was in the state I wanted it, but I could sense how thick and long it was, a marvellous penetrating instrument for pleasure. I squeezed my muscles the better to feel it and he groaned, clinging on to me.

'Do that again,' he said hoarsely.

I did, enjoying his reaction. There was an ache of unslaked desire in my loins. I could have come a hundred times and it still wouldn't have been enough. I'd never felt as insatiable as I did at that moment; primitive female mating with primitive male, for despite his costly leather coat and his silk ties there was something totally primitive about Pierce. He lived by the law of the commercial jungle and it was the same as the law of the natural jungle: kill or be killed. He'd

223

made his kills and that whole ridiculous, overblown ceremony today was the equivalent of the lion roaring out his pride of possession in his territory. Now I was a lioness mating with the top male. It was as basic as that.

I twined my fingers in his springy hair, kissing him devouringly, challenging his tongue with mine. He came back at me, thrusting his tongue deeply down my throat. I was in an erotic trance, possessed by delicious lust, taking and using him for my pleasure. I was glad for him if he enjoyed it. I really hoped he did. But frankly it was a secondary consideration. I was making sex because sex was what I urgently needed. And it was very, very nice.

I came, groaning and gasping, tightening my legs powerfully about him until my pleasure was complete.

'Now make me come,' he grunted.

'Wait,' I told him. I wanted to come once more before he did, and in this position I was in control because his hip movement was limited. I held off until I was ready, then I let him have it with both barrels, enjoying my moment before I let him have his, and enjoying it all over again when he came. I wasn't trying to dominate him the way I'd done with Leonard. I was asserting myself to let him know we were equals, because otherwise he'd walk over me, and I wasn't having that.

He slid out of me. 'What kind of woman are you?' he gasped.

I smiled. 'The kind you hoped I was when you went all out to get me.'

He gave a burst of laughter. 'You've finished me off, you know that?'

'Not you,' I assured him. I hoisted myself on to the bench behind me and tickled his cock with the tip of my big toe. It began to twitch again.

224

'You're right,' he said with gloating satisfaction. 'But you're more than I bargained for, just the same.'

'Well of course, some men can't cope with a woman who takes the initiative,' I teased, tickling him some more.

'I can cope with anything you throw at me,' he growled.

'That's good, because I plan to throw a great deal.'

I dropped my foot to the floor and leaned back, stretching both my legs straight out, one on each side of him. Still on his knees he came forward until his torso was between my thighs, and began to caress my breasts with both hands. The furnace heat of the sauna was still affecting me and my response was instantaneous. Desire rushed back in a great wave, and I wanted him again as urgently as if that ravenous, lusty mating had never happened.

He brushed my nipples with his thumbs till they were hard peaks. I moaned and tried to urge him inside me but this time he was in command and determined to stay that way. He wouldn't let me rush him. Curving his hands, he brought them closer so that my breasts were drawn together and he could bury his face between them, inhaling my scent and kissing them each in turn. His tongue was as great a weapon as his prick and he knew how to use it to attack and torment. He circled one nipple repeatedly, getting closer, retreating, advancing again, while I gasped and arched backwards, half demented with the sweet, poignant sensation.

He brought me to such a state of anticipation that when at last he touched the peaked nipple with the very tip of his tongue I lost control, writhing helplessly, gasping, 'Yes . . . yes . . .'

He dropped his head between my legs and I felt the tip of his tongue teasing me there, flicking back and

225

forth rhythmically so that I had no choice but to fall into the rhythm too, my hips rocking helplessly as my whole body was caught up in shuddering convulsions. Water was pouring off me from the heat of the sauna, making trickles down my neck, between my breasts and over my stomach. The whole world had become a furnace and my throbbing flesh was the fiery heart of it.

When he'd made me come again Pierce switched off the sauna and we sat there, waiting to cool down and get our strength back. We grinned at each other like conspirators, and he said, 'I hope you're not tired because I haven't started yet.'

'That's what I hoped,' I said.

'Let's get out of here.'

The sauna opened into the huge bathroom, and now that I had leisure to examine it carefully I had to whistle. It was entirely white and gold. The carpet was white as were the thick, soft towels, which also bore his monogram and coronet in gold thread. The sunken bath must have been twelve feet across.

'It's marble. I had to have the floor reinforced to take it,' Pierce announced with an air of pride. 'The taps and plug are solid gold. Get that? Solid. No gold plate. Same with the wash basins. Neat idea having two, isn't it? Saves arguments.'

I praised everything profusely and he seemed delighted. He was like a kid who wants every other kid to know that he's got the biggest toffee bar in the street. It was rather endearing.

Two walls were taken up by cupboards whose doors were floor to ceiling mirrors. I reckoned it was lucky I had a good figure otherwise seeing so much of myself might have been intimidating. High over the centre of the bath hung what appeared to be a golden birdcage, but when Pierce touched a switch on the side of the bath it showered water.

We stood under cool water, but instead of chilling our ardour it refreshed and reinvigorated us. Now I got a better look at Pierce's naked body and I liked its sturdy compactness, implicit with formidable strength.

We dried each other off. I was going to put on a bath robe but Pierce said, 'Wait,' and took my hand.

He led me into the bedroom, turning off all the lights as he went so that the whole place was in darkness. One wall was completely covered by a pair of curtains. Pierce flicked a switch and the curtains parted, revealing a huge window with a magnificent view over London.

We stood side by side, naked, gazing out over a world that couldn't see us. The brilliant lights of the city looked like jewels thrown down on black velvet and they hinted at magic and excitement. London has always thrilled me, but never more so than that night when it was laid out like a carpet at my feet.

'I had a view of London when I was kid,' Pierce said, 'but it wasn't like this. There were six of us and we lived in three rooms at the top of a housing trust. But I promised myself one day I'd have the best view of the city that money could buy. And now I have.'

'You always get what you want, don't you, Pierce?' I murmured.

'Always,' he said simply. 'I wanted London. I wanted you. Now I've got you I want to share my city with you.'

'*Your* city?' I teased him.

'The best of it is mine,' he said, either ignoring the joke or not understanding it. 'I can buy anything that's for sale, and I can get if for less than any other man could do. Let me give *you* the best, Honey – the best clothes, the best jewels, the best of anything you want. You deserve it.'

227

The next minute there was a chill of metal about my neck and Pierce was clasping something at the back.

'It's gold,' he said. 'Gold studded with diamonds. You should wear gold because you're a golden girl yourself.'

'Pierce – '

Before I could protest further he'd clipped two matching gold bracelets about my wrists. Even in the darkness I could see the polished mirror surfaces and the glitter of inlaid diamonds. Their perfection was breathtaking.

He touched a button and the curtains swung across the window. Then he put on the lights and lifted me high in his arms. 'You'll never believe what's going to happen now,' he said, laying me on the bed.

The mirrored ceiling threw back the reflection of a girl with heavy gold jewellery and golden hair. He was right, I thought in wonder. It was right for me. But he hadn't finished. He poured more jewels on to the bed and began to adorn me with them, wherever he could find a place, ear-rings, rings on my fingers and on my toes, bracelets on my ankles, a rope of pearls round my waist. My reflection was dazzling.

'Pierce, it's too much,' I protested, embarrassed at such generosity.

He laughed awkwardly, 'Well I have to admit I get them at cost price through the store, so I'm not being as generous as all that.'

He might try to pass it off but I knew better. I'd seen most of these jewels on display when we were in the store and I knew the ruinous prices. Even at cost they must be worth several hundreds of thousands, yet he'd decked me with them so matter-of-factly that I was lost for anything further to say. I didn't know how to cope with such a man. He laughed when he saw my face.

'Don't make too much of baubles. We should be enjoying ourselves. You do want to enjoy yourself, don't you, Honey?'

Here at least was a way I could make him feel appreciated. After all, my greatest skill was giving a man the time of his life, and if I couldn't produce something special for this generous man I ought to be ashamed of myself. I nodded eagerly and slipped the rings off my fingers, but he stopped me from taking anything else off.

'Stay like that,' he ordered, laughing. 'Those jewels are my brand. They say you're mine. It might be vulgar of me but I want to make love to you like that.'

Well, why not? It was a challenge to my ingenuity. 'Come on then,' I said.

He was kneeling between my parted legs. He placed his hands under my buttocks, lifting them so that he could slide a cushion underneath, then inched forward, aiming his swollen prick between my legs until he was ready to push. As he thrust he caressed my cunt with his fingers and the dual stimulation made me gasp with pleasure.

He put his head back to look into the overhead mirror. Intrigued, I looked up too and saw this girl loaded with jewels all over her body, and a huge penis entering and emerging from her. I'd never actually seen that part of me during sex before and I was fascinated.

'It's great when you get used to it,' Pierce laughed, 'and it gives you a whole new dimension.' He leaned back further so that I could see the size of his pumping organ more clearly. 'Look at that,' he cried triumphantly.

He was right, he *was* vulgar. But his vulgarity seemed to me to have an innocent, harmless quality about it so I just laughed, feeling fond and tender

229

towards him, and he responded with a huge, beaming grin.

I may have mentioned before that Pierce believed in great economy of effort. He told me later if he spent five pounds he always got six pounds value. In his sex life too, *everything* had to work for him. So while one hand was caressing me in front the fingers of the other were inching their way between my legs to the back and finding an entrance there. I've always found that stimulating, especially if the man is skilful, and Pierce was a tremendously efficient lover. He added one finger at a time until there were three, flexing his hand in time to the movement of my hips.

When his cock began to thrust faster I wanted to take hold of him, but he was too far to reach. I buried my fingers in my hair, writhing helplessly as my moment came. At the last moment I had a view of myself as I climaxed under Pierce's ministrations and saw that he too was looking up at my reflection. I thought it was an odd choice when he had the real woman there, but reckoned there was no accounting for tastes.

While I was still trying to get my breath back he grabbed the phone. 'Restaurant?' he barked into it. 'You can send supper up now.' He saw my look of surprise. 'I ordered our meal earlier. That's why I put a restaurant on the ground floor, so that it can stay open after the rest of the store's closed and cook my meals.'

'And you ordered for me without asking me?' I said, slightly nettled.

He laughed at my face and indicated the jewels that covered me. 'Sure. Same way I ordered these without asking you.'

When he put it like that it was hard to argue.

As with the watch, the meal came up in the lift and we drew out the wheeled table ourselves. This way there was no need for Pierce to see anyone. He was an impatient man who considered time spent talking to people he didn't need to talk to as time wasted.

We ate naked, sitting on chairs made, he told me, from toughened glass. And he was right. I did like the meal, especially the asparagus in butter. I'd never eaten it before but Pierce was fanatical about it. I watched him take an end in his mouth and draw it slowly in until it disappeared, then I did the same, noticing that he was watching the O of my mouth, riveted. When I'd finished I licked my tongue round my lips to catch the last of the butter and Pierce was so busy watching me that he momentarily forgot the asparagus stick in his hand.

As we were on the coffee he said, 'Have you got your passport with you?'

'Of course not. Are we going anywhere?'

'I'm flying to New York tomorrow. Fancy coming?'

'Do I *ever*?' I said, delighted.

'All right. My car will take you home now. Get your things together and come back.'

'Hadn't I better spend the rest of the night at home?' I said, thinking of all the preparations I'd want to make, like mud packs, which I could hardly do here.

'Nope. We start early and I like everything to hand well before I leave.' He grabbed up another phone. He had one in every room. 'Fred – have the car ready in ten minutes.'

I don't think I'd ever got dressed in that short a time before, but in ten minutes flat Pierce was ushering me into the lift and telling me that Fred would collect me at the other end. It made me feel a bit like the watch or the meal.

The lift descended to the basement garage and there was Fred, right by the lift, holding open the door of the Rolls whose engine was running.

In my flat I locked away my jewellery, thinking what an extraordinary man Pierce was, then hastily packed my cases and hurried out to the car. When I got back to the penthouse Pierce was talking business on the phone. I waved to him but he didn't notice me. I got into bed and waited for a while, but when he didn't come I fell asleep.

I discovered that this was typical of Pierce. Even while he was working on the Knightsbridge store half his attention was in New York and his internal clock worked on two time scales. The five hours difference in time was a godsend, enabling him to lengthen his working day.

He lived for success in business, and there were times when I thought he'd never leave off. But then something would click, he'd decide it was time to play and work would get pushed aside. He had the energy of a much younger man and sometimes it was all I could do to keep up with him.

He loved nightclubs and we'd dance the night away before going back to the penthouse to enjoy a different sort of exercise. Some of the floor shows were very raunchy.

Andy's Place in particular went in for 'specialized adult' entertainment with audience participation. Pierce took me there often, always insisting on the table closest to the performance. I saw people doing things I'd never even imagined before and he would whisper in my ear, 'I hope you're taking notes.'

I'll never forget one night, about two months after we met, just before one of our frequent trips to New York. We'd popped into Andy's for a couple of hours.

Pierce had to leave me for a few minutes. While I was sipping my drink I noticed an elderly man at the next table with a young girl, whom I recognised as one of the performers in the floor show, sitting on

232

his lap and petting him. But that's not all she was doing. With one hand she was twining her fingers in his hair and distracting his attention, while the other hand slid into his pocket, emerging with a wallet.

I moved quickly and grabbed her wrist just as she'd pulled the wallet right out. The old man stared at it in dismay.

'You should be careful about leaving this around,' I said, smiling. 'You might lose it.'

'I was just returning it to him,' the girl said sullenly.

'Of course you were,' the man said. 'Lana's a good girl, aren't you?' But he put his wallet firmly out of her reach, and every other man at the table checked his pockets.

I let it go at that. The old boy had had his warning. But Lana looked at me coldly and her eyes were very hard.

Pierce returned and a few minutes later the show began. The act was called 'Slavery' and consisted of Lana and another girl, naked except for sequinned G-strings, and a blond, muscular young man, naked except for a tiny black leather pouch that only barely contained him. The girls had their hands bound in front of them, the man, who was Andy himself, carried a whip.

They knelt before him, holding up their bound hands in supplication and a disembodied voice announced that the slave-master would set them a task that they must perform to have their bonds released. The task was that they must 'pleasure' one man from the audience.

About twenty men stood up eagerly but they'd already decided on their quarry and were hauling Pierce out of his seat before the voice had finished. Lana gave me a look of grim triumph to let me know this was aimed at me. I wasn't silly enough to beg Pierce not to go with them. They'd have loved that.

Instead I leaned back in my chair with an expression of amusement on my face.

Despite having their hands tied they managed to get most of his clothes off. I thanked heaven, for Pierce's sake, that he wasn't wearing comic boxer shorts or sock suspenders. They got him laid out on a low couch and really went to work on him. The other girl began kissing him with apparently feverish passion and Lana eased off his underpants, while Pierce made wild thumbs up signs that sent the audience into roars.

I couldn't blame him for enjoying himself, but I felt I should keep my end up. Andy had been prowling around cracking the whip theatrically and the next time he came near me I raised my leg, barring his way. He looked down at me with interest. He'd been casting brief glances at me for some time, and when I gave him my best slow, provocative smile the leather pouch leaped.

'Care to join the show?' he asked.

I nodded and got to my feet. I had on a one-piece, skin-tight pants suit of gold, and of course I hadn't spoiled the line by wearing anything underneath. The suit was elastic, showing off the shape of my bottom which I wiggled provocatively as I walked ahead of him on to the floor-space, looking over my shoulder to make sure he was following. He was.

The audience almost rioted and Pierce raised his head to see what had caused the cheers. When he saw me he made frantic gestures of protest but he couldn't do anything because Lana was sitting astride him, just about to settle herself on his upstanding cock.

I faced Andy and he let the whip snake around my waist. I grabbed one end and began to turn so that the lash wound round and round me until I ended up in the crook of his arm, my back to him, pressed tightly against his almost naked body. He dropped the end

234

of the whip. The top of my pants suit was very low cut and buttoned in the front. With one hand he held me against him, with the other he began to undo the buttons until it was open to the waist. He cupped one of my breasts in a large hand and began teasing the nipple.

Tremors of pleasure went through me but I kept them firmly under control. Pierce was watching us in agony, torn between his desire to haul me away and his ecstasy at what Lana was doing to him. I slipped my hands behind me and began to run them up Andy's leg. The hand that was on my waist undid some more buttons until he could slide his fingers down into the pants, just reaching the top of my legs. I smiled up at him.

That did it. Pierce couldn't stand any more. He jumped up so violently that Lana was sent sprawling over the floor. The audience rocked. It took all my resolution to force myself away from the man who was making me feel so good, but I did.

'Hey – ' Andy protested.

'Another time,' I said. 'Maybe.'

We retrieved Pierce's clothes and I got him behind the curtains at the back of the stage to help him dress. He was cursing furiously.

'Come on,' I rallied him. 'It was just a game.'

'A game? I've never seen a woman behave in such a disgraceful, immoral way in all my – '

'Where's your wallet?' I said.

And of course it was gone. There was a short sharp scene with Andy who swore he'd warned Lana to stop that sort of thing because this was a respectable club. Lana turned out to have vanished with all Pierce's money, but the wallet itself was found in her dressing room with his credit cards still in place.

In the car on the way home Pierce rehearsed his grievances against me, the chief one being that I should have kept an eye on his clothes and saved his wallet.

'Look,' I said at last, thoroughly exasperated. 'You made a fool of me, I made a fool of you. We're equal. The moral is, don't take your clothes off with strange women.' I spoke into the intercom. 'Stop the car please, Fred.'

When he did I opened the door. "'bye, Pierce. Call me when you're in a better mood.'

'Where are you going?'

'Home.'

'But you're coming to New York with me tomorrow.'

'Stuff New York!'

'We're going on Concorde.'

'Stuff Concorde!'

'But what about me?'

'Stuff you!'

I slammed the door and went in search of a taxi. I was fuming.

But next morning a packet arrived for me containing gold and diamond ear-rings engraved on the back. One inscription said, *To celebrate our first*, and the other, *and last quarrel. Pierce.*

What could you do with such a man? I made Heathrow with minutes to spare. He was waiting for me with open arms.

Chapter Sixteen

W hen Pierce and I had been together about four months I knew I had a problem. It would soon be his birthday and I was in a quandary about his present. After the expensive jewels he'd lavished on me my pride demanded that I give him something really stunning to demonstrate that I wasn't simply on the take. Yet a gift to fit in with his lifestyle would be right out of my price range, and I couldn't get it wholesale.

I wracked my brains for hours before the answer came to me: so simple, so obvious.

My Kamari pearl.

I'd had it valued by Mr. Edwards, a dealer in Hatton Garden, who'd offered me £20,000 for it, but, being an honest man, had also told me that if I hung on the price would rise. I'd taken his advice and put the pearl in the bank. Now I got it out, took it back to him and received £23,000 for it. I used the money to buy Pierce a set of matching diamond studded cuff links and tie pin.

Pierce was over the moon when he saw them. 'I can't believe you did this,' he said, turning his wrists so that the stones flashed. He seemed almost close to tears. 'People don't usually give me things. They think because I'm rich it's for me to give to them. But you – Honey, you're something special. How did you ever –? I shouldn't ask but – '

'I sold the pearl I brought back from Kamar,' I said, not boastfully, but because I wanted him to know I'd taken trouble for him. It was really moving to see this confident man so touched because someone had thought of him.

'You sold your pearl,' he said. 'Well, how about that.' He shook his head in wonder. 'I just can't get over it.'

I had another very special birthday treat for him that night. I'd ordered a meal sent up from the restaurant, including his favourite asparagus, and when it arrived I hid some before he saw it.

He was cock-a-hoop because he'd just driven some competitor into the ground, and I knew that meant our loving would be good. If he'd brought off a business coup he made love like a tiger. If he'd been defeated he wasn't so hot. Luckily he almost always won.

I fed him the half of the asparagus that I'd kept out and he told me everything that had happened that day.

'I've got them,' he kept saying. 'I've got them right where I want them. Lorrimers is mine.'

'But you don't own all the shares in Lorrimers, do you?'

'After today I own 90 per cent, which means I can force the owners of the other 10 per cent to sell to me.'

'You mean, once you've got 90 per cent they haven't got any choice?'

'Right. And today I reached 90 per cent. Ah, it's a good day to be forty-one.'

Actually he was forty-seven. I'd seen his passport, but I didn't remind him.

I let him get his New York calls over while I had a bath and made certain preparations. When he'd finished I stretched out on the bed and called, 'Pierce. . .'

'Yes darling?'

'Come and eat some asparagus.'

He came to the bedroom door. 'I've already eaten asparagus tonight.'

'Not like this you haven't.'

I saw his eyes light up with delight and wonder as he saw that stick of asparagus pointing up to the ceiling from where I'd lodged it.'

'You're right,' he said hoarsely. 'I've never eaten it like that before.'

He stripped off and dropped his head between my legs, munching happily away. 'Butter too,' he mumbled happily. He chewed his way down the stick until he reached where it was being held in place, drew the last mouthful carefully out, and demolished it. Then he licked up the remainder of the butter, but he didn't stop there.

'Hey, you've finished,' I pointed out.

He winked. 'No I haven't. I've just started.'

He teased me with his tongue until I was madly excited, then lay on top of me and we enjoyed good vigorous sex without any frills or fancy positions. Pierce was at his best that night, raw, lusty and urgent, staying hard for an incredibly long time, bringing me off again and again. It must have been a stunning victory in the boardroom.

We were dropping into a kind of routine, if you can ever use the word routine for a fire-cracker like Pierce. His plans for the New York store were

239

racing ahead and he went there more and more often. I accompanied him when I could but if I'd been offered work I stayed behind. He didn't like it because he couldn't see why I needed to work at all, but I preferred to keep some independence.

One night he called me from New York. He often did this but tonight he was in a bad way.

'You should be here,' he groaned. 'I really need you tonight, Honey.'

'*Imagine* me making love to you,' I suggested.

'That's what I *am* doing. It's why I'm suffering. Talk to me, Honey. Tell me exactly what you'd do if you were giving me a really special time.'

I put all my ingenuity into what I said, describing in detail all the cleverest things he liked me to do, and he gasped, 'Yes . . . yes . . . go on . . . make it a good one . . .'

'Well, then I'd let my fingers slide slowly down to – ' I stopped, alerted by a noise on the line that shouldn't be there. 'Pierce have you got a woman with you?'

'It's all right Honey, don't be jealous. She's following your instructions to the letter.'

I slammed down the phone, but when I'd cooled off I suddenly saw the funny side. In fact I wasn't jealous at all, chiefly because I wasn't in love with Pierce. That was lucky because he would have hurt anyone who loved him. I thought he was tremendously good fun, but my heart was intact.

I'd stayed in London this time because my new hobby was being a theatrical 'angel', investing in plays. Pierce said it was the fastest way of throwing good money after bad that he'd ever heard of but it fascinated me. I'd put a few thousand into *Dreams Of Evening*, and I didn't want to miss the first night even though it meant not going to New York. Pierce sulked a bit but I was adamant.

240

It was a fabulous occasion. Clive escorted me to the theatre and the party afterwards. It was a chance to wear a sapphire necklace Pierce had given me for Christmas and I wished he could have been there to see how good it looked on me.

Clive saw me home and dropped a heavy hint but I kissed his cheek and said goodnight. I was tired and only too glad to drop into bed. In less than a minute I was off.

I woke quite suddenly, sure that I'd heard a noise. I lay unmoving, straining every nerve, and then, faintly but surely, I caught the sound of breathing. Without a second thought I sat up and switched the light on.

I nearly jumped out of my skin at the sight of a young man standing near the window. He was dressed in a black stretch suit that was skin-tight on his slim figure, outlining marvellous taut thighs. Even his gloves were black. It could mean only one thing.

'You're a burglar,' I said furiously, grabbing for my bedside phone.

Quick as a flash he shot across the room and whipped the phone out of my hands. 'Now don't do anything hasty,' he said. 'Let's discuss this like civilised folk.'

'I don't discuss things with a man who creeps about like a thief in the night,' I insisted.

'But I *am* a thief in the night,' he pointed out with impeccable logic. 'Of course I creep about. I wouldn't get far knocking politely on your door and asking to be let in, now would I?'

'You'll get as far as a police cell,' I said reaching for the phone again. But the movement revealed a good deal of me and I suddenly remembered that I wasn't wearing anything. I crossed my arms over my chest and glared at him.

241

'Would you like to put something on?' he asked me.

'Yes I would,' I snapped ungraciously.

'Where do you keep your nightdresses?' he said, opening my chest of drawers.

'You won't find any there. I never wear them.'

'What's this pretty lacy thing then?' he demanded, holding up something he'd found.

'That's a slip.'

'Well it'll do.' He handed it to me and turned his back like a gentleman. In fact his whole manner was gentlemanly. His voice was educated and reminded me a little of Myles. But despite his civilised ways he kept his hand on the phone so that I couldn't use it. I wondered if I'd gone completely mad. This couldn't really be happening.

'My name's Frank, by the way,' he said when he turned round. 'I'm sorry I startled you. I didn't mean to.'

'Good of you,' I snorted.

'All I want is those pretty sapphires you were wearing tonight.'

I looked at him. 'And then you'll go?'

'Word of honour. And I'm a man of my word.'

I reckoned I could always call the police the minute he'd left so I told him where to find them. As he got the box out and raised them to the light I had the chance to study him. He was in his late twenties, tall and slim. That stretch suit outlined a pair of the nicest, firmest male buttocks I've ever seen. He also had a merry, handsome face and a pair of deep blue eyes. Under other circumstances I could have taken to him a lot. But I was on my guard.

To my amazement Frank gave a sigh of disappointment and dropped the sapphires back into their box, closing the lid.

242

'Don't tell me you've had an attack of conscience?' I demanded.

'Oh no. I'd take them like a shot if they were worth taking, but they're fake.'

You'd think I'd have had the sense to leave it there and usher him out, wouldn't you? But like an idiot I started arguing.

'Of course they're not fakes. Pierce gave them to me.'

'Then I regret to have to tell you that Pierce has been taking you for a ride. I've had a lot of jewels through my hands in a short but splendidly misspent life, and I know fakes when I see them.'

'I don't believe it,' I said mechanically.

'Did you choose these yourself in the shop and take them away with you? I bet you didn't.'

'No,' I admitted reluctantly. 'He just turned up with them one day.'

'So you don't actually know where they came from?'

'Well, no but – '

'Tell me, just how many times *has* he bought you something in a shop, with an assistant to vouch for its value?'

'There's my diamond watch,' I said triumphantly. 'He gave it to me at our first meeting and the assistant told me it was worth twenty-eight thousand pounds.'

'And he presented it to you there and then?'

'Well – no. I got it a couple of hours later because he wanted to have it engraved.'

'Or because he'd planned the whole thing and wanted to substitute a cheap imitation.'

I started to say, 'But he couldn't have known I was going to notice that particular watch . . .' when my voice trailed off as I recalled how Pierce had directed my attention to it. It was sleight of hand, like a conjuror's trick.

'Can I see the watch?' asked Frank.

'It's away being repaired or I'd never have told you about it,' I retorted. 'I'm not that silly.'

'Well have it valued. In fact have everything valued and see if I'm not right.'

'But – it doesn't make any sense,' I protested. 'He's an immensely rich man.'

'And how do you think he got rich? Not by giving valuables away.' He got to his feet. 'I'll be going now.'

Before I could say a word he vanished through the window and when I looked out I saw him swinging his way down to the ground like a monkey.

Next day I went to the bank, got out all the jewellery Pierce had given me and took it to Mr. Edwards. As he lifted out first one piece then another I began to have doubts. There was the diamond and emerald bracelet, identical to one I'd seen on sale in Lander's for £33,000, the diamond brooch shaped like the sun that had been priced at £29,000 in the shop – I'd demurred at the price but Pierce had urged me to choose it ('Hell, sweetie, what's a few extra thousand to me?'), then hadn't let me take it straight away because he wanted it engraved on the back.

I watched the dealer lift up the Art Deco diamond bracelet. Surely it *must* be worth the £16,000 Pierce had told me. And that huge flashing diamond set in a ring, it had to be real. And the satin-finish white gold brooch, and the gold necklet set with diamonds . . . fakes couldn't look like that, *could* they?

Finally Mr. Edwards finished examining every piece and looked up at me.

'If you really need to raise the money I could let you have two thousand pounds for the lot,' he said.

Two thousand! My hair stood on end.

'They've been very cleverly done,' he went on. 'These zircons are brilliant. At first they look exactly like diamonds.'

'And they're all fakes?' I demanded. 'Every single one?'

'Oh no. This one's quite real.' He held up a tiny brooch, shaped like a spider. 'It's worth about five hundred.'

Well thank you for nothing!

I gathered everything up and left the shop, seething.

Pierce wasn't due back for several days so I couldn't have it out with him. I'd have to swallow my rage until he returned.

A couple of nights later I woke in the early hours to hear a faint tapping on my bedroom window. I pulled back the curtains and when I saw Frank outside I realized that I'd been subconsciously expecting him to return.

'Come in,' I said. I wrapped a silk dressing gown about me and switched on the light. As he shut the window behind him I pulled out the drawer where I'd dumped my baubles and tipped them out onto the bed. 'You can have the lot.'

'Bad news?' he said sympathetically.

'Two thousand pounds.'

He tut-tutted and began going through them. 'If they'd been real they'd have been worth nearly two million,' he mourned.

'I had the watch checked this morning. That's worthless too, unless you like zircons,' I said bitterly. 'The lying skinflint! And you'll never guess what I did for his birthday.'

'I probably can,' he said sympathetically. 'I'll bet you gave him something really valuable because you were so touched by his generosity.'

'You've come across this situation before, haven't you?'

'More times than I care to remember. It makes my life very difficult.'

'I actually sold my Kamari pearl to buy him a super present. It fetched £23,000 and I spent the lot on him.'

I thought Frank was going to burst into tears. 'You had a pearl worth £23,000?' he said piteously.

'I did *once*.'

'And you got rid of it before I turned up?'

'I'm afraid so. It's not your day, is it?'

Frank groaned.

'I bought him diamond studded cuff-links and tie-pin. And *they* were real. No wonder he gave me such a funny look. Not conscience-stricken, you under-stand. Just funny. *Yeeow!*'

I finished with a screech of pure rage and Frank quickly put his hand over my mouth. 'Hush, some-one will hear,' he said anxiously.

'So what if they do? This is my home. I have a right to be here.'

'So you have. Sorry, I'm so used to being in places I've no right to be that I forgot.'

'It's not the money, it's that he deceived me. I don't like being made a fool of.'

'None of us does,' Frank observed sympathetically. 'Think how I felt when I made that dangerous climb up here only to find that your sapphires hadn't been worth the effort.'

His manner was so droll that I couldn't help laughing.

'You know, you're much prettier than your pic-tures,' he said, 'especially when you laugh. In fact I don't think I've ever seen a picture of you laugh-ing.'

'Nobody wants me to,' I explained. 'They all want me to come over all sultry and sensuous, like this.' I let my face fall into its standard lines, lips pouting, looking at him through half closed eyes.

'Don't do that to me,' he begged. 'I've got to climb

back down again in a minute and I need to be clear-headed.'

'I'll make you some coffee,' I said, going into the kitchen.

'I couldn't take a cold shower as well, could I?'

As we drank coffee together I asked, 'Are you often this unlucky?'

He shrugged. 'Off and on. It's a life with no security, but then so's yours.'

'That's true,' I said, feeling sorry for myself.

We sipped our coffee in an atmosphere of mutual sympathy. Then Frank said, 'Of course, success in this business depends a lot on your physical equipment.'

'I know the feeling.'

'It's easier if you're nippy on your feet. I trained as a gymnast, nearly got into the England squad. It comes in very handy.'

'Didn't you ever want to do anything else?'

'The trouble is I'm not very bright. I was always at the bottom of the class at Eton. My father's a banker and I was supposed to go into it too, but I couldn't get the hang of the figures. I know about jewels though. I can spot a fake at fifty paces. By the way you haven't asked me why I'm here.'

'Oddly enough it hadn't occurred to me.'

'I've just come back from another job, a country house in Surrey. Nice place. It's called Astleys.'

'But that's Pierce's home – his 'country seat' as he will insist on calling it. Don't tell me you cracked it. He's got the very latest in security.'

'Oh, there's plenty of security but it's all style and no substance. It was one of the easiest places I've ever done.'

'Did you pinch his gold signet ring? I'll bet that's not a fake.'

'I didn't go for jewellery. He keeps something a lot

more valuable in that house: papers that are presumably too secret to be left in his office. Here.' He pulled a tiny object out of a breast pocket. 'It's a microfilm of every paper in his desk.'

'But what use is it to you?'

'None at all, but there must be something in there that will give you a way to make him sorry.' He put the film into my hands.

'You got this just for me? Frank, that was very sweet of you, especially as I haven't anything worth stealing.'

'Ah, but the very nicest things aren't stolen,' he said with a twinkle, 'they're given free.'

Well, it was the least I could do when he'd taken so much trouble for me. Besides, that skintight suit was showing a significant bulge that had been interesting me for some minutes. I took hold of the zip fastening and drew it slowly down to his waist . . . down . . . down . . . he was completely naked underneath.

He had a disarming smile. On impulse I slipped my hands inside the suit, round to the back and down to where I could take hold of his buttocks, pulling him hard towards me. But I was stopped in my tracks by a yelp of agony.

'The zip,' he said painfully. 'Do you want to do me a permanent mischief?'

'Sorry,' I said guiltily.

'Look, I'm just a nice ordinary boy. Can we keep it simple?'

'Come on,' I said, taking his hand and leading him to bed.

He insisted on undressing himself ('I'll feel safer if you don't mind') and what came out of that wet-suit was well worth waiting for. I could see Frank was a trained athlete. His body was lithe, lean and firm like a panther's. I ached to caress those long elegant thighs and that neat muscular bottom. I slipped off my robe and lay on my stomach on the bed, facing the foot, with my chin resting on my arms, watching.

He grinned. 'Enjoying the view, are you?'

'Very much. And thinking what I'm going to do with it all.'

He sat beside me. 'Well, why don't we try a mutual exchange of ideas?'

He rolled me over and immediately lowered his head between my legs, inhaling my scent as if he loved it, and starting to kiss me. I reached for his cock which was now in just the right position to be drawn into my mouth. We worked on each other with lips and tongue, almost as if we were competing to see who could give the other the best time. He won. I came first. He laughed and said, 'Let me show you something I'll bet you've never done before.'

He sat astride my shoulders, supporting his weight on his own thighs. I felt them and the muscles were as hard as steel. I let his cock slip between my lips again, running my hands up his legs to feel his buttocks.

Then he did something only an athlete could have done. Keeping his cock in my mouth he bent right over backwards until his head came down between my legs and I felt the tickle of his tongue again. I gave his balls a soft squeeze of appreciation. I don't know where he got the strength to stay like that, but he managed it until he'd made me come again. It was quite a performance, and I couldn't think why he'd called himself an ordinary boy. This wasn't my idea of simple.

But when he'd straightened up he said, 'Now let me show you I'm not just an athlete.'

And he did. Superbly. If Frank wasn't very bright in the head it was because he kept his brains in his body. He had intelligent hands that could insinuate their way into just those places a woman most likes to be touched, and caress her with extraordinary sensitivity. He had a clever mouth and subtle lips that could tease and torment and fulfil, and an ingenious tongue that never ran out of new things to do.

But if the rest of him was bright, his prick was pure genius. It was strong and hard, not a blunt instrument battering away mindlessly, but a knight's lance held at the ready to do his lady service. It could thrust slowly, tentatively, easing its way in, giving me time to show by my response what I wanted. And when its patience was rewarded by the right signal, it could power into me fast and often so that I cried out with joy and clung to him and wanted more . . . and more . . . and more . . .

When he rose to go I helped him on with the suit and kissed him tenderly. After the discovery of Pierce's duplicity I'd felt used and foolish. Frank had made me feel like a desirable woman again. My heart was full of gratitude towards him.

'Wait,' I said as he moved to go. I held out the little spider brooch. 'This is the one thing that's genuine. The dealer said it's worth five hundred. I don't know what you'll get for it but it won't be a wasted trip.'

'I won't get anything for it,' Frank said. 'I'll never sell this as long as I live. And it's been the best trip I've ever made.'

He took me in his arms and we kissed each other. It had been a sweet meeting and we knew we'd never repeat it. I watched as he swung over my balcony and vanished into the darkness.

I got Clive to develop the film for me and when I received the prints I studied them carefully. I wasn't hoping for much because I thought the papers would probably all be written in Businessspeak which I couldn't follow. On the whole I was right. But I discovered one titbit that made the whole thing worthwhile.

Pierce had apparently been buying up all the shares of a firm called Hanning's, with a view to outright ownership. He now owned 85 per cent, 10 per cent was owned by another firm who flatly refused to sell, and the remaining 5 per cent belonged to someone identified only as 'Mr. X' who was willing to sell but was holding out for five times the market price. Obviously Mr. X knew the law Pierce had told me about, the one that said if he owned 90 per cent he could force the sale of the other 10 per cent.

Even so, he could hardly have known just how big a hold he had over Pierce. An internal memo declared that 'failure to secure total ownership of Hannings would be seriously prejudicial to the long-term future of Lander's. I couldn't follow all the ins and outs, but I could understand that Pierce needed Hanning's very badly indeed, and was almost ready to pay Mr. X's price.

I read the papers through three times to make sure I hadn't misunderstood anything. Then I made myself some coffee and settled down to do some hard thinking.

I'd had a very pleasant few years and gained something from each of the men I'd known; not necessarily material things, but experience and a broader outlook on life. But *they'd* all gained a great deal more.

Many of them had exploited me in one way or another. Clive's career had taken off. Randy got a new lease of life – after our public romance he'd started to be offered younger, more romantic roles again. Butcher got a million seller from our relationship. The least said about Abdul the better.

As for Pierce – my anger with him knew no bounds. He was a mean man who'd deceived me, basking in my gratitude for his 'generosity'. I hadn't asked to be showered with costly gifts. He'd insisted on giving me that load of trash because he wanted a reputation on the cheap. He'd made a fool of me, and that I wasn't going to stand for.

After everything I'd given – willingly in some cases, by trickery in others – I felt the time had come to claim something back. I had a chance that would never come again.

Because I knew the identity of Mr. X.

Chapter Seventeen

I called Leonard at the Foreign Office and told him I might need a favour.

'Let's meet and talk about it,' he said eagerly.

'Won't your lady friend mind that?'

'We don't see each other any more.'

That made it a lot easier. 'Well then, how do you fancy having one of our old get-togethers?' I suggested.

He was so excited he dropped the phone. 'Can it be tonight?' he pleaded. 'I've got an important debate in the House tomorrow.'

He came to my flat at eight o'clock. I met him at the door in a sedate dress, but as soon as he was safely inside I threw it off to reveal my kinky leather get-up. Poor man, he hadn't had any real fun for ages and he was all too ready for what I had to offer. I caned him soundly before tossing him on to the bed and practically taking him by force. Not that he put up any resistance.

'What can I do for you, Honey?' he asked me as we lay gasping in each other's arms.

'It's nothing really, just that I may need to talk to Freddie of the Inland Revenue. I promised him I'd never call him direct.'

'And you want me to make contact? Of course I'll do that for you.'

'I may not need him after all, but I'd like to know he was on standby.'

'No problem.'

'That's very sweet of you, darling.' I picked up the paddle. 'Now for your reward.'

He stayed the night and the next morning I treated him to a really special session. He went off humming happily to himself, and that afternoon he really trounced the opposition in the debate.

Next on my list to contact was Randy. The timing was lucky because his girl-friend had just left him for a younger man so I caught him at a vulnerable moment. It did wonders for his pride to think I was trying to come back to him.

But he wasn't so happy at the end of the evening.

He took me to dinner at the flashiest restaurant he could find and I'm sure he alerted the press because there were several of them there.

Over the caviare he grew sentimental. 'I've never forgotten you, Honey. I think often of the happy times we had together.'

Did he indeed? He must have forgotten a good deal then. But I just smiled sweetly and let him burble on.

'I've never known another man quite like you, Randy,' I said. Which was absolutely true.

He simpered, no kidding.

'I suppose a girl doesn't forget her first real love,' he sighed, 'the first man to show her the pure poetry of passion. Oh, I know technically Clive was before me but –' he took my hand and his voice throbbed with emotion '– we were *different*, weren't we, Honey?'

I don't know about 'we'. *He* was certainly different. I've never known a man who had such trouble getting it up and keeping it up. But I didn't spoil the atmosphere by saying so. I just looked soppily into his eyes and he was so vain he took it for agreement.

'I see you're going out with Lander at the moment,' Randy observed. 'He's always struck me as a bit of a flashy character.'

'Well, he's not the first flashy man I've been involved with,' I pointed out. I knew I was safe in saying that. Randy wouldn't get it.

'No, you've been around with a weird crowd, but we were bound to rediscover each other, weren't we?'

'You think that's what this is, Randy?'

He gave me his best 'warm' smile, eyes glowing with seductive intent, lips curved in wry appreciation of life's little ironies. It used to make me go weak at the knees on the screen. 'Well you certainly called me for a reason, didn't you?'

'That's true.'

His voice grew husky. 'And it wasn't just for a chat.'

'That's true as well.'

'Well then . . .'

'All right, I'll come clean. There is something I want from you. Something I want very much. In fact, I haven't been able to sleep nights for thinking about it.'

He took my hand, looking deeply into my eyes. 'Tell me.'

'I want to buy your Hanning's shares.'

He dropped my hand as if it had suddenly become red hot.

'What did you say?'

'Your shares in Hanning's. You own five per cent of that firm and I want it.

255

'Well, well, quite the little tycoon, aren't we? I must have educated you well. But no dice, darling. Pierce Lander has offered me five times their market value. I can make him increase that before I sell.'

'But you're not going to, *darling*,' I told him sweetly. 'You're going to sell them to me – at the market price.'

'The hell I am! Forget it, Honey. You're out of your depth.' He took my hand again and raised it gallantly to his lips. 'And who wants to talk about business when there are so many more pleasant things?'

I smiled. We were sitting at right angles to each other and I leaned over to whisper in his ear. My lips tickled him and he had to grip the edge of the table.

'Darling . . .' I murmured.

'Yes?' he said breathlessly.

Still in the same tone I cooed, 'How would you like to have all your tax affairs investigated?'

Randolph paled. I knew a tax investigation was the last thing he'd want. But he tried to bluff it out.

'You can't fool me that way.'

'I'm not fooling, Randy. I have friends in *very* high places.'

This time he gave a nervous swallow. My relationship with Leonard had never become public but it was suspected in certain circles (although not the precise details, of course), and Randy moved in those circles.

After a struggle he managed a ghastly smile. 'You wouldn't do that, Honey. You're not that kind of girl.'

'What sort of girl do you think I am?'

'You're a darling, an absolute little sweetie who wouldn't hurt a fly.'

'By "a darling" you mean a bimbo, someone whose only asset is her body. Someone who's docile, permanently available and too stupid to see when she's being used. Actually, you're right in a way. I *have* been stupid. But now I've wised up. I want your shares and I'll get tough if I have to.'

He choked as his wine went down the wrong way. I patted him on the back while he struggled to breathe and splutter curses at the same time.

'Market price,' I reminded him.

'Go to blazes!' he said violently.

'Randy, my pet, if I go anywhere it won't be to blazes – it'll be straight to the nearest telephone booth to send a message to my friend in the Revenue.'

He groaned and tore his hair. 'Why on earth did I let you wheedle so much out of me about my financial affairs?'

'I didn't wheedle anything,' I said indignantly. 'You wouldn't shut up about them. I spent hours listening to you wittering on about the tax fiddles you were pulling and how many bank accounts you had in different names. You wanted to boast how clever you were and you reckoned I was too dim to be dangerous.'

'Well I was wrong about that, wasn't I? I suppose Lander put you up to this?'

'You've got it wrong again, Randy. I thought of this all by my little self.'

'*You?*'

'Even bimbos have brains. And my days of doing things for the benefit of men are over. From now on I act exclusively for me. Do I get those shares?'

'All right,' he snarled. 'And I hope they choke you. *Delilah!*'

'My broker will call you in the morning.'

When Leonard had given me some shares he'd also put me in touch with George Brand, his own stockbroker. I'd had a chat with George earlier that day, and he'd explained that I didn't actually need

257

any money for what I was going to do. I could buy the shares on Monday but settling day wouldn't be until Friday. If in the meantime I could sell them at a higher price all I had to do was pocket the profit.

'Of course if you can't sell them you're in trouble,' he warned.

'Don't worry, there's no fear of that,' I said. 'I never knew you could do it this way.'

'There are lots of little ways and means if you know your way around,' he told me with a twinkle.

I bought Randy's shares at market price on Monday. On Tuesday Pierce returned from New York and I went to the Penthouse in the evening. As I stepped out of the lift I could hear him barking into the phone and suddenly realized I was faced with an unusual problem of protocol. At this point I normally undressed so that I was ready for him when the call finished, but considering how I was planning to take him to the cleaners, was that the right way to behave now?

Not to put too fine a point on it, should I screw him before I screwed him?

I decided to have one last fling to remember him by. I was feeling at my best that night, alert and vibrant. The knowledge that I was going to bring off a brilliant coup had reinvigorated me and I wanted to celebrate physically.

I went into the bedroom, stripped right off and threw back the quilt. A touch on the switch made the ceiling vanish, revealing the mirror, and I lay surveying myself. I was nearly twenty-one and I still had a fantastic body, but for how much longer? There were new sixteen year olds coming up all the time, and perhaps my face was a little too well known to the public . . . yes, I was doing the right thing.

Pierce came in and immediately started throwing off his clothes.

'That's right, sweetie. Everything ready for me. Just how I like it.'

He bounced on to the bed. 'I had a fantastic trip. I really murdered 'em left right and centre, and you know that turns me into a tiger, don't you?'

'It must be a heady feeling to know you've done someone down,' I said, looking at him thoughtfully.

'Heady? I couldn't begin to describe it. It's the biggest aphrodisiac in the world. Boy, could I have done with having you there! Never mind, you're here now and I'm going to make the most of you.'

He was big and hard already, though whether from the effect of seeing me naked or from thinking about how he'd 'murdered 'em' I wouldn't like to guess.

What we did together that day was done selfishly on both sides. With him it had always been selfish, and perhaps it was naive of me not to have seen it sooner. But now I felt entitled to be selfish too. I used him for my pleasure, just as he'd used me, and I think I had the most enjoyment out of it because I knew something he didn't. And that made a nice reversal of our usual positions.

He looked a little surprised when we'd finished. I'd been more insistent than usual on having things my way. But he put a brave face on it, sighing with exaggerated satisfaction and saying, 'I missed that. You missed it too, didn't you, Honey?'

'I've certainly been waiting eagerly for you to return,' I said truthfully. 'The fact is, I have some news for you, Pierce.'

'Tell me.'

'I've started to dabble in the stockmarket.'

He grinned. 'You should have talked to me first. What do you know about it?'

'Enough to buy Hanning's shares.'

The grin faded abruptly. 'What do mean, "Hanning's". The only Hanning's available are – *where did you get them?*'

'From Randolph Berrick. All 5 per cent,' I said calmly.

Pierce stared at me, then he let out a *'Yaaah – hooo!'* of triumph that made me put my hands over my ears.

'You little beauty!' he yelled. 'You got Berrick's shares – all 5 per cent. You genius. How did you know I wanted them?'

'Perhaps I didn't know,' I said, nettled by his presumption. 'Perhaps I got them for my own sake.'

He roared with laughter at that. 'Oh, that's rich!' He saw me looking at him wryly and stopped laughing. 'Hey, come on! You *are* going to sell them to me, aren't you?'

'Oh, yes. That's what I bought them for.'

He gave a sigh of relief. 'That's all right then. For a moment you had me worried.'

'Not half as worried as you'll be in a minute,' I promised.

'Oh-hoh, I see what it is. You want to make a little on the deal. Well, that's only fair. I'll pay you 5 per cent over the market price. Never say I don't know how to be generous.'

'What I say is that you're a miserable cheapskate.'

'What?'

'I want six times the market price.'

He tried to laugh again but I think he must have seen something in my eye made him nervous because it didn't come out right.

'You don't mean that.'

'I do mean it,' I said.

'But that's robbery.'

'No, it's just what all my jewellery would be worth if it were real.'

260

His jaw dropped and it took him a moment to recover. 'I don't know what you – how did you find –? There's obviously been a misunderstanding –'

'The only one who misunderstood is you, Pierce. Now watch my lips and try to take this in. I want six times the market value of those shares. Considering that you'll get the whole of Hanning's in the end it's cheap at the price. You'll pay me.'

'I'm damned if I will. Hanning's can go to hell.'

'And so will you if the Revenue starts looking through your books.'

I didn't have to explain that. Pierce knew of my 'connections' even better than Randy did. He'd once tried unsuccessfully to persuade me to ask Leonard to fix him commercial favours overseas. Perhaps because he was more of a realist than Randy he gave in sooner. But he staged one last effort.

'Five times the value.'

'Six. And if I have any more argument it'll be seven. Come to think of it –'

'All right, six,' he said hastily. 'Thank God you're not in business full time. It would be like having Lucrezia Borgia in the City.'

'My broker will call you tomorrow.'

I knew I'd really outwitted Pierce because he was as limp as a dishrag in front, the infallible sign that he was wounded to the heart.

That was the last time we saw each other. I called George next day and by Friday afternoon I was worth two million pounds.

I couldn't get used to the idea of having all that money. My Dad would have called it the wages of sin, but he'd have touched me for a hand-out in the next breath. And it was a sight better than I'd have done if I'd gone to university.

That set me thinking. University. Why not? I was still young, I was ready for a new way of life, and my

261

first experience of business had left me with a taste for more.

With a bit of research I found a university that did a degree course in business studies. I wrote to them and was invited for an interview.

I wore my 'power' clothes on the day I went there, but that wasn't the only reason I was thinking of Leonard as I got dressed. It was in all the papers that morning that he'd resigned suddenly and left the country without explanation. I was the only person who knew where he was and why, because he'd called me on the way to the airport last night to say that he couldn't live without the new happiness I'd shown him. He'd turned his back on Whitehall and chosen freedom. He still writes to me from Hawaii where he ended up, and where he married a very understanding local girl. He sounds terribly happy and I have a permanent invitation to go and stay with him and his wife. He says she and I have a lot in common.

The interviewers were inclined to view me as a comic turn at first, but when I told them about the deal I'd just pulled (minus certain details) they grew more interested. At my suggestion they called George, and after that one of them asked me if I was sure I had anything to learn from them.

'I want to learn everything,' I said firmly. 'After all, two million pounds won't last forever.'

They accepted me. I floated out in such a state of euphoria that I didn't look where I was going and cannoned straight into a young man.

'I'm terribly sorry,' he said as he steadied me.

Then he stared at me in amazement and I stared back, feeling a burst of disbelieving joy in my heart.

'*Steve!*'

We threw ourselves into each other's arms, laughing and crying and trying to talk and kiss each other

262

at the same time. Some people came out of a door behind us and we had to move out of the way. Steve grabbed my hand, said, 'Come on,' and in five minutes we were in his flat.

He pulled me into his arms again for a long, deep kiss and this time there was no-one to disturb us. There was nothing to fear now either, just our two selves in peace and privacy to love each other as we'd always been meant to. We hurried to take our clothes off and get into his bed which was a single one, but wide enough for two people who wanted to be close.

We'd had so few lovings but they'd been the ones that mattered and I remembered every inch of his beloved naked body. I remembered the deep golden hair of his crotch and the beautiful strong prick rising from it. I recalled my own throb of happiness at the thought of taking it into me, and felt that throb again. I wanted him so much, not just to be united with him, but almost to *be* him, for we were two halves of a whole and neither of us was complete without the other.

He savoured me slowly first, touching every inch of my body with his lips as he rediscovered it, giving me the caresses that pleased me from him as from no-one else. He kissed my throat, my breasts, my nipples, letting his tongue make leisurely circles around them until it reached its destination. I twined my fingers in his hair in an ecstasy of abandon as he teased each one to a firm peak. I loved this man so much.

His hands strayed downwards to my waist and over my hips, relishing the roundness he found there and the firm flesh of my bottom. But I couldn't wait any longer and I pulled him over me, wanting him, craving for him with all my being. I lay beneath him and circled him with my legs, gasping at the poignant beauty of his entry and the long, deep thrusts that sent flames through me. If I could, I would have kept him in me forever.

But no-one is allowed to hold on to total happiness forever. It must be given up, if only that it may be renewed and enjoyed again. We shared our moment of passion and afterwards lay together tenderly, holding each other as though fearful of another separation. But I wasn't going to let that happen again.

'I love you, Steve,' I whispered.

He kissed me. 'I love you, darling Honey. You're the only woman in the world for me. I wanted to come and find you when I returned to England, but you were being seen around with Sir Pierce Lander. I know how wealthy he is. I'm just an archaeologist. I have a research fellowship here for the next two years, but after that I have no security.'

'Two years? Funny, that's just how long I'm going to be here.'

I told him about my course and his face lightened. 'Then we'll be able to see each other.'

'We can do better than that,' I told him. 'We're going to get married.'

'I can't offer you the kind of life you've been used to. Can you be happy with a poor man?'

'I could be happy with you anywhere, any time,' I said.

It wasn't the right moment for explanations. There'd be plenty of time to tell him everything later. I'd found the love of my life and just then I had other things on my mind.

'Come here,' I said softly, 'we have so much lost time to make up.'